IN THE DARK

Also by Brandon Massey

Novels
Thunderland
Dark Corner
Within the Shadows
The Other Brother
Vicious
Don't Ever Tell
Cornered
Covenant

Collections
Twisted Tales

Anthologies
Dark Dreams
Voices from the Other Side: Dark Dreams II
Whispers in the Night: Dark Dreams III
The Ancestors (with Tananarive Due and L.A. Banks)

IN THE DARK

BRANDON MASSEY

Dark Corner Publishing
Atlanta, Georgia

For more information:
Email: support@darkcornerpublishing.com
Web site: www.darkcornerpublishing.com

When Reggie King stepped inside the rental house on that rainy Saturday evening, the first thing he did was draw his Glock nine millimeter and begin searching from one room to the next, opening doors and flipping on lights as he moved.

He had to make sure the place was empty.

It was a three-bedroom, two-bathroom ranch in East Atlanta. A few pieces of no-frills furniture occupied the rooms, only the essentials needed for simple living. His real estate company advertised the place as "fully furnished, utilities included," which helped to maintain a steady stream of new tenants, mostly transient types who needed a pad for a few months.

As he searched each room, he kept one hand wrapped around the gold crucifix that dangled from his necklace. His other hand was steady with the gun, a good sign. He'd been so terrified the past three days that his sure grip gave him confidence that he was regaining control of his life.

The only sounds in the house were the rain drizzling on the roof, and his labored breathing. He didn't hear the noises he feared: the whispers and the soft laughter that had been following him like his own shadow.

He scratched the back of his neck. A monster mosquito—he'd assumed it was a mosquito but hadn't really seen it—had bitten him a few days ago, and the swollen sore itched like a mother. He'd dab some hydrogen peroxide on it whenever he got a chance.

The house was clear. Every room and closet was as vacant as he'd hoped. It was a safe place for him to spend the night, and, he prayed, at least the next few days. Until he could figure out what the hell was going on.

He returned to the front room. He'd dropped his suitcase in the entry hall and left his bag of Chick-fil-A sitting on an end table. He grabbed the paper sack and headed into the kitchen.

He'd bought five chicken sandwiches and four large orders of waffle fries. After twenty-four hours without eating, he was ravenous.

He had a big appetite under normal circumstances. He was six-three and two-fifty, heavily muscled, his physique almost as solid as it had been twelve years ago, during his days as a starting defensive linebacker at Morehouse. He still hit the weights and the track six days a week, determined to stay fit as he crept through his mid-thirties; his grueling workout routine demanded he consume a high amount of calories.

In spite of his obsession with physical fitness, he'd been unprepared to handle the terror that had begun three days ago. He would have been better prepared, in fact, to deal with the zombie apocalypse.

He sat at the table, gun at his side, and devoured three of the sandwiches and two of the sleeves of fries, before he even bothered to check his new cell phone. It was a prepaid he'd picked up and activated earlier that day. He'd discarded his Blackberry yesterday— had taken a hammer to it and smashed it until the electronic guts leaked out.

No one had his new cell number. That was critical. It was safe from tampering. He needed to call a few folks in his inner circle and let them know how to reach him.

He wiped his greasy fingers on a napkin, and slipped the cell out of the inside pocket of his windbreaker jacket. He thumbed on the power button.

Two text messages were already waiting for him.

The first one was a welcome message from the wireless provider, explaining the rates for sending and receiving texts.

The second text came from a familiar source: the number of his own Blackberry that he'd pounded to bits yesterday.

The text read:
Vengeance is mine i will repay

Reggie dropped the phone onto the table as if it had given him an electric shock. Rising out of the chair, he picked up the Glock and swung it around the kitchen, his heart thudding.

He was alone.

How the hell had the guy used his Blackberry? How had he gotten this new number? Reggie didn't even know the number yet for his new phone.

His stalker seemed all-knowing, godlike. Did he know where Reggie was hiding, too?

Delicious aromas drifted from the opened bag, but Reggie had lost all semblance of his appetite. He needed to search the house again.

Gun held in front of him, he crept from the kitchen, into the brightly-lit hallway.

The lights flickered, and went out.

"Shit," Reggie said, under his breath. He bumped against the wall, and stopped. He wasn't familiar enough with the property to navigate in the dark, needed to wait a few seconds for his vision to adjust.

A second later, a noise came from the area of the house where the bedrooms were located. Someone speaking in a low but intense tone.

A chill slipped down Reggie's spine.

No, Reggie thought. *He can't be here.*

He turned around, to face what he thought should be the front door, the way out, but he had become disoriented. The house was nearly pitch-black. It didn't seem possible for a home located on a well-lit residential street to be so dark.

Heavy footsteps dragged across the tile floor.

"Brought you into this world, little man," a raspy voice said, in what was close to a whisper. It was the voice of a man ravaged by lung cancer, the result of forty years of smoking two packs of Newports a day. "Brought you into this bitch . . . I will take you out."

Cold sweat saturated Reggie's face. It was the voice of his father, Ronnie King.

But his father had been dead for seven years.

It was still too dark for Reggie to see him clearly. He saw only a hulking, shadowy figure, larger than him. Ronnie, or Ruthless Ron as he was known on the gridiron, had three inches and fifty pounds on his son, and a fearsome reputation on the college field. He'd specialized in hitting the opposing team's quarterback so hard that the poor saps often left the game on a stretcher.

Reggie remembered, too, how it had felt for his father to hit him. Growing up, he'd been on the receiving end of those brutal fists many times.

Knees quaking, Reggie backpedaled in the direction where he believed the front door lay. The back of his leg knocked against a table, and he stumbled.

His father chuckled.

"Told you to train up on that footwork, little man."

Reggie regained his balance and hustled to the doorway. He snatched open the door. Thin light sifted inside from a streetlamp, and cold raindrops hit his face.

He remembered his luggage. He had valuables in there that he couldn't easily replace—and he didn't know how much longer he would be on the run.

He turned, searching for the bag, and saw it only a few feet away, beside the sofa. As he stepped toward it, the thing that was his father shuffled into a shaft of watery light.

Reggie looked away, but not fast enough.

This was not the first time he'd seen the nightmarish thing from the grave. It had been haunting him since this madness has begun three days ago. But each time he caught another glimpse, he edged closer to plunging into total, irrevocable insanity.

That fleshless skull full of wriggling maggots might be forever imprinted on his memory.

Reggie tucked the suitcase under his arm as if carrying a football. He bolted out of the house.

He'd parked his black Mercedes sedan in the driveway in front of the attached garage. He tossed the suitcase onto the passenger seat and scrambled behind the wheel.

He was shivering so badly that it took him four fumbling attempts to fit the key into the ignition.

His dead father didn't appear in the house's doorway. He wouldn't. He never chased him. He was always *waiting* for Reggie, wherever he happened to go.

Reggie knew what would happen if he dared to stay behind and confront his father. His father would kill him. After all, he'd wanted to kill Reggie before death had taken him. The last time Reggie had seen his father alive, they'd come to blows about how to best handle a hundred acres of family property in Alabama that had fallen into their hands with the death of an older relative. His dad had wanted to sell the land on the cheap and pocket the money. Reggie had seen opportunity and wanted to build a subdivision. Dad didn't like his son implying that he was a fool, and the fight was on.

Reggie had landed one punch, purely in self-defense, and then fled the house, but not before his father had promised him: *If I ever see you again, I'm gonna kill you.*

By some devilish turn of fate, his father had been given another chance to accomplish his final wish.

He stomped on the accelerator. The tires screeched on the wet pavement briefly, and then found purchase. He peeled out of the driveway.

The stereo was on, blaring music. He'd switched it on while driving earlier, attempting to calm his nerves. Stevie Wonder was singing his classic, "Superstition."

Steering the car onto the road, Reggie punched the button to switch off the radio. He needed to figure out his next move.

Hiding out in one of his vacant rental properties had been his best idea thus far. But that had worked for barely fifteen minutes.

He considered leaving Atlanta. He had family in Alabama, California, and Texas.

Even better, what if he left the country for a while? He could go somewhere he loved, like Brazil. Surely, on another continent, he would be safe from this nightmare.

He had his passport in his suitcase. He could book a flight into Rio tonight. He had the funds. Owning a real estate management company for the past ten years had been a highly lucrative endeavor for him. He'd managed to turn a hefty profit regardless of market shifts, because he hadn't been afraid to bend—or break—the rules as needed. Survival of the fittest. That was a lesson his dad had taught him that he'd mastered.

He had decided that he was going to drive to the airport, and was about to turn in another direction, when he saw the tall, slender figure about a hundred yards ahead. The man stood under the boughs of an elm tree, as if waiting for a taxi.

It was Reggie's torturer. The one who had launched this living nightmare in the first place.

Reggie's fingers tightened on the steering wheel. He gritted his teeth.

Vengeance is mine, *asshole,* he thought. *I'm ending this.*

And then he floored the gas pedal . . .

Part One

1

It was a peaceful Sunday morning in April, full of sunshine and promise, until the stranger arrived at the front door.

When it happened, Len and Olivia Bowden were unpacking boxes in the parlor. Or rather, Len was unpacking boxes. His wife, he assumed, had other things on her mind.

"I feel as if I'm dreaming," Olivia said. She placed her hands on her waist, gazed out the bay windows at their new neighborhood, and released a sigh of pure satisfaction. "We did it, babe. We're really here."

Here was a hundred-and-ten-year-old Queen Anne Victorian in Candler Park, one of Atlanta's prized historic districts. They'd had their eye on the community for years. That past March, when the rambling, five-bedroom house hit the real estate market after the owner lost the property in foreclosure, they'd "pounced," as Olivia liked to say when she related the story to their family and friends.

"Glad we're finally moving in," Len said. He mopped sweat from his brow with a wad of paper towels. "It took long enough to square things away."

Getting on his knees on the hardwood floor, he prepared himself to face the next unopened box. A fresh round of sweat trickled from his receding hairline. For the past two days, he'd been slinging boxes around as frantically as a postal worker during holiday season. He wore a support brace for his back while doing the work, a necessity due to a nasty lumbar injury he'd suffered two years ago, but he still planned to end that day, as he had last night, with a generous dose of Advil and an ice pack pressed across his lower spine.

He pushed up his glasses on the bridge of his nose. *Parlor --*

3 of 6, was written on the box lid in black marker. Olivia's handiwork. The woman was a logistical maestro, had coordinated this move from their townhouse in Midtown with a precision that Len simply didn't possess, so he did what any smart husband would do: got the hell out of the way and followed his wife's orders.

This box, he found, bulged with photographs: shots of grinning family and friends, mostly Olivia's people. Len came from a small clan and wasn't in the habit of collecting printed photos. But Olivia, who hailed from a sprawling family that had roots from Harlem to Haiti, had a pic of everyone she'd known over the past thirty-five years.

Lips pursed, Len flipped through the shots and glanced around the living room—*parlor,* he corrected himself—wondering how they'd arrange the pictures. One of the photographs was taken fifteen years ago, on his graduation day at Georgia Tech. He stood with his mom and dad, all of them cheesing hard, even his sour-puss father. *I'm so happy you've finally graduated, Lenny,* his dad had told him over a beer later that evening. *Now I can stop supporting your ass and get my new 'vette.* Dad had died only a year later of a heart attack while waxing his coveted sports car in the driveway.

Sighing, Len moved to the next photo. Seeing it immediately brought a blush to his cheeks.

It was another picture from his college days. He was at a party with Todd, his best friend at the time, and his then-girlfriend, April Howard. All of them hoisted beers and wore the easy grins of the pleasantly buzzed. Len remembered what happened later that night, too: after he and April had left the party and gone back to his dorm room, they'd enjoyed an erotic episode straight out of his wildest teenage fantasies.

The memory brought a tingle to his spine.

But it was a bittersweet recollection. Six months or so later, he and April broke up, and not long after, April—a brilliant mathematics student who came from a troubled background—had climbed into a bathtub and slit her wrists.

Len tucked the photo into his back pocket, glanced at Olivia to see whether she noticed what he'd done. She had no idea he'd been in a relationship with the girl in the picture, and sure as hell knew nothing of their bedroom adventures. It seemed disrespectful to have such a photograph standing proudly on an end table in their new home, and he decided he would place it in his office, probably in the deepest reaches of a desk drawer.

Olivia was still gazing out the window, her back to him.

That morning, she was dressed in her knockabout clothes—a white tank top, pink lounge pants, and flip flops. Her long, ebony hair was wound into a ponytail. Nevertheless, she looked as good to Len as she would have if she'd been posed for a glamour shot in her finest evening wear. Even after six years of marriage and one baby, his attraction toward her was as strong as it was on the first day they'd met on a blind date.

Len was a video game director, a life-long geek and late bloomer who hadn't gone on a date until he was eighteen years old. He'd lucked up and married a woman far more beautiful than any he'd ever expected to find. Only in fevered nerd fantasies did the Olivia DeJeans of the world actually settle down with a guy like him.

Briefly, he thought of walking over to his wife, placing his hands on her narrow waist, sliding his fingers down to caress her shapely derriere, and kissing the smooth nape of her neck. The idea made his pulse race. He was thirty-eight, but lately he had the raging hormones of a teenager.

But you know she won't like that, he thought. *You'll get swatted away like a house fly.*

The sudden crackle of the baby monitor sitting on the fireplace mantel drew both of their attention.

"Great," Len said. "Sounds like Miss Kennedy is waking up."

Kennedy was three years old, or as Len told friends and colleagues, "three going on thirty." Moving into a new home while attending to the needs of a restless toddler—was there any other kind?—had been a challenge, to say the least.

Olivia crossed the room and plucked the baby monitor speaker off the mantel. She placed it against her ear, her attention shifting to the cathedral ceiling, as if she could see their daughter upstairs with x-ray vision that only mothers possessed.

"Go back to sleep, sweetie," Olivia whispered to the speaker.

"Please," Len added, though the handset was not a two-way radio and could not transmit their voices.

They had just spent their first night in the house. It was a few minutes past eight o'clock, and Kennedy typically slept in till around nine on weekends. Len expected she'd need time to adjust to the new digs, but he hoped this wasn't a sign of things to come. He was an early riser, even on weekends, and cherished those couple hours of blessed silence.

Another cry issued from the speaker, softer than the first.

Len rose, knees popping. "Want me to go check on her?"

"I don't think that's necessary." Olivia read her sports watch, her honey-brown eyes sharp. "We should get another forty-five minutes or so of freedom. She went to bed later than usual last night because she was so excited to be here, and I think she needs the rest, or she'll be intractable when I get her up."

Within a few seconds, the cries faded. Olivia returned the receiver to the mantel.

"See?" She smiled at him. "Back to work, *mon amour*. Chop, chop."

Len scratched his head and looked around. The spacious parlor—apparently a primary activity area in traditional Victorian homes—had doorways that led to the entry hall, and dining room. Many more rooms lay beyond those. The three-story house had over five thousand square feet of living space, not including the unfinished basement.

And at the moment, moving boxes lay everywhere, some opened, some still taped shut. Where had all of this stuff come from? You didn't realize how much crap you'd accumulated until you moved.

"Sorry. I need a break, Liv. I've been at it since six o'clock."

"Babe, I can't relax with these boxes sitting all over the place. It's chaos. We need to keep pushing."

"We've already set up our bedrooms. The kitchen is in decent shape, too. It's going to take more than a weekend to get the entire house in order exactly the way you want."

"Right." She smirked. "I'd expect to hear a reply like that from the guy whose bachelor pad was full of boxes he hadn't unpacked in two years."

"I knew how to find everything I needed."

"Bringing a hot date to an apartment full of junk isn't the best way to make a positive impression."

"You married me. My impression must've been positive enough."

"I saw the *potential*." She rubbed her hands together. "Like I see a lot of potential in this house once we've got everything unpacked and arranged in its proper place." She pointed outside the room. "For example, I was thinking of replacing that chandelier in the entry hall with a better period piece, and we could put some nice armchairs in here, too. Also, like I said before, I think we need to seriously consider updating these hardwoods."

Len felt like clapping his hands over his ears. When Olivia started gathering steam on a topic, she'd talk you into a state of bleary-eyed submission. It was little wonder that she'd found success as a trial attorney.

She continued: "We definitely need new crown molding in all of these rooms, too. And don't forget the wainscoting. I've got big plans for painting as well. And you know what? We've *got* to tear down the rest of this terrible wallpaper. Seriously, it gives me a migraine to look at it."

"I'm getting a migraine thinking about all of the work you want to do here."

"We discussed all of this, babe, many times." She stared at him, brows knitted. "Remember our list?"

"When are we going to have time to complete all of these major home improvement projects? We barely have time for each other anymore."

He hadn't planned to speak those words to her; they just rolled out of him. Olivia's eyes sharpened like daggers. He braced himself for a lacerating remark.

Then, two things happened simultaneously: Kennedy screamed. And someone knocked on the front door.

"Jesus." Len's heart leaped. He looked from the baby monitor handset, from which Kennedy's screech blasted in an ear-grating wail, toward the ceiling. "What the hell's going on up there?"

"Get the door, please, I'll check on the baby." Olivia grabbed the handset and hurried out of the room, flip flops clapping as she raced around the maze of boxes.

Len considered following her upstairs. Kennedy had cried out as if she were terrified. He didn't care about who might be knocking. They weren't expecting visitors anyway.

But another series of knocks came, harder and more insistent: *thump-thump-thump-thump-thump.*

Len slipped off his back support brace, placing it on one of the boxes. Then he moved to the bay windows. Who would be visiting their home on a Sunday morning? They hadn't met any of their neighbors yet, but it seemed too early in the day for a neighborly greeting. As far as Len was concerned, if you knocked on someone's door at this hour you were liable to get cussed out.

The hardwood blinds that covered the windows were half-open, allowing a partial view of the world outdoors. He lifted a slat of the blinds and peeked outside. A black Cadillac Fleetwood

Brougham, circa 1985, was parked in front of their house. The pastor of his mom's church had used to drive a Caddie like that, but that was a long time ago. He had no idea who owned the car.

He glimpsed someone sitting behind the wheel, face concealed in shadows. A chauffeur for their impromptu visitor?

The Victorian had a wraparound front porch that extended from the turret that housed the bay windows, to the other side of the residence. Len craned his neck to get a better look at the region of the front door . . . and could make out a tall, lean gentleman dressed in a black suit and matching top hat.

He frowned. *Who the heck is that? A Jehovah's Witness?*

The visitor knocked again. The raps were impatient. In Len's experience, religious solicitors didn't usually present themselves in such a brazen manner.

He didn't know the stranger's purpose, but the urgency of his knocking had piqued his curiosity.

He backed away from the windows and entered the hallway.

Let's see what this is all about.

He disengaged the deadbolt, and opened the door.

2

The first thing that struck Len about the visitor was his height. Len was about five-ten, not short, not exactly tall. He pegged the stranger's height at about six foot six; Len worked with a similarly-sized giant and was accustomed to feeling like a dwarf in his colleague's presence. The stranger's formal top hat—*who wears a hat like that anyway these days,* Len thought—made him appear even taller.

Involuntarily, Len took a step backward.

The gentleman was clean-shaven, with russet skin so smooth it looked like a plastic mask. He had high cheekbones, and an aquiline nose that gave him a hawkish appearance. The only evidence of the stranger's age was the fringe of curly, snow-white hair under the brim of his hat. He might have been sixty, or ninety. Len had no way to be sure.

The man wore darkly-tinted, wraparound sunglasses that concealed his eyes. Len also noticed that he gripped a wooden cane in one gnarled, gigantic hand. The cane was black, matching his suit and hat, but had a string of bright, multi-colored jewels embedded along its length.

Len cleared his throat. "May I help you, mister?"

The man inhaled deeply, head cocked, as if he were drawing in every scent in the vicinity, separating them out like threads, and making an assessment. After a moment, his lips twisted into a sour expression.

Do I stink or something? Len thought, and then a realization hit him: the stranger was blind. He didn't look directly at Len, only in his general direction, but Len got the feeling that this man's olfactory perception was profound.

The man said, "You gonna let Dr. Laveaux come in now, boy? Respect your elders, know better."

Len paused. The man spoke in a nasal tone, with a strong hint of a Haitian accent. Olivia's family was from Haiti, and they had visited the island nation together once, in the first year of their marriage. This guy—this Dr. Laveaux, as he called himself—sounded like a few of the elders Len had met during his visit.

"I'm sorry, but we can't accept visitors right now." He offered a chuckle to soften the blow of his refusal. "Still unpacking, you know. What can I do for you?"

Dr. Laveaux's gaze moved into the space above Len's head. Len could see his own face reflected back to him from the shadowed mirrors of Laveaux's sunglasses, and he found the vision strangely disturbing.

Upstairs, Kennedy released a shriek that made Len cringe. Laveaux's head snapped upward. He sniffed the air again. His lips curved into a soft smile.

Len felt his stomach knot. He decided he didn't like that smile, not one bit; a snake might grin like that.

"How old that little girl?" Laveaux asked.

Len had no idea how Laveaux knew Kennedy was a girl. Had he smelled her?

"She's three," Len said.

"Ah, precious child, precious." His grin broadened. Len noticed his teeth: large, white, and as perfectly formed as a display model sitting on a dentist's desk. They looked genuine, too.

"So," Len said, clasping his hands together. "We're kind of busy here, as I said. Can I help you?"

Laveaux's smile vanished. He lifted a bony index finger that looked as long as a surgical probe, and pointed at Len.

"You and this family in Dr. Laveaux's house," he said. "Dr. Laveaux wants it back."

Len blinked. "Excuse me?"

"The people, boy!" Spittle flew from his lips and sprayed Len's forehead. "The people took it from Dr. Laveaux! Dr. Laveaux gonna get it back, he sure is, mark that."

Len wiped his forehead with the back of his hand, comprehension sweeping over him in a cold wave. This man was the former owner of the Victorian. He'd lost the property in foreclosure. The "people" of whom he spoke was presumably the lender that had initiated foreclosure proceedings.

Len didn't know how to reply. The guy might have a legitimate beef. Over the past several years, a lot of terrible things had taken place in the mortgage industry. Len had friends whom had lost homes in foreclosures due to bad contracts, or had been so deep underwater on their loans that they had simply walked away. It was a difficult time for everyone.

But Laveaux losing his property wasn't Len's fault, and coming to threaten the family who had moved into your former home was hardly the action of a rational human being.

"Listen, I'm sorry for whatever happened, mister," Len said. "I know losing a home in a foreclosure is a painful experience. I wish I could help you."

Laveaux coughed, spat on the veranda floor. The phlegm landed close to the tip of Len's sneaker.

"But there's nothing I can do," Len continued. "I'm sorry."

"Eh?" Laveaux sneered. "Dr. Laveaux ain't done here."

Cold sweat had begun to gather in Len's armpits. He should have gone to check on the baby, and Olivia should have handled this visitor. She was much better at confrontations than he was, thrived in heated debates and arguments.

"I don't know what else to tell you, mister," Len said.

"Do Dr. Laveaux need to talk to your wife? She wear the pants, boy, huh? Bring her to Dr. Laveaux and we'll talk proper business now." He made a shooing gesture. "Go on now."

Len's throat clicked dryly as he struggled to reply. Laveaux smirked at him, and stepped forward.

Len shifted, purely by instinct, and blocked his entrance. At closer proximity, Laveaux smelled of exotic, musky herbs, and raw earth, and in the back of his mind, Len wondered what sort of doctor Laveaux happened to be.

"Out the way," Laveaux said.

"We bought this house," Len said, pleased by the conviction in his voice. "We have a legal contract on this property. We're staying here, mister."

Laveaux laughed at him. He drew back, and deftly flipped his cane from one hand to the next, with the flair of a magician performing a sleight of hand trick. The jewels on the cane glinted in the sunshine, and Len noticed that the handle of the walking stick was carved into what was, unmistakably, a huge phallus.

Dirty old man, Len thought. *I'll be damned if I let you inside.*

"Boy got a little heart," Laveaux said. "A little strength in the blood, Dr. Laveaux says. But it don't matter."

"I'm asking you to leave," Len said in the firmest voice he could muster.

"You don't know Dr. Laveaux's house. Nobody knows Dr. Laveaux's house like he does. Don't know what you got into. Don't know what be deep down there, eh."

"Leave," Len said. "Or I will call the police."

Laveaux laughed again. "Dr. Laveaux gave you a chance to be good, he did. He gave you wise counsel. *Bouch granmoun santi, sak ladan l se rezon.*"

"Pardon me?"

In one quick, fluid motion, Laveaux extended his long index finger—*that thing really does looks like a surgeon's probe,* Len thought—and jabbed it against Len's chest.

Len rocked backward on his heels, nearly losing his balance.

"Three days," Laveaux said. "Three days and you be gone from Dr. Laveaux's house, you know what good for you and that family."

"Are you crazy? We're still moving in, for God's sake."

Laveaux held up three fingers and waved them in Len's face.

"Three days, you be gone," Laveaux said. "*Apre bal, tanbou lou.*"

"Excuse me?" Len scowled. "What the hell does that mean?"

As Len stared at him in bewilderment, Laveaux made a series of quick gestures above Len's head, hand slashing through the air, while he whispered something in a mysterious language. To Len, Laveaux's actions and words had the air of a ritual, and a superstitious part of him thought, *he's casting a magic spell on us to make us leave.*

Of course, that was silly. Magic wasn't real. Everyone knew that. Laveaux was just a kooky old man.

Laveaux concluded the odd display by snapping his fingers, a sharp sound that made Len's heart skip a beat. Chuckling, Laveaux turned away. He ambled down the veranda steps. In spite of his blindness, he found his way easily with the cane, his posture as straight as a man's half his age.

A young man dressed in a rumpled navy-blue suit had gotten out of the Cadillac parked at the curb. He moved in a slow shuffle, as if every joint in his body ached. He kept his gaze averted from Laveaux, opening the passenger door in the solicitous manner of a slave serving a cruel master.

Dr. Laveaux took one last look in Len's direction, and flashed his reptilian smile. He ducked into the car. His driver shut the door and returned to the other side of the vehicle, walking as carefully as he had before.

The Cadillac started with a rumble and a belch of black fumes. It grumbled away down the street and vanished from sight.

Finally, Len exhaled. His chest still burned from where Laveaux had poked him with that freakishly long finger.

And he kept thinking: *what the hell have we gotten ourselves into?*

3

Len closed the door, engaged the deadbolt lock.

Silence had fallen like a heavy veil over the house. Kennedy must have finally calmed down. He didn't hear her crying.

He needed to tell Olivia everything that had happened, and check on the baby, but decided to grab a drink of cool water first. His mouth was dry, his heart still knocking.

The floor creaked under his feet as he walked down the main hallway toward the kitchen. He hated those noises; they reminded him of the property's old age. He preferred new things. He was the first in line when the new iPhone came out, leased a new vehicle every two years, pre-ordered new video games and DVDs months before their release.

But Olivia loved her antiques. She had pushed them to purchase this house, when frankly, Len had been more interested in buying new construction. He hadn't put up much of a fight. Like most husbands who desired a peaceful household, he believed it was his duty to give his wife what she wanted. Happy wife, happy home, as the saying went.

In spite of his preference for contemporary design, he had to admit the Victorian was impressive, inside and out. It had those soaring vaulted ceilings, wainscoting, and crown molding throughout many of the rooms. Heart pine hardwood floors. Those long, double-hung windows. Considering all of the classic features the home offered, he could understand why Olivia had fallen in love with the place—and why Laveaux wanted it back.

If they allowed the old man to kick them out, it would crush her.

He entered the kitchen. From Len's understanding, it was a larger room than was typical in a Victorian—a good thing, because Olivia had a million things to cram in there. They'd brought in all of their ultra-modern, stainless steel appliances. The refrigerator chugged away on the other side of the room, next to the door that led to the basement.

That door, to Len's surprise, hung wide open.

He approached the doorway. He didn't recall leaving this door ajar, though he supposed it was possible that Olivia had ventured into the cellar that morning. The huge basement was entirely unfinished—a bit like a dungeon, actually, and accessed via a steep, narrow staircase.

His long-term plan was to renovate the basement into the ultimate man cave. He envisioned a huge media room, billiards table, workout area, and mini-bar. But that expensive project would take years to complete. In the meantime, they needed to keep the door shut. Those stairs were treacherous, and with a toddler running around, they couldn't take any chances.

He closed the door, locked it with the security chain. He found it odd that the chain was included on the cellar door—as if it were intended to keep something contained downstairs—but for his purposes, it came in useful.

He grabbed an empty Dixie cup from a stack of them on the counter, filled it with cold water from the refrigerator's dispenser, and took a long, satisfying gulp. Then, he headed upstairs.

The house had a sweeping spiral staircase, the balustrade fashioned of rich oak. As he ascended, the steps groaned under his weight. A cat burglar would have no chance of creeping undetected on those old stairs.

Several doors opened off the wide second floor hallway. The first room, on the left, was going to serve as his home office. He went inside.

It was a spacious room, sunlight filtering inside through the two windows. Several unpacked boxes stood within, along with his desk, bookcase, and a floor lamp.

At some point that day, he needed to root through those boxes and finish up in here, or else Olivia was going to nag him about it.

He withdrew his old college party photo from his back pocket. April's perfectly preserved smile beamed back at him. Such a damned shame what had happened to her—and whenever he allowed himself to dwell on those old memories, guilt inevitably surfaced, like heartburn.

Shaking his head, he opened the bottom desk drawer and dumped the photo inside.

He entered Kennedy's bedroom. The shadowy room was larger than his office, but fully unpacked. Olivia sat in the glider in the corner, gently rocking as she clasped Kennedy to her bosom. Still dressed in her pajamas, Kennedy clung to her mother. She was tall for a three-year-old, her long legs dangling over the armrest.

A couple of months ago, they had transitioned Kennedy from her crib to a full-size, "big girl" bed as they called it. The bed was positioned against a far wall, a wooden railing on the opposite side protecting Kennedy from rolling out. She was a wild sleeper.

"Hey." Olivia looked up. "Who was at the door? I heard you talking to someone but didn't catch the words."

"Long story," Len said. Leaning against the bed's railing, he ran his fingers through his daughter's thick, curly hair. "Is she okay now? How you feeling, pumpkin?"

"Okay," Kennedy said, and grinned. Everyone said their daughter looked like a young, female version of him, and while Len admitted to a strong resemblance, he could see characteristics of Olivia in her, too. In his mind, their child was the perfect blend of the best of them, inside and out.

"She had a nightmare, from what I can figure." Olivia shrugged. "She was so upset that she was still screaming after she woke up."

"Monter," Kennedy said, her brown eyes widening.

"Monster?" Len had to keep himself from smiling at how his child mispronounced the word. "There are no monsters in here, honey."

"That's what I keep telling her," Olivia said. "You need to stop letting her watch you play your crazy video games. That's where she gets these ideas from, in my opinion."

Grumbling, Len turned away. The bedroom had two windows: one overlooked the street; the other was above the detached two-car garage on the right side of the house. The blinds had been drawn on both. He pulled the cords to open them, letting sunlight flood into the room.

"See?" Len said. "It's bright and safe in here, honey. No monsters."

"Okay." Kennedy sat up in her mother's lap, looked around. "Monters all gone?"

"All gone," Len said.

"So back to the visitor," Olivia said. "Was it a neighbor?"

"Not exactly." Len pushed up his glasses, blew out a heavy sigh. "Unfortunately, we've got a major problem."

He told her what happened. With every sentence, Olivia grew more agitated. She set Kennedy down, rose from the chair, and paced the floor, fists bunched on her hips.

"I don't believe this," she said in a low voice taut with anger. "He thinks he can force us to move out by threatening us?"

"He gave us three days," Len said.

"And then what happens? He's going to call the police? What's he going to do?"

In his mind's eye, Len imagined Dr. Laveaux kicking in the door, stomping inside, grabbing both him and Olivia by the scruffs of their necks with his gigantic hands, and tossing them onto the street as if they were little more than rag dolls.

"I have no idea what he intends to do when we're still here after his deadline," Len said. "But my gut tells me that he's not the type of guy to run to the cops."

"He doesn't have any legal recourse whatsoever. Everything about our purchase of this house was legitimate. There was nothing underhanded about it."

Freed from her mother's arms, Kennedy attempted to dart out of the room. Len caught her by the sleeve of her pajamas. Kennedy tugged to escape, giggling at the simple game.

"The old guy lost his house, fair and square," Len said. "It sucks, but it's not our fault."

"It took a lot of nerve for him to show up banging on the door, too," Olivia said. Her eyes narrowed. "I don't like that at all. That was far out of bounds."

Len lifted Kennedy off the floor and shuttled her through the air in a great, sweeping arc. She screamed, a cry of pure joy.

"Can we double check our paperwork on the house?" Len asked.

"Don't you think I did that before?" Olivia glared at him. "Don't you think I *thoroughly* researched everything about the sale of this house before we signed those contracts?"

"I'm just saying, Liv. In light of this new development, another review might not hurt."

"Shit." Olivia folded her slender arms over her chest. "I wish I'd talked to Laveaux. I would have set him straight."

Len didn't take offense at her implication that he didn't handle the encounter properly. A working marriage required that each partner utilize their strengths for the benefit of the entire family. Olivia was the one who led the confrontational conversations, because she was relentlessly rational, able to keep a laser-minded focus on facts, and didn't fold under pressure. Len tended to step in when a softer touch was needed, or when they needed a creative approach to solving a problem. The unofficial arrangement usually worked out fine.

"I didn't really know what to say to him," Len said. "But I made sure I told him that we aren't moving out."

"*Out*," Kennedy said, mimicking him as he set her back on the floor. She attempted to flee the room again, but Olivia beat her to the doorway, and shut the door. Kennedy reached up on her tiptoes and grasped the bottom half of the doorknob. She tried to turn it, but was still too short and lacked the dexterity to twist it all the way around.

"Go out," she said, and looked from Olivia to Len, expectantly.

"You can't run around the house, sweetie," Olivia said. "We have too many things left to unpack. You might get hurt."

Kennedy whined and continued to test the doorknob. She was a strong-willed child and would soon succeed in turning those knobs all the way. Len made a quick mental note to pick up some child-proofing covers to foil her attempts.

He turned back to Olivia. "So what if his lender did something shady, and he lost his house because of it? I mean, that sort of thing has happened. I'm no fan of this guy, but he was seriously pissed, said *the people* took his house."

"I don't know," Olivia said. Her shoulders slumped; it looked as if her anger had drained out of her, to be replaced by worry. "I've got to dig through everything again, for starters, see what I can find. We can't lose this house, baby, not after it took us so long to get in here in the first place."

Len didn't need to be reminded of all the headaches they'd suffered in order to close the deal on the property and move in. Fighting through a bidding war that had dragged on for two nerve-wracking weeks. Losing their financing with the first lender, due to a silly error on Olivia's credit report. A home inspection that had revealed several alarming issues that they'd needed to resolve before they could move in.

And after all of that, the final straw: the former owner was demanding they move out.

On impulse, Len pulled Olivia into an embrace. Both of them had been so busy lately, it was the first time they'd shared such physical contact in days. His wife's body molded to his, and the familiar feel of her, firm and soft in all the right places, made his heart pound.

But her muscles were tense, her spine rigid under his fingers. It was going to take a lot more than a hug to set her mind at ease.

"We aren't going to lose the house," he whispered in her ear. "Trust me. We aren't going anywhere."

"I hope you're right."

4

While Len took Kennedy downstairs to feed her breakfast, Olivia went searching for their records on the property.

She kept all of their documentation—for the house and everything else—in a file cabinet in her home office. She crossed the hallway and entered the room, flipped on the light switch.

Her office was slightly larger than Len's—and currently, much better organized. She'd unpacked all of the boxes yesterday. The desk, floor lamps, lounge chair, filing cabinet, bookcase, photographs, and even her potted plants all occupied their proper places. The room had two long windows, the partially-open blinds letting in bands of golden sunlight.

It would have been an inspiring view, if she had not been so agitated.

She couldn't believe this Laveaux character had the *nerve* to show up at her door and demand they get out. Instead of unpacking and getting settled into their new home, she had to worry about a legal battle brewing on the horizon.

The lateral file cabinet stood adjacent to the desk, the elegant, two-drawer cabinet finished in dark cherry wood, matching the other pieces of office furniture. A framed photo of her baby brother, Michael, stood atop it, next to a wireless printer.

Olivia knelt and pulled out the bottom drawer.

She thumbed through the typed labels affixed to each folder. She found the legal-size folder for the property exactly where she expected.

She lifted the thick bundle of documents out of the drawer. She eased into a sitting position on the cool hardwood floor, folded her legs, and placed the records on her lap. Before she headed downstairs, she wanted to confirm all of the paperwork was in place.

She flipped open the flap and scanned the collected docs. Reviewing the papers was the equivalent of studying a timeline of every step in the lengthy transaction. She'd printed out the seller's listing for the Victorian. Their pre-approval authorization from their lender. Copies of their bids. The good faith estimate. The purchase agreement. The home inspector's report. A termite inspection report. The appraisal. The invoices from the contractors who had to perform repairs before they could move in. Proof of title search and insurance, and proof of homeowner's insurance. A copy of the certified check they'd used to pay the closing costs, the HUD-1 settlement statement, the mortgage note, the deed of trust . . . every piece of paper she expected to find was included, and she felt a flush of pride at her organizational skills.

In that respect, she'd been totally unlike her brother, Michael.

Sighing, she plucked the old photo off the file cabinet. It was a shot of Michael in his Marine dress blues. He looked handsome, dignified, and in control of his life. It was the way she preferred to remember him.

But at that time of year, it was hard to avoid dwelling on the truth.

Michael had died on April fifteenth; tomorrow was the tenth anniversary of his untimely death. While she had been filing taxes, her brother had been overdosing on heroin in a shithole apartment in College Park that he shared with his equally drugged out girlfriend, choking to death on his own vomit after he passed out.

Her stomach clenched.

She still felt responsible for what had happened to him, though no one blamed her. After he'd been dishonorably discharged from the Marine Corps for drug use, she could have done more to help him get his life back on track. She'd been so focused on getting through law school and establishing herself as an attorney, that she had left him behind to flail away on his own, and in the deepest pieces of her heart, she believed she could have done *something* that would have kept him alive.

A floorboard creaked in the hallway. She turned. Beyond the door, she saw only formless shadows.

"Babe?" she asked. "Is that you?"

No reply. But she heard another creak. The noise seemed to have weight behind it; a foot applying pressure against a floorboard.

She replaced the photo on the cabinet, slid the folder off her lap, and walked to the doorway.

She heard Kennedy downstairs, yelling incoherently and banging what sounded like a utensil against the table, while Len spoke to her in a calm tone about being patient. She smiled to herself. *Good luck with that, babe.*

But she was alone upstairs. The long, shadowed hallway was empty.

It had absolutely sounded as if someone had been creeping along the corridor. But that was a foolish thought.

What she'd heard, she concluded, were undoubtedly the natural settling noises of the old home. She hadn't lived in a place this old since she'd been a child, when her family had moved from a cramped Harlem apartment to a rambling Victorian in Decatur. That ancient house had used to sigh and groan as if it were a living creature, but it held a fond place in her memory. It was the last time in her life that all of her family had been together, and happy.

In some idealistic way, perhaps she hoped that moving her family to this old Victorian would ensure their happiness, too.

But first, she'd have to make sure they could keep hold of the place.

She went back to her office, grabbed the folder, and headed downstairs.

5

Olivia entered the kitchen as Len was attempting, without much success, to prevent Kennedy from dribbling milk all over the floor. Gripping the plastic Dora the Explorer cup in both hands, Kennedy swung around in her high chair, spraying droplets of milk with each wild revolution and giggling with malicious pleasure. Len knew he should take away the drink, but also knew that doing so would trigger a temper tantrum. After the screaming she'd already done that morning, he wanted to give his eardrums a respite. As a parent, you had to choose your battles.

"Join the party, Liv," Len said. He got up, grabbed a roll of paper towels off the counter. "Looks like you found the house records?"

"Of course." Olivia placed a long folder on the round dinette table and sat in a chair opposite Kennedy. "I did a quick review to confirm everything was here. I want to take a closer look to see if anything stands out, though I highly doubt it will."

As Olivia began to thumb through documents, Len mopped the milk off the tiles around Kennedy's chair, and tossed the wet towels into the trash can. He picked up the bowl of banana slices off the counter. Kennedy clapped when he placed the fruit in front of her, the milk promptly forgotten for the moment. Strategic distraction, another parenting trick he'd acquired.

With Kennedy safely preoccupied, he went behind Olivia and scanned the paperwork from over her shoulder.

He must have been in a horn dog mood, because almost immediately, his attention flitted from the tedious legal documents to his wife's cleavage. Her scoop-necked tank top gave him a tantalizing glimpse. His groin tightened.

37

Back in their dating days and the early years of their marriage, it had been nothing for them to satisfy a surge of lust with a quickie. Olivia had been just as likely to initiate sex as he'd been, had been downright insatiable on some days. But those carefree times were gone—understandably so, with a three-year-old romping around the house. They planned their sex in advance, as if it was merely another item on a weekly To Do list, and lately, that section of the list had been noticeably blank. The ordeal of buying and moving into this place had consumed any of the time and energy that Olivia might have held in reserve for him. That was what she said to him, anyway.

He settled for placing his fingers on her bare shoulders. He massaged the flesh gently, and bent to kiss the nape of her neck.

"Knock it off." Without looking back, she brushed his hands away as if batting aside a bothersome fly. "I need to focus on this. So do you."

His face burned. "Damn, it's not as if I ripped your shirt off, Liv. Relax."

"Relax?" She swung around in the chair to face him. "Are we going to review the records, or are you going to start foreplay? You were the one who asked me to pull out the paperwork."

He expelled a breath between clenched teeth. "You're right. My bad. I was thinking with the wrong head. Let's review the papers."

Olivia rolled her eyes, but turned back around. Gripping the back of her chair, he forced his attention to stay focused on the long sheets of paper crammed with legal jargon. It was a lot of official-looking documentation that seemed as if it would withstand a legal challenge in court, but what did he know?

"I'm going to call Kim," Olivia said. She turned another of the stapled pages. "I'd like to get her perspective. All of this paperwork is looking fine to me, as I knew it would. We need more background."

Kim Spalding was the realtor who had helped them discover the home. Her assistance had been invaluable in scooping up the Victorian.

Len crossed the kitchen and poured himself a fresh mug of coffee from the coffee machine. Kennedy had gobbled up most of her banana slices and was squishing the remaining fruit between her fingers, a sure sign that she was done eating.

"When are you going to call her?" he asked.

38

"This morning. I'm not putting this off."

He nodded. "We've got three days, according to Dr. Laveaux. Day one is today. That means our deadline is Tuesday."

"Why are you concerned about his deadline?" Olivia frowned. "You described him as a blind old man. He sounds as if he would be harmless, maybe more of a pain in the ass than anything else."

In his earlier retelling of the encounter with the old doctor, Len had left out the weirdest parts, such as Laveaux making those bizarre gestures in the air and muttering his unintelligible incantations. He didn't really know how to describe it, and none of it seemed relevant to their real issue of needing to confirm that their claim on the property would hold up in a court of law.

Len shrugged. "He was . . . strange. You would've had to meet him yourself to know what I'm talking about. Anyway, I want to help out here. What can I do?"

"We're definitely low on milk. Can you also check how much yogurt we've got, too? Last time I looked, I thought we had only a couple of cups, and you know Kennedy will work through those by tomorrow."

That's not what I meant when I offered to help, he thought. *I can do more than run errands to fetch food for our kid.*

But he kept his mouth shut, and opened the refrigerator. Of course, Olivia was right. A trip to the grocery store was in order.

"I'll take care of it," he said. "Make a list of anything else we need."

6

Grocery list stored on his iPhone, Len pulled on his Georgia Tech baseball cap, and stepped outdoors onto the front porch.

The morning was sunny, the temperature in the mid-seventies, and the sky free of clouds. A cool breeze whispered through the city, carrying the fragrance of flowers in bloom. He loved spring time in Atlanta, and much preferred this season to the blistering summers.

He descended the veranda steps. The short staircase ended at a flagstone path that led to the long driveway. A detached two-car garage stood at the end of the drive. The garage was not original to the house, had been built about forty years ago, but the deep blue shingles and white accents perfectly matched the Victorian's exterior.

Len had parked his silver Lincoln Navigator outside, while he used the garage to store various items (all stuff that belonged to him) for which they'd not yet found a place in the house. Of course, Olivia, Queen of Organization, was displeased. She worried it would become a glorified storage facility instead of a place for parking their vehicles, and was pressing him to clear out everything by the end of the day. Item one thousand and one on his endless To Do list.

He noted with a sour smile that his truck was coated in pine tree pollen. The yellow powder was an unfortunate complement to spring time in the South. He would need to set aside some time that day to rinse off the vehicle.

Before heading to the supermarket, he strolled to the sidewalk. He hadn't formally met any of their neighbors, though a handful of them had waved at him in passing over the past couple of days. It was time to go out and meet someone.

Ideally, he wanted to talk to someone who could tell him about Dr. Laveaux. For all he and Olivia knew about the guy, Laveaux had escaped from a psychiatric hospital, his threats backed up by no credibility whatsoever.

Their property was located on Page Avenue. Old Craftsman and Victorians lined the block, the houses framed by elms, maples, and magnolias. Many of the homes were under renovation, with building permit signs posted near the front doors and large Dumpsters full of construction debris standing at the curb. In-town properties in historic Atlanta neighbor-hoods were in high demand, with affluent professionals moving in and driving up property values, but Len wondered what happened to the original residents who couldn't keep pace with the rising tax rates.

A few doors down, a shirtless guy with a hairy chest washed a vintage Mustang in his driveway. A young blonde-haired woman jogged past on the opposite side of the street, a Golden Retriever padding along at her side. She smiled and waved, and he returned the greeting.

The house to the left was a Craftsman with a crepe myrtle growing near the front porch. Kudzu ran rampant across the front, too, vines entwined throughout the wooden porch railing. Len glimpsed someone in the shadows of the covered porch: a man with a long white beard who appeared to be reclining in a wheelchair.

The guy was looking at him.

Len waved. "Good morning!"

His neighbor wheeled back inside his house without so much as a grunt in reply. The door banged shut behind him.

Nice guy, Len thought. *I don't think he and I will be tossing back beers on the patio anytime soon.*

He looked around at the other homes. He was reluctant to approach a stranger's residence and knock on the door. But he thought he heard the bass line of a familiar song drifting through the open front windows of the bungalow directly across the street: "That's the Way of the World," by Earth, Wind & Fire.

Well, anyone with such good taste in old school music had to be friendly.

He crossed the road. The house was well-maintained, the grass and shrubs neatly trimmed. It had a carport, not a garage. Two vehicles were parked underneath: a black Chrysler 300 with tinted windows, and a cherry-red Mercedes convertible with a vanity plate that read DYMPIEC.

As Len started along the cobblestone path to the entrance, the door swung open.

A bald-headed bear of a black man emerged. He had a frost-colored goatee that probably put his age in his late fifties or early sixties. He wore paint-stained overalls, a plaid shirt, and work boots. His wire rim glasses glinted in the sunshine.

I'll be damned, Len thought. *He looks like Bishop T.D. Jakes.*

Len paused on the walkway, concerned he had picked the wrong time for a neighborly introduction. But the man came forward and flashed a broad grin that revealed a sizable gap in his front teeth.

"There he is!" the man said. He had a booming voice that undoubtedly carried down the entire block. "I was telling myself, if that young man doesn't come over here and talk to me this morning, I was gonna walk over there myself to greet him, yes sir."

He offered an enormous mitt of a hand that swallowed Len's grasp whole, and shook vigorously.

"Nice to meet you," Len said. "I'm Len Bowden."

"Jacob Parks," he said. "Been up doing some painting in the kitchen this morning. Work on an old house is never done, if you know what I'm saying. I've been living here for almost twenty-five years and I still haven't run out of things to do, yes sir."

"I heard that." Len hooked his thumb behind him. "We're still getting settled in over there. We haven't had a chance to meet any of our neighbors yet."

"Aww, man, you'll get around to that." Jacob took a handkerchief from his pocket and wiped a rivulet of perspiration off his shining dome. "This is a great neighborhood, most everyone's friendly and takes good care of their property. You couldn't have picked a better place to raise your family. How many kids you got?"

"My wife and I have a three-year-old daughter. Trust me, she's more than enough for now."

"I hear ya, brother, I hear ya. I got three sons, they're all grown and spread across the country." He laughed. "Shoot, those boys 'bout to drove me and Nettie crazy back in the day."

"Nettie's your wife?"

"Yes," Jacob said with a slow nod. In a soft, reverent tone, he added: "She passed three years ago. Cancer took her."

"I'm sorry," Len said.

"Hey, every day we breathe is a blessing, am I right?" Jacob grinned. "Cycle of life, yes sir, cycle of life. Gotta make the most of every moment. What kind of work you do?"

"I design video games," Len said.

"Is that so?" Jacob gazed at him as if seeing Len through fresh eyes. "That's not something you hear every day. I'm not gonna stand here and pretend that I've ever played anything like that, but my grandkids do. Big business, huh?"

"It's a nice industry to work in," Len said. "How about you?"

"Architecture," Jacob said. "I work out of my home. I've also taught part-time at Tech for many, many years." He nodded at Len's hat. "You're alumni?"

"Yep. I didn't take any architecture classes, though."

"Nah, you're a techie," Jacob said. "The design and history of properties has always been an abiding interest of mine. In fact, your Victorian is the oldest home on the block. Did you know that, man?"

It was a perfect segue into the topic that Len had most wanted to explore.

"I had no idea," Len said. "How well did you know the former owner of our house, Dr. Laveaux? He stopped by this morning for a . . . chat, I guess you'd call it."

Jacob's demeanor shifted: he looked both ways along the road, as if worried someone was watching, and when he spoke, it was at a lower volume, almost a whisper.

"I didn't know him well, no, not well at all," Jacob said. "The gentleman minded his own business, I respected that."

Len nodded, unsure how to interpret Jacob's abrupt mood change. He had a lot of questions he wanted to ask about Dr. Laveaux. But Jacob, who had been as loquacious as a talk show host only a minute ago, seemed visibly uncomfortable with the topic of his former neighbor.

"The property was in foreclosure," Len said. "There's always a story behind that sort of thing. Laveaux gave me his side, but I suspect there's more to it. Know what I mean?"

"Sure, sure." Jacob used his handkerchief to swipe another bead of sweat from his forehead. "The gentleman traveled abroad quite often, I believe. I don't know what happened with his home, I didn't ask. Like I said, he minded his own business, and I didn't meddle."

"Was he good friends with any of the neighbors?"

"No, no, no, absolutely not." Jacob's eyebrows gathered into a deep frown. "Was that unusual here? Sure it was, sure. But not

43

everyone wants to be your friend. He lived over there, he kept to himself, we kept our distance, and that was that."

"Was there ever any trouble going on over there?" Len asked.

"No," Jacob said, in a tone of finality.

Instinct told Len that Jacob was being evasive. But he wasn't going to push it. Jacob seemed like a decent guy, someone who might become a trusted neighbor and perhaps even a good friend. Maybe later, he could coax the guy into sharing more information.

"Anyway," Len said with a shrug, "we love the house. We're looking forward to staying here for a long time. We'll need to live here for at least thirty years to finish the list of renovations my wife has in mind."

"Indeed." Jacob laughed heartily, once again the jolly giant of a man who had first greeted Len.

A gorgeous young woman appeared in the doorway of Jacob's house. She wore a green tank top that exposed her taut midriff, and blue jeans so tight they looked shrink-wrapped on her long, slender legs.

Len did a double-take. The woman was at least thirty years younger than Jacob. Brushing a strand of long hair away from her eyes, she stuck out her bottom lip in the pout of a spoiled teenager used to always getting her way.

"Boo, when you coming back inside?" she said in a throaty voice that sounded fake, an affectation she might have learned from watching too many porno flicks. "You got me working in here all by myself."

"I'm meeting my new neighbor, sweetheart," Jacob said. "Come say hello."

The girl sashayed across the porch as if strutting down a runway. Jacob glanced at Len, and winked.

As she approached, Len noticed she wasn't wearing a bra. Her nipples strained at the fabric of her tank top. He saw a tattoo of a red butterfly on one of her large breasts.

Len was convinced he had recently seen this girl pole dancing in a hip-hop video on YouTube, to the song of some Atlanta rapper whose name escaped him. She had that video vixen look about her: an almost cartoonishly shapely body, lots of makeup, a weave that probably cost more than their monthly mortgage.

How the heck had Jacob managed to land a woman like her? Old head must've been a playa from the Himalayas, as they used to say.

"Hey, new neighbor," she said to Len. "I'm Simone."

"Nice to meet you, I'm Len."

But she had already turned away from Len and had grasped Jacob's hand. She pulled him toward the door. Len was reminded of when Kennedy tugged on his fingers to try to convince him to do something.

"Duty calls," Jacob said, allowing the woman to lead him away. "Sometime soon, I'd like to drop by and meet your wife and daughter so we can all get acquainted."

"Come by later this afternoon," Len said. "We'll be around."

"I'll do that," Jacob said.

Len crossed the street, heading toward his truck.

He noticed his next door neighbor, Mr. Friendly in the wheelchair, watching him from his front porch again. Watching him intently. But not waving, and not speaking.

7

Alone with their daughter, Olivia continued her work on defending their ownership of the home.

She brought Kennedy into their temporary safe zone: a cleared out section of the family room, complete with flat-screen TV, coffee table, a sofa and chair, and some of Kennedy's favorite toys, the space separated from the rest of the house by a child-safety gate. After popping in a DVD of *Happy Feet,* an animated film Kennedy loved, Olivia settled onto the upholstered chair with her iPad.

She preferred to limit the amount of time her daughter spent watching TV. Typically she liked to fill Kennedy's weekends with enriching activities outside of the house. But that day had brought an unusual challenge, and she needed to focus. She promised herself they would take Kennedy to the park sometime that afternoon.

So far, she had already left a voice mail message for Kim, their realtor. In her message, she described the basic details of the situation and asked Kim to return her call as soon as possible. She was anxious to get Kim's suggestions on next steps.

While Kennedy danced and sang with the cartoon penguins, Olivia poked around online, aiming to dig up information on actions to take if a foreclosure sale was challenged. From her prior research, before they'd bought the Victorian, she'd already learned that foreclosure laws varied by state—and that Georgia had some of the most unforgiving foreclosure guidelines in the entire country. Georgia had a non-judicial system, whereby lenders could foreclose on a property without court approval. Commonly, the time from notice of default to a house being sold was only ninety days. In other states, such as New York, where a judicial process was required, it could take well over a year before a delinquent owner was evicted.

Not surprisingly, foreclosure fraud was high in Georgia. There was easy money to be made if an unscrupulous lender or real estate pro knew how to work the system.

But Olivia was unsure how the laws would affect her own situation. She was an employment attorney, and spent her days litigating sexual discrimination lawsuits and the like. Beyond a couple of classes she'd taken in college a decade ago and her prep for the bar exam, she understood little of the intricacies of real estate law.

After about twenty minutes of mostly fruitless research, she set aside the tablet. She needed to take a break.

Outside of the gated area, the unpacked boxes beckoned.

A cynical part of her was reluctant to continue with moving into the house. What if they really did have to vacate the property? Then they'd need to pack all over again. Why waste her time?

But she entertained those doubts for only a few seconds. Unpacking would be a step of faith toward their future here. She pushed off the chair, opened the gate's child-proof latch, and stepped outside of the area.

Kennedy barely noticed that she'd left. She was enraptured by the movie.

A couple of large, unopened boxes lay outside the gate. Both were designated for the family room. She couldn't remember what they'd placed in them, but guessed they contained pictures, table lamps, and other furnishings intended to turn the house into a home.

As she knelt to pull open the flaps of the nearest box, she heard, very clearly, a door slam shut upstairs.

She straightened. Cocked her head. Listened.

She didn't hear anything else. The music issuing from the television drowned out most of the ambient noise.

But she was certain she'd heard a door close—and Len hadn't returned home yet.

She glanced at Kennedy. Her daughter sat Indian-style on the area rug, her attention totally riveted on the TV screen.

I'll go upstairs for just a minute and see whether I'm imagining things or not.

Olivia padded out of the room and entered the hallway. She approached the bottom of the spiral staircase, looked up to the second floor.

The upper level was thick with shadows, and silence.

Every riser creaked under her footsteps as she ascended the steps. When she reached the top and looked along the hallway, she saw the door to Kennedy's bedroom was shut. All of the other doors stood open.

Lips pressed into a firm line, she opened the bedroom door.

Both windows were wide open. A cool breeze stirred the cords of the venetian blinds, plastic knobs batting against the walls.

I know damn well I didn't open the windows in here. Or did I?

She couldn't remember. Since Len had told her about this Laveaux character, her morning had been a blur.

If she hadn't opened the windows, perhaps Len had. He'd complained on more than one occasion that the house smelled old. He liked to let in fresh air.

She closed both windows. She tried to lock them, too, but the old latches were stuck.

Add new window locks for Kennedy's room to the list of home improvements.

Outside the room, she heard another door slam.

She whirled and went into the hallway.

Before, the door to her office had been open. It was closed now.

What the . . .

Quickly, she crossed the hallway, twisted the knob, and shoved the door open. No one was inside her office, of course, and the windows were shut, as they should have been.

Drafts, she thought. *This house is drafty and could use new insulation, like most older homes.*

As she stood on the office threshold, a patch of cold air slipped by her. It brought goose bumps to her flesh. She rubbed her hands against her forearms, but found her palms were clammy, too.

She told herself that she'd better get back downstairs. Kennedy had been placed in the safe zone, but she thought it unwise to leave her child unattended for more than a minute or so, even in their own home. Call her a helicopter parent.

Casting one last glance around the hallway, feeling vaguely uneasy, she returned to the staircase and hurried down the steps.

8

Around noon, they took a family outing to Candler Park.

Going to the park was Olivia's suggestion, but Len readily agreed. Kennedy hadn't done anything outside of the house all weekend and was going stir-crazy. A romp outdoors would burn off some of her pent-up energy and ensure she took a nice nap later in the afternoon.

The park that shared the name of their neighborhood was only two blocks away from their new residence. They buckled Kennedy in her canopied stroller, and the three of them ambled along the sidewalk, Len pushing the stroller and Olivia beside him, both of them greeting neighbors they encountered on the way.

Len noted that their next-door neighbor, the guy in the wheelchair, had vacated his porch and was nowhere to be seen. Not that he would have said anything to them anyway. Mr. Bizzaro.

Earlier, Len had told Olivia about his chat with Jacob. She agreed that Jacob probably knew more about Laveaux than he was willing to admit, that it would be in their best interests to probe deeper when they got the opportunity.

On the other front, their realtor, Kim, had yet to respond to Olivia's message. Olivia promised to call her again later that day if she didn't hear back soon.

Candler Park spanned dozens of acres, and included a golf course, swimming pool, fields for playing soccer and football, basketball and tennis courts, a paved walking path, and most importantly to them, a playground. It was a well-equipped one, too, with a separate group of slides, swings, and monkey bars for older kids, and little ones. Leafy elms, maples, and magnolia trees provided shade at strategic spots, metal benches sitting in the cool shadows.

Kennedy squealed with excitement as they drew closer and she saw other children clambering on the play equipment. She tried to squirm out of the seat.

"All right, little girl, give us a second," Len said.

"I've got it," Olivia said.

She knelt and unsnapped Kennedy's seat belt. Kennedy bolted out of the stroller like a liberated prisoner and raced across the grass toward the playground, her afro puffs bouncing. Olivia had to pour on the speed to keep up with their daughter.

Len smiled to himself. He could remember when Kennedy successfully taking two steps without stumbling was a huge achievement. But these days, his little girl was sprinting like Jackie Joyner-Kersee.

He caught up to his family at the little kids' swing set. Olivia was getting Kennedy situated on the seat, while their daughter grasped the chain handles and swung her legs impatiently.

"Push, push!" Kennedy said. "Push, Mommy!"

"You're so impatient, kid," Olivia said. "Jeez."

"She takes after her mother," Len said.

Olivia rolled her eyes at him. She got behind Kennedy, drew her back, and gave her a good shove. Kennedy cried out with glee as she swung through the air.

Len's heart swelled with emotion. Seeing his daughter happy always pushed his buttons, and he could understood, on a level so deep it had to be pure human instinct, why a parent would do anything within their power to ensure their child's safety and happiness. That knowledge hadn't come to him until Kennedy had emerged into his world. Fatherhood had changed him, irrevocably.

He watched Olivia as she pushed Kennedy through each arc. Marriage had changed him, too, but he wasn't convinced that all of the changes were positive. Olivia had slipped on a pink halter top, white capris, and sneakers, and she wore only light make-up. She looked like Spring personified, and his physical attraction to her never wavered.

But she was so damned moody. And she nagged him to death when she wanted something—and often ignored him otherwise. When he observed his married buddies, all of whom had been wed for as long as he had, or longer, he noticed similar behaviors.

He was becoming like his father. Hiding out in his man cave with his toys, interacting with his wife only when pressed to perform some onerous duty, a simmering tension running like an ocean current underneath all of their interactions, either of them ready to explode at the slightest provocation.

He wanted to do something about it, wanted to restore harmony to their marriage, but he didn't know *how* to do it.

Olivia tired of pushing after a few minutes, so Len switched places with her. A few minutes after that, Kennedy was ready to hop off and tackle the next challenge.

"All right, pumpkin." Len slowed the swing to a stop. "What do you want to do now?"

Kennedy leapt off the seat and raced forward, sandals slapping against gravel.

"Slow down!" Len said.

Kennedy ignored him. She darted around a thicket of trees and flowering shrubs, out of sight.

Sighing, Len glanced at Olivia. She was taking a sip from the water bottle they had packed in the stroller's rear compartment.

"Your turn to chase, Daddy," she said. "I'll catch up to you guys."

Len shrugged, and ran after his daughter. He loved her more than life itself, but sometimes, she frustrated the hell out of him.

He found Kennedy on the other side of the trees. She had slipped her thumb into her mouth and stood as still as if she'd been caught in suspended animation.

She was staring at a man who sat on the nearby bench.

It was Dr. Laveaux.

Len's heart felt as if it had crawled into his throat. What the hell was he doing here?

The old doctor sat alone, his bejeweled, phallic cane leaning against the bench. His lips were curved in a gentle smile, as if he were amused at some private joke.

At Len's approach, Laveaux shifted in his direction. His masked eyes gazed sightlessly.

"Dr. Laveaux is enjoying the fresh air at his favorite park." He pulled in a deep breath, nostrils flaring. "Hmm. Your child smells of sweetness and innocence. Like a flower, eh?"

Len grabbed Kennedy's arm and pulled her behind him. Kennedy offered no resistance; her eyes were dazed, but she sucked on her thumb eagerly. She did that when she was frightened.

Why was she afraid of this man? What had he done or said to her?

"Come on, sweetheart," Len said. "We don't speak to strangers."

"The precious little one is no stranger to Dr. Laveaux." He chuckled. "She lives in his house, sleeps in his rooms."

"What's going on here?" Olivia said, catching up to them.

"He's here," Len said, and motioned toward the doctor. "Laveaux."

Frowning, Olivia sized up the old man. Her jawline tightened.

Dr. Laveaux had turned in Olivia's direction, too. "Mmm. The daughter smells like her mother, yes, mostly. Sweetness, but there is a bitterness there, too, Dr. Laveaux knows. You have not lain with your husband in some time . . . while he gives off an odor like a dog in heat."

The old doctor laughed heartily. Len stared at him, amazed at the man's uncanny insight, but Olivia dug her fists into her waist.

"Listen, I heard about your visit to *my* house this morning," Olivia said in her lawyer tone, a crisp delivery that usually squashed all debate. "We're not moving out, mister. You have no legal footing. We *will* win this fight."

But Laveaux had shifted his attention back to Kennedy. Len picked up his daughter, and her limbs immediately wrapped around him tightly. She would not stop sucking on that thumb.

"Wanna go home . . ." Kennedy said, in a thin voice.

Laveaux rubbed his long, bony hands together. "Dr. Laveaux could use a child like her. She's perfect for the house, he thinks, most suitable."

Len didn't understand what Laveaux was talking about, but a chill gripped him.

"Let's get out of here," Len said. "Come on, Olivia."

But Olivia stepped forward, in full attack mode.

"If you continue this harassment, we're contacting the police," Olivia said. "You've been warned. Do you understand?"

Dr. Laveaux paused—and then he rose off the bench. As he unfolded to his full height, Len had to increase his estimate of this guy's size. He was probably six-foot-nine. The top of his hat brushed against the overhanging tree branches.

Laveaux grinned, displaying those huge, perfect teeth. It was a smile a shark might have favored you with before it ripped you apart.

"*Bel fanm pa di bon menaj,*" Laveaux said, and followed his comment with a snicker. "*Mache chèche pa janm dòmi san soupe.*"

Olivia took a couple of steps backward, as if Laveaux's words had hit her like a physical blow. The resolve had faded from her eyes. Some terrible realization seemed to have come to her.

"What is it?" Len whispered. "What did he say?"

"Go," she said in a faltering voice. She grabbed Len's arm, her fingers digging so deeply into his flesh that he winced. "We've got to go. *Now.*"

Without waiting on his response, she snatched Kennedy out of his arms. Kennedy went to her limply, without protest, her thumb buried in her mouth. Clasping their daughter to her chest, she hurried away across the grass.

Len located the baby stroller that Olivia had deserted behind them. He wheeled it after Olivia's rapidly retreating figure.

"*Ravèt pa janm gen rezon devan poul,*" Laveaux said behind them.

He was laughing.

9

"Now, can we please talk about what happened?" Len asked.

They had just put Kennedy down for her afternoon nap. Kennedy had snapped out of her strange, dazed state when they'd arrived back at the house, and with a healthy appetite, had eaten a lunch of fresh peaches, string cheese, and graham crackers. Whatever weirdness had occurred at the park had passed.

But all along, Olivia had refused to tell Len why she was so troubled by what Dr. Laveaux had said to her.

"I've got to pick up Mom," Olivia said. She closed the door to Kennedy's bedroom and walked to the stairs. "We're visiting my brother's grave today."

"Liv, we need to talk about what happened at the park." Len followed her to the staircase. "What did Laveaux say to you? Why were you so freaked out?"

"It doesn't matter." She shrugged. "It's over."

"What did he say? Something in Haitian Creole, right?"

"We aren't having this discussion."

"You're being ridiculous, you know that? This isn't like you at all."

"Drop it, Len." A warning flickered in her eyes.

Len slipped off his glasses and pinched the bridge of his nose. Hot blood had flushed his cheeks. He mentally counted to five.

"All right," he said. "I'll let this go—for now. But this is not over."

"I'll be back around four," she said. "Please pick up the phone if Kim calls."

She went downstairs. Watching her go, Len ground his teeth.

He didn't understand her behavior at all. But she could be as stubborn as the proverbial mule. He might never convince her to open up and disclose what had bothered her.

Maybe he needed to drop it, like she'd told him. But Dr. Laveaux's disturbing remarks about Kennedy kept circling in his thoughts.

Dr. Laveaux could use a child like her. She's perfect for the house, he thinks, most suitable.

What the heck had the old man been talking about? He could use her for what? For what purpose was she suitable?

Len couldn't imagine. But he didn't like the tone of those comments, and his daughter's response to encountering Laveaux worried him, too.

As far as he was concerned, the old man was never coming within a hundred feet of Kennedy, ever again. He was positive he and Olivia could agree on *that*.

He heard Olivia exit the house via the side door.

He was exhausted from all of the unpacking, but if he lay down for a nap, he'd wind up sleeping for a couple of hours and would feel groggy for the remainder of the day. It was as good a time as any to set up his gaming PC. A bit of leisurely game play would pull his thoughts away from what had occurred at the park.

He went downstairs and grabbed a beer. His current favorite was Georgia Brown, an unpasteurized ale from Sweetwater, a local Atlanta brewery. He slipped the cold bottle into his Georgia Tech drink koozie, and returned upstairs.

His gaming desktop computer and all of the accessories were stored in three of the large boxes standing in his office. He carefully unpacked each component and set it up on his desk. He'd invested an obscene amount of money in his customized "rig," as they were called, and handled each piece of the system as gently as if it were a newborn kitten.

About fifteen minutes later, he had the rig up and running. The high-performance processors hummed at a whisper, the premium speakers and sound card broadcast theater-quality audio, and the graphics card produced an eye-popping array of images on the large, flat screen display, at HD resolution levels.

Len eased into his swivel chair and nestled his beer between his legs. His fingers danced across the keyboard as loaded *Skyrim*, an older title that remained one of his guilty pleasures. It was an open world, fantasy role playing game in which you created a unique character and embarked on various adventures, slaying dragons, battling wizards and bandits, and plundering dungeons filled with treasures.

It was easy to lose track of time while engrossed in the detailed virtual world. He had no idea how long he'd been playing when he heard Kennedy scream.

10

Len bolted out of his chair, his beer bottle flipping out of his lap and landing on the floor. The koozie protected the bottle against breaking, and fortunately, he'd consumed all of the brew anyway.

He put the bottle on the edge of his desk and hurried out of his office. A glance at his watch revealed that Kennedy had been napping for about forty minutes. On weekends, she usually napped for at least an hour, often times longer.

He cracked open her bedroom door.

The room was steeped in shadows, the blinds drawn against the afternoon sun. He saw Kennedy cowering on one corner of her bed. She clutched her blanket. Her eyes were wide with fear as she stared at something across the room.

Len stepped inside. "What's wrong, sweetheart?"

"Monter," Kennedy said. She pointed. "Monter over there."

Not this again, Len thought, but he turned to the area she indicated. She was pointing at the closet.

Len noticed that the door hung partially open.

"In there?" he asked.

"Monter in there." Kennedy nodded. Her breath hitched in her throat.

"There are no monsters in here," he said. "I'll show you, and then you can go back to your nap. Okay?"

He approached the door. He closed his hand around the brass knob. He pulled it open, the hinges squeaking softly.

Have to oil those later, he thought. Creaking doors reminded him of the house's old age.

There was nothing in the closet, of course, except for

Kennedy's vast collection of clothes. She had a larger wardrobe than he did, and she was only three.

"See, pumpkin?" he said. "No monsters. Only your clothes."

"Saw the monter," Kennedy said.

"There was never a monster in here." He closed the door. "You had a bad dream. Okay?"

Kennedy shook her head. "No, saw monter."

She was as stubborn as her mother. He pushed up his glasses on the bridge of his nose, and approached the bed.

"Let's go back to nap time." He pulled her blanket out of her fingers. "Come on, lie back down, pumpkin."

"Monter gone?" she asked.

"Yes, it's gone. It's gone forever. You will never see a monster again. I promise."

Studying his face, Kennedy nodded slowly. She crawled out of the corner and lay across the mattress. He covered her with the blanket, and then bent over the railing and kissed her forehead.

She closed her eyes. He stepped quietly to the doorway, shut the door behind him.

He hoped they could soon put an end to this monster obsession of hers. But he reminded himself that it was common for young children to be convinced that bogeymen were real, to see shapes lurking in a closet that, in reality, were no more harmful than an ordinary pile of clothing. He remembered his own childhood fears of such things. He could easily dismiss them as an adult, but as a kid, he'd nearly pissed his pants on a few occasions.

Suddenly, he heard a crashing sound downstairs, as if a plate or glass had shattered against the floor.

What the hell is it now?

Frowning, he descended the staircase.

He discovered the source of the noise in the kitchen. A plate had shattered on the floor, near the dinette table.

And the basement door was wide open.

Had Olivia left a plate precariously balanced on the table— and forgotten to close the cellar door, too? Why would she have gone down there anyway?

Weird.

He didn't understand what had happened, but he swept up the broken shards, and closed the door, and locked it.

11

True to his word, Jacob dropped by later that afternoon. He arrived on their front porch cradling an expensive-looking bottle of red wine.

Len was glad to see him. Since Olivia had returned from visiting her brother's grave site earlier that day, she was even moodier than usual, though in that instance, Len could empathize with her. But they still were barely talking to each other.

"Hey, Jacob," Len said. "Thanks for dropping by. Come on in."

"I come bearing gifts," Jacob said. "Please accept with my compliments."

He offered Len the bottle. Len checked the label, whistled.

"Pinot noir, nice," Len said. "Appreciate it."

Smiling, Jacob entered. Before Len closed the door, he glanced across the street and noticed the red Mercedes that belonged to Jacob's girlfriend was gone.

"Where's your lady friend?" Len asked. "Simone, was it?"

"She left." Jacob grinned and rubbed his hands together. "But Keisha is coming over tonight, yes sir."

"Keisha?"

"I have several select young ladies in *heavy* rotation, if you know what I mean, brother," Jacob said.

"So it's like that, huh? I'm scared of you, man."

"I don't get a night off." Jacob winked. "I'm going through my Viagra prescriptions like nobody's business, yes sir. Last time I visited my doctor, he was so impressed, he wanted to know my secret."

"What *is* your secret?" Len asked, only half-joking.

"That's classified, brother." Jacob chuckled. "I'd tell you, but I'd have to kill you."

Kennedy raced into the hallway, undoubtedly curious about the new visitor with the booming voice. Olivia had taken down her Afro puffs that afternoon, letting their daughter's thick, long mane of hair go free in all its glory.

Predictably, Kennedy got shy when she came closer. Smiling, she took Len's hand and wrapped herself behind his leg.

"What an adorable little girl you've got," Jacob said.

"Kennedy, say hello to Mr. Parks," Len said.

"Hello, Mr. Parks," Kennedy said in a soft voice.

"Don't be fooled by her shy act," Len said. "She's wild as a banshee once she gets to know you."

"Hey there," Olivia said. She entered the corridor from the dining room, where she'd been sorting out items they'd unpacked. She offered Jacob a warm smile and shook his hand. "I'm Olivia. Len told me you might stop by."

"It's a pleasure to meet you," Jacob said. He looked around the house, eyes twinkling. "I've lived in this neighborhood for twenty-five years—but I've never seen the interior of this home. I'm truly impressed. It's in fine condition."

"Jacob's an architect," Len said to Olivia.

"I've also a deep interest in historic houses." Jacob raised his gaze to the chandelier that hung in the entry hall. "That crystal chandelier, for example, must be original to this home. And the stained glass in the transom above the front door is a wonderful example of period detail."

"It's nice to meet *someone* who appreciates an older place." Olivia gave Len a sharp look.

"Of course," Jacob said. "As I mentioned to Len earlier, this is the oldest property on the block. May I look around?"

"As you don't mind navigating an obstacle course," Olivia said. "We haven't finished unpacking."

"I'll mind where I step," Jacob said.

"While you guys do that, I'll go crack open this wine," Len said.

Len walked to the kitchen. Kennedy remained behind with Olivia and Jacob, listening to Jacob gush over the Victorian's authentic details as if she had any clue what he was talking about.

Len set the bottle on the counter and dug the rabbit wine opener out of the drawer. As he was preparing to fit the tool onto the cork, something buzzed past his ear.

He whirled around at the noise, the wine opener clattering onto the counter.

He didn't see the insect. It had sounded like a fly, and a large one, too. But it had vanished.

Then he felt a hot, stinging sensation on the side of his neck, near the edge of his collarbone.

Cursing, Len slapped his hand against his skin.

But he hit nothing. The enemy insect buzzed around his head. It was a fly for sure—it looked like a horse fly. A blood sucker. It must have slipped inside when he'd let Jacob in.

He searched the counters for something with which to swat it. He found a women's clothing catalogue that had arrived in yesterday's mail, rolled it up tightly, and revolved in a slow circle in the kitchen, listening and looking for his foe.

The damned fly had disappeared.

But the bite hurt like hell, and was already beginning to itch. He craned his neck, but couldn't get a good look at the damage. He left the kitchen and went into the powder room at the end of the hallway.

Standing in front of the mirror, he peeled away the collar of his t-shirt.

"Jesus," he said.

There was a red, quarter-sized welt forming on his skin. Was he having an allergic reaction to the bite? The damned things carried all kinds of diseases.

He grabbed a cotton towel off the nearby rack, dampened it with cold water, and pressed it against the wound. It felt better, but he'd need to apply some anti-itch ointment for true relief.

After another minute, he went back to the kitchen. The fly had traveled to parts unknown.

He poured three glasses of the pinot noir Jacob had brought, and glasses in hand, went to track down his wife and neighbor. He found them in the parlor. Jacob was remarking on the period details displayed in the spacious, high-ceilinged room. Olivia listened intently, while Kennedy had finally lost interest and had opened one of her talking story books on the coffee table.

"Watch out for a sonofabitch of a horse fly, guys," Len said.

He distributed the wine to Jacob and Olivia. "The sucker bit me good."

Len scratched the bite again. Olivia stepped closer to examine his neck, and her brows crinkled with concern.

"We've got some Benadryl cream in our bathroom upstairs," she said. "I'd apply some on that, dear."

"I definitely will," Len said. He turned to Jacob. "I wanted to ask you. The guy who lives next door to us, the bearded fellow in the wheelchair. Do you know him?"

"That's Bill Knox," Jacob said. "He's lived in that house for a long time, yes sir. Fifteen years, perhaps?"

"He doesn't seem very talkative," Len said. "Earlier today, I waved at him and said 'hi' and he ignored me."

"Don't take it personally, brother." Jacob shrugged. "Things changed for Bill after his accident. He's not the man he used to be, physically or psychologically."

"What happened to him?" Olivia asked.

"This was about five years ago. He was outdoors walking his dog. His dog saw some creature—a squirrel, or some such thing. The hound chased after it, running right across the road. Bill chased after his dog. But there was some teenage kid barreling down the street in a Ford F-150, and neither Bill nor the teenager saw each other, until it was too late."

"That's awful," Olivia said.

"He was fortunate to survive," Jacob said. "Blessed, truly. Although I doubt he feels that way about it."

"What do you mean?" Len asked.

"Bill and I used to chat with each other quite often, once or twice a week. Since the incident, he's become a bit of a recluse. He lost his job. His wife divorced him. He has an adult daughter who checks in on him a couple of days a week, but mostly, he keeps to himself."

"I won't bother him, then," Len said. "That's a sad story."

"Very much so, very much," Jacob said. He swirled the wine around the glass and took a small sip. "Hmm. This is good."

"You've never tried it before?" Len asked.

"I don't imbibe," Jacob said. He grinned. "The young lady I met at the package store recommended it."

"She has good taste, then," Olivia said.

"Indeed she does, in men, too." Jacob laughed. "She gave me her phone number."

"Oh?" Olivia's eyebrows arched.

"Jacob here is a bonafide lady killer," Len said. He patted Jacob's meaty shoulder. "I may have to study up on his moves."

"Is that right?" Olivia said.

"Only so I can use them with you, of course," Len said.

"Nice save, brother, nice save," Jacob said.

"One other thing I wanted to ask you, Jacob," Len said. "It's about Dr. Laveaux."

He noticed, immediately, that Olivia frowned; he figured she would not want to discuss Laveaux. He didn't care. The topic of Laveaux was the elephant in the room and he wasn't going to avoid it any longer.

"What about him?" Jacob said. The warmth had faded from his voice. His smile flickered, like a faulty light bulb.

"To your knowledge, has he always been blind?" Len asked.

"Blind? No, not always." Jacob shook his head, sipped the wine. "No, sir. He wasn't always blind."

"What happened?" Len asked. "Did he have an accident?"

"He might have had glaucoma," Olivia said. Len was surprised that she had any interest in the conversation.

"I don't know what happened, exactly," Jacob said. He looked around the room, as if worried about an eavesdropper, and his voice was a near whisper. "He traveled abroad quite frequently, as I mentioned to you before. After one of these trips, he returned home, and he was blind. I don't know what occurred. That was perhaps twelve years ago, I believe, yes, about twelve years ago. I remember because it was the same summer that my youngest son finally moved out, hallelujah."

"He could have gone to get eye surgery in another country," Olivia said. "That's fairly common. Medical procedures are prohibitively expensive here in the United States, especially if you don't have insurance. It could be a third of the cost somewhere else."

"He may be blind . . . but his senses are *keen*," Jacob said. He glanced around the room again, and then he hunched over, and beckoned Len and Olivia closer. Behind the lenses of his glasses, his eyes, normally full of mirth, were utterly serious.

In a tense whisper, Jacob said, "Take heed. This is all I can say. Do. Not. Underestimate. Him."

Len nodded, and was about to ask another follow-up question, but Jacob set his wine on an end table and clasped his hands together.

"I've had a nice time visiting," he said, in his regular megaphone tone. "I'll let you fine folks resume your afternoon. I've got to prepare to meet a lady friend later this evening."

And with that, Jacob walked to the door and let himself out.

12

Olivia was preparing dinner when their realtor, Kim Spalding, finally returned her call.

So much had happened since that morning that she'd almost forgotten she was expecting Kim's callback. She'd spent the afternoon refusing to think about the incident at the park with Dr. Laveaux, and avoiding conversation about it with Len, and instead, busied herself with other concerns. Such as visiting her brother's grave with Mom, always a saddening experience. Then coming back to the house and resuming the endless work that she needed to complete. Unpacking. Sorting. Arranging. Cleaning.

The unexpected visit from their neighbor, the charming Jacob Parks, had been going fine until the subject had turned to Laveaux. In spite of herself, Olivia had been interested in what Jacob had to say. She hadn't anticipated his guarded manner of speaking about the old blind man, as if afraid someone would overhear—and she sure hadn't expected his warning.

Do. Not. Underestimate. Him.

Predictably, after Jacob abruptly ended his visit, Len had wanted to talk to her about it. But talking about it further was exactly what she wanted to avoid. Len was frustrated with her, but she could live with that. He would get over it.

Trust me, you don't want to know, babe, she wished she could tell him. *You don't want me to blurt out what I'm afraid of and open that door. You don't want us to go there . . . 'cause that way lies madness.*

When Kim called her back, Olivia was still sipping wine from the bottle Jacob had brought, in between chopping up fresh

65

vegetables for dinner and listening to Maxwell's Urban Hang Suite album on her iPod, the music streaming through the pair of portable speakers she'd placed on the kitchen counter. Weekends were her time to cook, since during the work week, Len got home earlier than she did and either picked up take-out somewhere or whipped up a simple meal. As she prepped the ingredients, Len and Kennedy were in the now totally-unpacked family room, building fantastical structures with the set of Lego blocks she'd gotten for Christmas.

Olivia dropped the music's volume, slipped on the wireless headset, and answered the call on the third ring.

"Hey, Livia," Kim said, her South Georgia accent dripping like syrup through the phone. "Y'all done moving into that big, pretty house now?"

Every time Olivia talked to Kim on the phone, she found it easy to imagine the woman sitting on the veranda of an antebellum mansion like Tara from *Gone with the Wind*, wearing a fancy hat and sipping mint juleps. In actuality, Kim was a hard-working agent who spent her days crisscrossing metro Atlanta in a red Mustang convertible; Olivia heard the muted rumble of an engine in the background.

"We're getting there," Olivia said. "Unfortunately, we've run into a serious problem and I wanted to get your advice."

"Oh, Lord," Kim said. "I was hoping you had good news. What happened?"

"We had a visit from the former owner. Dr. Laveaux. He lost the house in the foreclosure."

"What'd he want?" Kim asked, her tone wary.

"Long story short, he said he was scammed out of the house by his lender. He's challenging our ownership of the property. He demanded that we move out in three days."

Kim sighed. "Goodness, I hate when this happens. This isn't the first time I've had to deal with this, Livia, you know. When you work in a market that's seen so many foreclosures, you're gonna have some unhappy folks who've lost their houses disputing the sales."

"Sour grapes," Olivia said. "I get it."

"Uh huh. Folks get emotionally attached to their homes, it's tough to see it go under normal circumstances, but especially when you lose it in a foreclosure or something like that. He say anything about slapping a lawsuit on you?

"He hasn't said anything about hiring a lawyer. I'm not sure he's going to use that route. So far, he's tried to intimidate us. He showed up at the house this morning and was very threatening to Len." She omitted mention of the encounter at the park.

"I bet he was," Kim said. "Len's such a sweetheart, he doesn't seem to be the kind of fella who likes confrontation."

"Does this man have any legal rights to the property? I did some research on my own, of course. I can't see that he has any legal recourse. We have the deed, our closing attorney conducted a title search. Everything is in order from what I can tell."

"He can't do a thing to y'all, honey, but fume and sue and make your lives miserable," Kim said. "Your real estate lawyer knew the situation when they drew up the closing papers, they researched the title like you said. Your claim on the house would stand up in court. But that doesn't mean this gentleman's gotta accept it."

"That's what I'm concerned about." Olivia leaned against the counter, took another sip of wine.

"You remember what happened to Tyler Perry a few years ago?" Kim asked.

"Can you refresh my memory?"

"Honey, he had a terrible dispute over a mansion he bought in Buckhead. Huge, beautiful home, a friend of mine helped him find it. Anyway, the place had been owned for years by an attorney, fella who made his money with a hotel that was popular back in its day. The lawyer hit hard times, lost his property, and Tyler came in and scooped it up. That's when the lawsuits started. Lawyer kept filing one suit after another claiming that he was still the rightful owner. When Tyler had the house demolished so he could build the place he wanted on the land, the lawyer even had the police show up once to remove the work crew from the property."

"What a nightmare," Olivia said.

"The lawyer was an old guy, too, almost ninety I believe," Kim said. "Old and ornery and had nothing better to do than be a big pain in the rear."

"Sounds like the guy we're dealing with," Olivia said, though she was unsure of Laveaux's age. He could have been any age between sixty and eighty-five, but her gut told her that he was at the upper range of her estimate.

"Eventually Tyler got fed up with all of it, I guess," Kim said. "He moved up to John's Creek."

"We're not going anywhere," Olivia said firmly.

"I hear you, honey, and I agree," Kim said. "But I hope you and your family are prepared, 'cause this situation might go on for a while. If this guy is anything like the fella that Tyler Perry was dealing with, he's gonna be pretty darn stubborn. You might need to call the police if he keeps showing up at the house."

"So we're looking at possibly filing a restraining order against a former homeowner," Olivia said.

"If it comes to that, sure," Kim said.

"Almost half the time, those orders are violated anyway. And given the circumstances, I doubt the cops will take our situation seriously." Olivia ran her fingers through her hair. "Is there anything else we can do? I want to be able to sleep peacefully at night knowing I don't have to ever worry about us losing the house."

"Hmm." Kim clucked her tongue. "Okay, there's one thing that might give you a little peace of mind."

"What is it?"

"Get back in touch with Hodges and Klein, the law firm we used for the closing. See what they can find out about the seller and how they came to hold the property. Since you and Len bought the house from a real estate investor, not the bank who originally foreclosed on the home, there could be something there you can look into. I honestly doubt it, Livia, I think you'll be wasting your time for no good reason, but if you want to be able to sleep at night like you say, I think you'll need to dig a bit deeper into the history of the house."

"I'll call them first thing tomorrow."

"At the end of the day, I'm afraid you and your family are just gonna have to dig in your heels until this poor old fella gives up—or dies off."

Olivia thanked Kim for the tips, and ended the call. She slipped the headset off and tossed it onto the counter.

Dig in their heels. Wait it out. Get a restraining order if necessary. Investigate the seller. That wasn't the advice she'd hoped to receive. Naively, she'd been assuming Kim might have some startling insight into their predicament that would magically make the man go away.

You can make him go away if you move out of the house, girl.

But financially, moving out wasn't the least bit feasible. They'd dropped a hefty amount of cash on the down payment and on improvements that had been essential for them to move in, such as buying a new water heater and repairing other critical issues. If they put the house on sale tomorrow and sold it for market value, they wouldn't get their money back. They would be deep in the red.

Besides the monetary challenges, giving up was not in her nature. *When the going gets tough, the tough get going* was one of her closely held beliefs. Her unswerving focus had gotten her through undergrad and Georgetown Law, helped her land a job at a top firm and make partner by age thirty-five. She didn't quit merely because things got difficult.

This isn't the same thing, and you know it, Laveaux might be a ...

She slammed that door before it opened.

She picked up the chopping knife, and went back to slicing vegetables. Turned up her music again. Sipped her wine.

She might as well get comfortable. This was her home, and she wasn't going anywhere.

13

Carrying an empty cardboard box, Len went outside after dinner. It was almost eight o'clock in the evening, but he still had work to do.

They had made good progress with unpacking and arranging items throughout most of the house, but he'd left several boxes sitting inside the garage. A few days ago, he'd promised Olivia that by the end of that weekend, he'd find a permanent spot for the stuff—and at dinner, she had pointedly reminded him of his promise.

Don't you have some junk to sort through in the garage, Len?

He was in no mood to argue and wanted to clear out space to park his SUV anyway. The high levels of pollen circulating in the air made it impossible to keep his truck clean.

Outdoors, dusk settled over the city. Soft lights glowed in the windows of the neighboring homes. A few houses down, someone mowed grass, and the aroma of barbecue flavored the cool air. It was only April, but when the weather was temperate, folks loved to fire up the grills.

Len scratched the bite mark on his neck. He'd applied a generous amount of anti-itch cream, to little effect. The guilty fly had managed to evade him and he wondered if it was still lurking inside the house.

Walking along the path that led to the driveway, box bouncing against his thigh, he pressed the button on his key fob that activated the garage door. The sectional door began to rise.

As he waited, he saw a silver BMW convertible veer onto their block, music throbbing from the stereo. The coupe nosed into Jacob's driveway and parked beneath the carport.

Was this the next lady in Jacob's "heavy" rotation?

A stunning young woman slipped out of the BMW and strutted to the front door, heels clicking on the pavement. She could have been a body double for Gabrielle Union. She wore a tight, black leather mini-skirt, stilettos, and a see-through red blouse.

Shaking his head, Len flicked on the overhead fluorescents in the garage.

The space was large enough to accommodate two vehicles, and an assortment of tools. Built-in shelves lined the far wall, beside Olivia's black Audi sedan. Several hooks hung from the back wall, above a work table. The vehicle bay on the right contained five large cardboard moving boxes, the side of each marked with the words, "Len's junk."

Funny. Olivia and her sarcasm.

Dropping the empty box on the floor—it was going to serve as his Stuff to Keep container—he approached the small mountain of boxes and opened one at random.

It was packed to the gills with empty manila file folders, staplers, coffee mugs he'd picked up at electronics and game conventions, mouse pads, pencils, pens, Post It Notes, an old radio, computer *diskettes* for crying out loud—none of his current machines could even read those old disks—and he was forced to admit that he didn't know what to do with half of this crap. He wondered why he'd brought most of it in the first place instead of trashing it.

Perhaps he was something of a hoarder, like Olivia always said.

He inventoried the other packages. One of them contained a yellowing collection of science-fiction paperbacks and comics, and various promotional giveaways he'd picked up at conventions. One of the items was worth keeping: a small but ferocious-looking stuffed kitten that was clothed like a samurai warrior, complete with a plush sword. It was a character from a video game that had been hot some time ago. He set the toy aside in his Stuff to Keep box. It might be a nice surprise for Kennedy.

The next package held dog-eared manuals on various programming languages and game design concepts. A couple of the books were references worth having around; he dropped them into the Stuff to Keep container.

Yet another package was stuffed with old, irrelevant documents from his job that he'd been holding onto for no apparent reason—and a thick wad of color photos crammed in an envelope.

He thumbed through the pictures. These were old, all right. They dated back to his college days. All of them were shots of his ex-girlfriend, April Howard. She had loved to pose for photos, and he'd been an eager photographer.

Sometimes, he imagined how his life would have turned out if April had been emotionally stable and hadn't committed suicide. Would they have gotten married? Would they be happy? Would they have had children? On the other hand, her impulsive personality had been part of what had attracted him to her. He never knew what she might do from one moment to the next. That was fine for a college relationship but would have created havoc in a marriage. For all Olivia's faults, she was as reliable as the sunrise.

Many of the photos were innocent: April making a goofy face or posed while gazing out a window. But a few were risqué. In one, he'd snapped the shot while lying on bed, underneath April while she straddled him, her large, bare breasts hanging above him. In another, she wore a GA Tech football jersey, and had peeled down her panties, mooning him, her tattoo of the Greek letter *Pi* winking from the small of her back. A third shot displayed a fully nude April sprawled across the bed, head tilted back in ecstasy as she caressed her vagina.

Len's mouth went dry. He couldn't dare let Olivia catch him with these. He returned the photos to the envelope, sealed it, and stuffed it underneath the other items in the Stuff to Keep bin. When he brought it into his office, he'd hide those pictures in his bottom desk drawer.

The fifth box was full of CDs of old video games and hip hop albums, a PlayStation, and an obsolete Motorola cell phone as large as a brick and about as heavy as one. He would keep the albums and rip them to MP3 files. The rest of the items were garbage.

He had to reluctantly admit that Olivia was correct. With the exception of the pictures he'd discovered, the toy samurai kitten, and a few other things, the majority of what he'd packed was junk.

But he couldn't trash anything that evening. The garbage collection trucks didn't make their rounds until Wednesday. He glanced around the room, looking for a corner in which he could temporarily stack the boxes and free enough space to park his SUV.

He caught a faint glimmer of an object lying on the uppermost shelf of the built-ins, on the other side of the garage. He walked around Olivia's car, and stood on his tiptoes to get a closer look.

It was some kind of statue, lying on its side on the shelf.

He picked it up—it weighed perhaps a pound—and brought it into the light. It was coated in dust. He used the edge of his t-shirt to wipe it clean.

It was about a foot tall, carved from wood. Age had worn away the details, but to Len's eye, it portrayed a slender man with hands shaped like spoons, and stubby legs. A furry collar, clearly sourced from an animal's pelt, hung around the figure's neck, and it wore a leather belt from which dangled various, tiny metal charms.

The head was striking, too. It had deep-set holes for eyes, a lumpy nose. Its disproportionately large mouth yawned wide, in a grimace of either pain or terror.

But what stood out the most were the three rusty nails embedded in the figure's back, the nails positioned in a straight row along the spine.

Immediately, Len thought about vodou, and felt a shiver pass through him.

He knew virtually nothing about vodou, in spite of being married to a woman whose family came from Haiti. Most of what he associated with vodou had come from Hollywood movies, which tended to exaggerate and sensationalize for the sake of creating an entertaining story.

Besides, weren't vodou dolls normally made of cloth, to facilitate being stuck with pins? The statue was wood.

He wasn't quite certain what purpose the figure served, but it seemed to be a ritual object of some kind. He placed the statue on one of the lower-level shelves, and stood on his tiptoes again.

He'd seen one more thing on the top shelf.

He swept his hand farther back along the dusty space. His fingers closed around what felt like a picture frame.

He wiped off the grime and studied the photograph. It was a five-by-seven, black-and-white shot of Dr. Laveaux standing beside a much shorter, brown-skinned man. They appeared to be in a courtyard. An enormous white mansion—it could actually be considered a palace—dominated the background, the majestic building flanked by immense palm trees. Both men wore dark suits and shaded glasses.

Both men had faint smiles, too, as if they shared some private joke.

Len had no idea when the picture had been taken, and he didn't know the identity of the other man, but one impression struck him: Laveaux looked *exactly* the same. As if he hadn't aged a single

73

day from the time the photo had been snapped, to when he'd shown up at their front door that morning.

It disturbed him, but he wasn't sure why.

"What's going on in here?" Olivia said.

Startled at the sound of her voice, Len almost dropped the photo.

"Hey," he said, and exhaled a deep breath. "I'm sorting through the so-called junk in here, like you asked me to do."

Olivia had brought Kennedy outside with her. Their daughter viewed every large box as an object to climb upon and leap from, and when she saw the scattered boxes in the garage, she squealed with excitement and raced to them.

"Be careful, honey," Len said. He turned to Olivia. "I actually found some stuff in here that I wanted to show you, if you're willing to take a look."

"Is that a photograph?" she asked.

"Check it out." He offered it to her, and she accepted it. "I found it on the top shelf in here. Obviously, the cleaning crew who went through the house after the foreclosure overlooked it. Any idea of the identity of the guy standing beside Laveaux? Looks like they're in front of a presidential estate or some important place."

"That's Papa Doc." She scowled.

"That name sounds familiar. Who is he?"

"He became President of Haiti back in the 1950s." She turned over the photograph in her hands. "When the heck was this picture taken? I swear, Laveaux looks as if he hasn't aged a day."

"My thoughts exactly."

"Papa Doc died in 1970 or 1971." She pursed her lips. "My family had left the country by then, thank goodness. He was a dictator, a terror."

"Even if this picture was taken at the end of this guy's life," Len said, "that still makes it over forty years old. What fountain of youth has Laveaux discovered? Weird, huh?"

Shaking her head incredulously, Olivia handed the picture back to him. He tried to give her the statue he'd found. She took one glance at it, and pushed it away with a sharp look.

"Throw this crap in the trash," she said.

"Are you serious? It's a photo and a piece of art."

"Get them out of here. Or I will."

"This is some kind of vodou thing, isn't it?" He held up the wooden figure to the light. "It looks authentic, not like some cheap trinket you would pick up in a gift shop. It's some sort of ritual item, I think."

Olivia sucked in air, her nostrils flaring, fists bunched on her waist. She looked prepared to knock him flat on his back if he didn't comply with her demand.

But Len wanted her to talk to him. Her behavior on the topic of Laveaux had been downright bizarre that day, and he was sick of her shutting down on him.

"Talk to me," he said. "Please. I want to understand. I need to know."

"Don't push it." The heat in her gaze could have seared his skin.

She's afraid, he thought. *She's not as angry as she looks, but acting pissed off is her way of dealing with the fear. What is she afraid of, and why won't she tell me?*

He shrugged. "All right, fine. I'll throw them away."

She nodded tightly. "After you do that, please come inside for a minute and help me move a couple of things in the family room. I want to try a new furniture configuration."

"I'm here to serve," he said.

Rolling her eyes, she took Kennedy by the hand, and they left the garage.

Len gathered up the photo and the statue— and deposited each in the Stuff to Keep box.

Olivia had left him no choice. If she wouldn't give him answers, he would find them on his own.

14

Olivia gave Kennedy a bath, and then prepared her for bed. It was a familiar routine, and Olivia had learned to cherish those private moments with her child. There would come a time, not too far off, when Kennedy would bathe and dress herself and would scoff at the idea that her mother had once done such things for her. Olivia knew, because she had used to think the same naïve thoughts about her own mother. Parenthood had opened her eyes in more ways than she could have imagined.

Len came into the bedroom as she was standing Kennedy upright so she could zip up her pajamas. He carried something hidden behind his back.

What does he have now? Olivia wondered, and felt an uncomfortable tightening in her stomach. The photo Len had found of Laveaux posed with Papa Doc had rocked her. Her parents had shared terrifying stories of the atrocities Papa Doc had engineered in Haiti. To see Laveaux on friendly terms with such a man was confirmation of her worst fears about the old, blind doctor.

And he'd discovered the statue, too . . .

"What have you got there?" Olivia asked. Her tone came out sharper than she'd intended.

"Something for the big girl." Len grinned. "Are you a big girl, Kennedy?"

"Yes." Kennedy sat on her bed. She nodded solemnly. "I'm a big girl."

"Then look." Len revealed what he'd been hiding: a stuffed kitten dressed like a warrior. It gripped a little sword, too.

"Oooh." Kennedy clapped and reached for the toy.

"His name is Kitty-san," Len said. "He's a samurai warrior. He keeps *all* of the monsters away."

Kennedy clasped the stuffed toy to her chest. She gazed upon Len with adoring eyes, as if he'd just given her the best gift ever.

Even Olivia had to smile.

"Good job, Daddy," she said.

Len winked at her. "I have my moments."

He kissed Kennedy on the forehead, and Olivia tucked her in. Kennedy yawned and turned over, but she kept her arms wrapped around Kitty-san.

Olivia switched off the light. She followed Len out of the bedroom, closed the door quietly behind them.

"Where did you get that toy?" she asked.

"From my *junk* in the garage," he said. "Imagine that."

"Well, nice move. It should help her get over this recent fixation on monsters."

"It's a new house to her. She'll need time to adjust. Hell, it's an adjustment for me. The way this house groans and creaks . . ."

"It's a little unnerving, I admit," she said. "I grew up in an older home, you know. Those noises are typical."

"It sometimes sounds as if someone is creeping around." He shrugged. "I'll get used to it."

He seemed about to tell her something else, but then he shrugged again, as if dismissing the thought. She was about to divulge her experiences from earlier that day, of hearing what sounded like a footstep in the hallway, and later, hearing a door slam for no apparent reason . . . but she dismissed both incidents as unimportant and not worth discussing.

"It's an old house, full of quirks," she said. "We all need time to adjust."

"Right." He pushed up his glasses on the bridge of his nose. "What're you going to do now?"

"Shower, then turn in. I'm exhausted."

"I'll be in my office for a while. Don't wait up for me—unless you planned to surprise me with a session of hot, kinky sex."

"Let's put it this way: I won't be waiting up for you."

Len looked away and muttered something under his breath.

"What did you say?" she said.

"Nothing. Good night."

He shuffled into his office and closed the door. Sighing, she went into the large bathroom at the end of the hallway.

Probably, he'd made a snide comment about how she was always too tired for sex. She admitted that their marriage had experienced a severe drop off in the intimacy department. But the past several weeks, she had been consumed with purchasing, and then moving into, the Victorian; when she wasn't working eleven-hour days at the firm or tending to Kennedy, she was poring over a detail related to the property. She'd had to initiate and plan *everything*. Len was a sweetheart, but he was so passive that if she'd left matters up to him, they would have lost out on the deal from the very beginning.

She would make it up to him soon, she promised herself.

The bathroom had a vanity, commode, porcelain claw foot tub, and a shower stall. It was the largest bathroom in the house, but by modern standards, would have been considered small. She didn't mind, because she'd claimed it as hers; Len had picked the other one, at the farther end of the hallway.

She switched on the shower head and peeled out of her clothes, grimacing as she moved. Her body ached from all of the lifting and twisting she'd done the past few days. She was a runner and in good shape, but the work of moving in had awakened muscles she had forgotten she possessed.

Something buzzed past her ear.

She flinched, swung toward the noise. Len had warned her earlier about a nasty horsefly that had gotten inside and bitten him. The bite mark on the side of his neck looked as if it hurt something awful.

But she didn't see the insect. It had disappeared in the thick layers of steam issuing from the shower.

Pain pierced the back of her left thigh.

"Shit!" She swatted the back of her leg.

But her hand came away empty. The fly buzzed to her right. She whirled and saw it dart into the open shower stall.

The bite wound throbbed. It felt as if someone were jabbing a sewing pin into her flesh.

She tried to put the pain out of her mind, and yanked a fistful of tissue from the roll beside the toilet. Balling up the tissue in her hand, she peeked inside the enclosure.

The fat fly clung to the wall opposite the stall door.

She reached up, grabbed the shower head, and twisted it, redirecting the jet of scalding hot water to the wall. Struck, the fly dropped onto the stall floor, wings flailing.

Using the tissue, Olivia picked up the weakened insect and flushed it down the toilet.

Good riddance, she thought. *Now, let's assess the damage.*

She propped her leg against the lip of the sink and used a hand mirror to view the back of her thigh. A crimson lesion as large as a quarter had formed.

Gently, she ran her fingers across the wound. She winced.

It was beginning to itch, too.

15

Locked inside his home office, Len booted up his gaming PC, but he had no intentions of playing a video game. He was going to research the items he'd discovered in the garage that Olivia had demanded he trash.

If she wouldn't talk to him, he'd find out answers on his own. He could be as driven as she was when there was something he wanted.

And all he wanted was to learn more about the man who'd given them three days to get out of the house.

He had hidden the old photo and the wooden statue in a lower desk drawer, along with the pics of April he'd uncovered. He opened the drawer, brought out both pieces, and placed them on the edge of his desk, next to his bottle of water.

He was briefly tempted to linger over those revealing shots of April again, too. It wasn't as though he was having sex anytime soon. Olivia had made that clear, in her typical, direct way.

Using his foot, he nudged the drawer shut.

He could fantasize later. He had to stay focused.

He began his research with the guy standing next to Laveaux in the photo: Papa Doc. He typed "Papa Doc" into Google, hit "Enter" and scratched the bite mark on his neck, waiting.

The search engine retrieved almost one million results.

The top page was a Wikipedia entry. He clicked on the link.

The web page included several photos of the man, and an extensive article. Len glanced from the computer screen, to the framed photo beside him. It was the same dude.

He began to read.

François Duvalier (14 April 1907 – 21 April 1971) was the President of Haiti from 1957 until his death in 1971. Duvalier first won acclaim in fighting diseases, earning him the nickname "Papa Doc" ("Daddy Doc[tor]" in French).

He opposed a military coup d'état in 1950, and was elected president in 1957 on a populist and black nationalist platform. His rule, based on a purged military, a rural militia and the use of a personality cult and vodou, resulted in the murder of an estimated 30,000 Haitians and an ensuing "brain drain" from which the country has still not recovered.

Len shook his head as the factoids jumped out at him. A physician had directed the murders of thirty thousand people? What about the pledge in the Hippocratic Oath to do no harm?

The mention of vodou intrigued him, too. A hunch told him that vodou was the thread that tied Laveaux and Duvalier together.

He took a sip from his bottle of water, and continued to read.

The article didn't delve into much detail in regard to Papa Doc's interest in vodou, other than how he'd claimed to be a *houngan*, or priest, and that he'd, "deliberately modeled his image on that of Baron Samedi. He often donned sunglasses to hide his eyes and talked with the strong nasal tone associated with the *loa*."

The mention of this Samedi guy intrigued Len, too. Based on the old photo, Dr. Laveaux habitually wore sunglasses *before* he was blinded, and he spoke in a nasal tone. Just like this dude.

Len clicked the hyperlink under "Baron Samedi" and was routed to another Wikipedia entry.

Baron Samedi (Baron Saturday, also Baron Samdi, Bawon Samedi, or Bawon Sanmdi) is one of the Loa of Haitian Vodou. Samedi is a Loa of the dead, along with Baron's numerous other incarnations Baron Cimetière, Baron La Croix, and Baron Kriminel. He is the head of the Guédé family of Loa, or an aspect of them, or possibly their spiritual father.

Sipping water, Len leaned forward in his chair. His heart knocked with excitement. He was finally getting somewhere.

He is usually depicted with a top hat, black tuxedo (dinner jacket), dark glasses, and cotton plugs in the nostrils, as if to resemble a corpse dressed and prepared for burial in the Haitian style. He has a white, frequently skull-like face (or actually has a skull for a face) and speaks in a nasal voice.

It was obvious to Len that Dr. Laveaux had modeled himself after this *loa*. The old man wore the entire ludicrous getup for the most part, looking like a cast member from a low-budget horror film.

Len pushed up his glasses on his nose, tilted back in his chair.

What did he know at this point? Dr. Laveaux patterned his appearance after this *loa*, Baron Samedi, the *loa* of the dead. What that meant, Len couldn't say for sure.

More important, however, he'd learned that the former president of Haiti, Papa Doc, had a predilection for vodou, and at some point in his presidential reign, Laveaux had earned an audience with the man. The bloodthirsty dictator would not have granted a sociable visit to his palace to any old fool who called himself a *bokor*, which Len had learned was a general term for a vodou sorcerer. Dr. Laveaux must have enjoyed a high level of prominence in that world, such that even a feared tyrant had respected him.

Len glanced at the wooden figure standing on his desk. Studied the metal charms hanging around the statue's waist, the nails protruding from the spine.

Bouncing forward again, he typed a new search query: "vodou statue."

The search engine returned over two million results, including images. Len selected the image results.

A bevy of striking photos filled the screen. Images of skulls, of figures with fantastic features, such as a man with three heads, of fearsome wooden statues bearing human teeth, of the traditional vodou doll bristling with pins, of grinning heads carved in stone and studded with cowrie shells . . . Len continued to scroll down the page, until he found one of the graphics that closely matched the statue that stood on his desk. He clicked on it.

He was routed to, of all places, a product page on eBay.

It was described as an "entity fetish" and "power figure" from a tribe in the Congo. The nails were hammered into the back in order to "activate" the statue. The piece was sourced from the library of a gentleman who collected ancient artifacts.

Len's guess was that Laveaux had picked up the statue in one of his many journeys abroad. A man like him would have been interested in such things.

He picked up the photograph of Dr. Laveaux.

He'd learned a little more about the man. This man steeped

in vodou, whose prowess in the field had brought him to the palace of a ruthless dictator.

Len swallowed thickly.

He wondered what they should do next.

He wondered if they should be afraid.

Part Two

16

Sometime that night, Len snapped awake from an erotic dream about his ex-girlfriend.

He lay in bed in a tangle of sheets, face tilted toward the dark ceiling. His pulse raced. His mouth was dry. Cold sweat dampened his chest.

And his pajama bottoms felt wet.

He exhaled deeply and dragged his hand down his face. His heart rate began to settle.

The glowing numerals on the bedside clock were too fuzzy to read. He fumbled out his glasses from the case on the nightstand, slipped them on. The room shifted into sharp focus. It was 2:39 in the morning.

Beside him, Olivia slumbered quietly, her back facing him. She was a deep sleeper.

Len swung his legs out of bed. The hardwood floor was cold underneath his bare feet. He was bare-chested, and the cool air in the room prickled his flesh.

Or it could have been that his skin was still tingling from his dream.

He found his slippers next to the bed, slid them on. Quietly, he shuffled out of the bedroom, shutting the door behind him.

The house was silent. On a side table at the end of the hallway, a small Tiffany-style lamp glowed with soft light. Olivia loved those lamps and had positioned a ton of them at strategic spots throughout their home, but Len was grateful for this one; he was still so new to the place that he didn't trust his ability to navigate in the dark.

In the Dark

He went into the bathroom at the end of the hallway.

In the bright fluorescents, his worries were confirmed. He'd had a wet dream. Like a sex-starved teenager, for crying out loud.

But what a dream it had been. Damn. He could not recall the last time he'd experienced such a vivid fantasy.

He also noticed that the bite wound on his neck looked worse. He leaned closer to the mirror over the sink. The welt had grown darker, had become nearly purplish. It still itched, too.

Could he have been allergic to the fly? Or perhaps it carried a disease? If it got any worse, he might have to go to the doctor.

Using a wad of tissue, he wiped himself clean, and blotted the wetness from the pajama bottoms. He washed his hands and left the bathroom.

The hallway was dark. The lamp had been extinguished.

Had the light bulb blown, maybe?

He wasn't going to worry about it at this hour. The bed was calling him. He could attend to the lamp in the morning.

A floorboard creaked near the top of the staircase.

Len paused.

The house is just making noises again, he thought. *I've got to get used to those sounds.*

But a familiar fragrance drifted to his nostrils, borne along by the cool air. It smelled like the body lotion that April would use, a soft, floral scent. Chanel, from what he recalled. The lotion was expensive but April had come from a family of means, had worn the stuff the way other women applied cocoa butter.

Am I still dreaming? Is this round two?

The staircase creaked. As if someone were descending.

Len wiped his fingers across his dry mouth. Slowly, he moved down the hallway. His eyes had adjusted to the darkness, but the corridor was still little more than a pattern of vaguely defined lines.

He reached for the lamp, and by mistake, knocked it over on the table. The clatter seemed unnaturally loud. He fumbled for the base of it, set it upright, found the switch. He pressed it once, twice. The lamp remained off.

Forget it, then.

There was a ceiling light installed in the hallway, but he didn't remember where the switch was located, and didn't feel like bumbling around to find it. The fragrance of the perfume was heavier in the air. He was closer to the source.

88

He reached the head of the staircase and peered over the balustrade.

Darkness flooded the first floor, relieved only by the weak trickle of street lights that filtered in through the blinds. He heard a floorboard groan down there, and caught a streak of movement in the main hallway as a shadowy figure darted out of sight.

He heard someone down there giggle. A woman.

"April?" he said. "Is that you?"

He realized how crazy the words sounded after he'd spoken them. April had been dead for fifteen years. She wasn't in his house.

No one could possibly be in his house except for him and the two members of his family, and both of them were asleep in their rooms on the second floor.

What was going on here? Was he truly dreaming again? If he were dreaming, why did he feel wide awake?

He looked back along the corridor, to the door to his bedroom. He could go back to bed and forget about this, whatever it was that was happening.

Soft laughter rippled from downstairs.

Or he could follow it through, like Alice plunging down the rabbit hole.

"Honey bear, where are you? Won't you come play with me?"

The voice sounded exactly like April, and one of her pet names for him was "honey bear." No one else knew that little piece of trivia about their relationship.

Len headed down the staircase.

At the base of the stairway, he caught a piece of clothing lying on the floor. He picked it up and ran his fingers across the material. Silk panties, scented with Chanel.

A chill traveled down his spine.

"April?" he said. "Where are you?"

"I'm in the kitchen, silly."

Len pushed up his glasses on the bridge of his nose. He walked down the hallway, and into the kitchen.

Like the rest of the house, the kitchen was full of blackness, the darkness broken only by faint bands of light from outdoors. But he clearly noted two things.

One: April was not in the kitchen.

Two: the basement door hung wide open.

He tried the light switch beside the refrigerator. It didn't respond. That made no sense to him at all. He *knew* that light worked.

"Where did you go, April?" he said.

A giggle. Then: *"Come downstairs, honey bear."*

On shaky knees, Len approached the doorway. He paused on the threshold. The scent of Chanel was thick in the air.

But below, the basement was as dark as a bottomless abyss. Len swallowed.

April's voice came to him from deep in the darkness: *"Stop being a fraidy cat. Come down here with me. I'll make it* better *than your dream."*

Len blinked. Better than his dream? Did that mean that what was happening to him, right now, was real?

"Come down here, Lenny. Let me suck your cock and then show you how I died."

Coldness washed over him.

"You left me to die, you son of a bitch. I loved you and you left me. Let me show you how much you meant to me."

Slowly, Len shook his head.

"This is where the adventure ends," he said, more to himself than to whatever awful thing was down there. "I can't do this. I'm not that guy."

He shut the basement door, and locked it.

His heart pounded furiously.

The kitchen was silent. He heard no more taunts from . . . whatever that had been. The scent of perfume had faded, too.

He returned upstairs. On the side table in the hallway, the lamp glowed with pale, soft light.

Frowning, he scratched the welt on his neck.

What just happened? Did I imagine all of that?

He went inside their bedroom and crawled back into bed, but it took him a long time to drift back to sleep.

17

Olivia liked to sleep in on weekends, but on weekdays, she was an early riser. She awoke promptly at six o'clock in the morning and hit the button to switch off the bedside alarm clock as soon as it started to buzz.

Yawning, she stretched her arms above her. In spite of her immediate wakefulness, she hadn't slept well. The itching of the bug bite had annoyed her all night, and she'd experienced a terrible nightmare about her brother, Michael. The memory of it gave her chills.

As difficult as it was, she had to force it out of her mind and get going with her day.

She flung aside the sheets and pushed out of bed. In the shadowed room, she saw that Len continued to sleep, curled in fetal position, pillow clutched against his chest. He looked cute when he was deeply asleep, and she couldn't help noticing that sometimes, he and Kennedy slept in the exact same positions, like twins.

She slipped on her terry-cloth bathrobe and left the bedroom. She'd wash up quickly and then hit the road for her morning run.

After she rinsed her face, she propped her leg on the sink and checked the bite wound with the hand mirror. Her lips curled in dismay. The lesion had turned purple, like a bruise. She would need to monitor it closely.

Leaving the bathroom, she noticed that the door to Len's office was partly open, and a light burned inside. Had he forgotten to switch it off before he'd come to bed last night?

She bumped open the door.

The floor lamp beside the desk burned brightly. She went to

switch it off, and happened to glance at the desk. An envelope lay on the corner, one of those packets they gave you at the pharmacy when you had photographs developed. A couple of photos peeked out of the stack.

Olivia picked up the pile of pictures and thumbed through them. Her breath caught in her throat.

Who the hell is this *woman?*

She flipped to the other side of one of the pictures, and saw the date the photo was developed printed on the back. The pics were fifteen years old.

She was relieved, but only slightly. Why was Len looking at these? In a few of them, the woman was nude. She had to assume it was Len's girlfriend, presumably from his college days. She was a lot prettier than Olivia had thought any of Len's girlfriends had been, with an amazing body. Perhaps it was Olivia's own egotism talking, but she'd always believed that *she* had been the most attractive woman that Len had ever been intimately involved with; but this woman had bigger boobs and a lighter complexion.

Stop it, girl. Don't let your own insecurities surface.

Still, why had Len dug out these photos? Was he reminiscing about his ex? Thinking about speaking to her again? Talking to her on Facebook?

What if he's already having an affair?

She'd always taken comfort in her belief that of all the men with whom she'd ever been involved, Len seemed the most unlikely to cheat. He wasn't a ladies man; he liked video games, comic books, sci-fi movies, and college football. He didn't hang with his boys at strip clubs; his buddies were as geeky as he was and liked to go to Dragon Con and play multi-player games online. He was a great father and a loving husband, as easygoing and honest as any guy she'd ever met.

She studied the photo of the pretty girlfriend stretched across the bed, her lean, shapely body on full display as she pleasured herself.

But perhaps she didn't know Len as well as she thought she did. Had she ever expected to discover he had stashed a collection of nude pics?

She crammed the pictures into the envelope, switched off the lamp. She took the photos with her as she left the room.

Len had some explaining to do. Lucky for him that she needed to get her run in and prepare for work. But later that evening, they were going to chat about this "discovery" of hers.

The sun was still in hiding when she stepped out the front door attired in her exercise gear. She wore a neon green visibility vest over a tank top, white capris, and custom-fitted running shoes. Her hair was tucked underneath a baseball cap that matched her safety vest. When you ran the city roads before dawn, you had to take the proper precautions.

She did a series of warm-up stretches, and then took off down the side of the street.

The cool air was crisp and clear, as if the world had been cleansed overnight. Only light traffic circulated on the neighborhood streets. Early mornings were her favorite time of the day to run. The city was still quiet, slowly revving up to the next day.

She had already plotted her route. She would wind through the nearby park, and several blocks of their neighborhood. The entire circuit should encompass about two and a half miles, and she would rip through it twice, for a total of five miles.

Her arms and legs pumped smoothly as she hit her stride. She'd been running five miles a day, five days a week, for over a decade. Participated in the Peachtree Road Race every July and had traveled to several other cities to run marathons. She was addicted to the runner's high—and determined to avoid the high blood pressure and diabetes that plagued her family.

Typically, when she ran, she let her thoughts drift, and usually wound up thinking about the mountain of work waiting for her at the office. That morning, she thought neither about work, nor the photos of Len's ex-girlfriend—she was good at compartmentalizing and had filed that topic away for a later conversation with Len. She thought about her dead brother.

That day, April fifteenth, was the tenth anniversary of Michael's death.

The nightmare she'd experienced last night still chilled her. She had dreamed that Michael had knocked on the front door at their new house. When she opened the door, she found him standing on the porch, barefoot, dressed in a dirty grey Georgetown hoodie (she had given it to him as a gift), and ripped jeans; the same clothing he'd been wearing when his body had been discovered. Green vomit oozed down his chin, and tiny syringes were stuck between his fingers, dripping blood.

But his eyes were the worst. They were rimmed with red—and seethed with accusation.

Why did you let me die, sis? he had asked in a ragged voice clogged with vomit. *This is all your fault, you selfish bitch . . .*

Swinging her arms, shoes slapping the pavement, Olivia sucked in a breath and gritted her teeth.

Stop thinking about it, she told herself. *Stop it right now.*

She might have succeeded in putting the hellish memory out of her mind if she hadn't noticed the guy across the street, about fifty feet ahead of her.

The man sat on the curb, in front of a brick Craftsman with a For Sale sign stuck in the front yard. He wore a grey hoodie, the hood covering his head, and a pair of jeans with holes in the knees. He was barefoot.

Seeing him brought her to a halt as surely as if she'd run into a wall.

Michael? She thought. Then corrected herself: *no, it can't be.*

The man rocked back and forth, nodding to a beat only he could hear. His arms were clasped around his knees. She couldn't see his face because he wore the hood, and it was still dark outdoors.

But she didn't need to see his face, she decided. He was a stranger. Possibly a homeless man, which was, unfortunately, a common sight in Atlanta. There was nothing for her to do but keep moving.

She started forward, in a jog, to slowly build up her speed again.

The man lifted his head. He snatched away the hood.

It was Michael.

He was bald, like he'd been the last time she had seen him alive. Even from a distance, she could see the vomit oozing down his chin.

She screamed and broke into a sprint.

Michael bounced off the curb and came after her, bare feet slapping against the street.

"You bitch!" he shouted.

Oh, my God, this can't be happening, she thought

But she kept running anyway. Adrenaline flooded her system. Her heart felt as if it had risen into her throat.

Michael's footfalls clapped behind her. He was getting closer. He was taller, faster, and stronger. Driven by righteous fury. He'd died of a drug overdose because *she* had ignored his appeals for help.

She reached the end of the block, and cut to the right. She leaped over the curb and onto the sidewalk. A dog barked at her. An

Asian woman was loading an infant into a minivan and turned to glance at her, eyebrows arched in alarm.

It was the realization that she was making a spectacle of herself that made her slow. She didn't look like a well-balanced woman out for a healthy morning run; she looked as though she were running for her life.

And how was that even possible? Michael was *dead.*

She forced herself to stop.

Heart banging, she looked behind her.

Leaves stirred in a cool breeze. A cyclist zipped past on a bicycle.

Michael wasn't there.

She snatched off her cap and ran her fingers through her hair.

What the hell's the matter with me? How could I have imagined such a thing? Is the anniversary of his death affecting me so deeply that I'm hallucinating?

She needed to get a grip. She had a busy day ahead, and couldn't afford to lose control like that again.

She resumed her run. Looking around warily the entire time.

18

Len woke up late. He liked to be up by six-thirty, to lift weights, eat breakfast, and arrive in the office by eight-thirty. But when he awoke, Kennedy was fully dressed for school and standing beside the bed. She traced her tiny fingers across his face and grinned.

"Wake up, sleepyhead," she said, mimicking a phrase Olivia often used.

Yawning, Len wiped his eyes. He put on his glasses and checked the clock. It was a quarter to eight.

"Shit." He bolted upright and tossed away the bed sheets.

"Shit," Kennedy said, as clear as if she'd been using the word her entire life.

"Don't say that," Len said. "That's an adult word, honey."

"Shit." Smiling, she clapped her hands. "Shit, shit, shit."

"What is she saying?" Olivia asked. She entered the bedroom, heels clicking on the hardwoods. Like Kennedy, she was already dressed. She wore a sky-blue business suit, black pumps, and a pearl necklace. Her makeup and hair were done, too.

"She heard me use the s-word," Len said. He crossed the room to the chest-of-drawers, and searched for clothes. "I must've forgotten to set my alarm last night. Why didn't you wake me up, Liv?"

"I decided that you needed your sleep. Considering that you were up late in your office studying these."

She thrust an envelope toward him. The moment he saw it, he got a sinking feeling in the pit of his stomach.

She found the photos of April. How?

96

He caught the envelope before it dropped to the floor.

"Were you digging through my desk?" he asked.

"Those were on *top* of your desk, Len," she said in a crisp tone. Her "no bullshit lawyer voice," he called it. "I found them because when I woke up this morning, the light was on in your office. I went in there to switch it off and discovered those."

"That's . . . impossible. I put this in a drawer last night."

"Did you?" Olivia dug her fists into her waist. Barely-restrained anger simmered in her eyes. "We'll discuss this when I get home tonight. I suggest you create a more plausible story to explain those pictures."

"They're fifteen years old, for God's sake."

"Come on, Kennedy," Olivia said, ignoring him. She nudged Kennedy toward Len. "Give Daddy a kiss good-bye, it's time to go."

Kennedy attended a preschool program at a Montessori school in Midtown. The tuition cost about as much as a college education, but it was a highly rated program and she seemed to love her teachers and classmates. With their move to the new house, the facility was actually closer to them, which Olivia appreciated since she was usually the one who dropped off Kennedy in the mornings. Len would pick her up late in the afternoon when he left work.

Kneeling, Len kissed Kennedy on the forehead, hugged her.

"Did Kitty-san keep away the monsters last night?" he asked.

"No monter." Kennedy smiled.

"Let's go." Olivia took her by the hand. She cast a glance at Len that promised an ass-chewing to come, and hurried out of the room with Kennedy in tow.

Len removed his glasses and pinched the bridge of his nose. His day was off to a roaring start, wasn't it?

He shuffled into his office. Morning sunshine sifted inside through the partially opened blinds, bands of light and shadow striping the floor.

He didn't understand how he could have left the photos on the desk. He *knew* he had stored them in a drawer—precisely because he hadn't wanted Olivia to find them.

What if Olivia had been lying? What if the truth was that she'd been searching through his personal items?

He pulled open the bottom drawer where he'd placed the envelope. The old wooden statue and the framed shot of Laveaux and Papa Doc lay inside, as expected.

If Olivia had been digging through his stuff, wouldn't she

have found those items, too? Wouldn't she have said something to him about it, especially since he had promised her he would throw these things away?

Maybe she had found them, too, but had felt the pics of April were more worthy of discussion.

He didn't know. He didn't understand how any of this had happened. But the only feasible answer was that Olivia had been rummaging through his personal possessions, and she was wrong to do that. That was going to be his side of the story, and he was sticking to it.

He slid out one of the photographs. It happened to be the shot of April, nude, stretched across the bed and fingering herself.

His groin tingled pleasantly. Talk about morning wood.

His thoughts looped back to what had happened last night. The erotic dream. The trip downstairs. The silk, scented panties. The obscene taunts.

Was all of that really a dream?

Dropping the envelope on the desk, he went downstairs to the kitchen.

He didn't find the panties anywhere—imagine if Olivia had found *those*—and the basement door was closed and locked.

From what he recalled, April had been trying to lure him into the cellar. He was running late for work, but for his own peace of mind, he needed to debunk the notion that anything threatening lurked in the basement. This was his house. He had to prove he was master of his domain.

He grabbed a utility flashlight from a drawer. Then he unlocked the basement door, pulled it open.

A dank, dusty odor filled his nostrils. He found the light switch, flipped it.

Brightness streamed from an exposed bulb, flooded the narrow, steep staircase. He remembered April's spiteful words, spoken from deep in the darkness.

Let me suck your cock and then show you how I died . . .

And felt a shiver.

He was self-aware enough to realize that he had unresolved issues related to April's suicide. She'd come from a wealthy but dysfunctional family and had been screwed up way before they had started dating, but when he'd broken off their relationship after nine tumultuous months, it had sent her spiraling over the edge. She'd stalked him. Sliced his tires. Hurled a brick through his dorm window. Called him at all hours of the night. Threatened to kill herself.

Eventually, when her appeals failed to win him back, she made good on her promise to end her life.

Sighing, he pushed up his glasses on the bridge of his nose.

He carefully descended the staircase. There was no hand rail. He had to trail his fingers along the cold stone walls to maintain his balance.

It was a musty cellar with a low-ceiling, about eight-feet high. Old spider webs hung in the rafters and wrapped the pipes like faded holiday tinsel. The floor was concrete. There were no windows.

But it was a vast space that matched the square footage of the upper floor. It had several niches and nooks that could be walled off into separate rooms and storage spaces. The potential was unlimited.

He walked around, pulling on light bulbs when they were available, and sweeping the beam of the flashlight around when they were not, which was usually the case. The light panned across the brand-new water heater they'd needed to have installed before they could move in, the gleaming appliance looking totally out of place in the aged, dusty room. There was plenty of additional electrical and plumbing work that would need to be completed down there before the area would be suitable for his purposes.

He reached the spacious chamber that he'd pegged as one day serving as his home theater room. It was a wide open space with a huge wall that could accommodate a massive flat-screen television. Currently, a set of rickety, built-in wooden shelves occupied the wall. All of the shelves were empty, no doubt wiped clean by the crew that had scrubbed the property before their move-in.

As he swept the flashlight beam across the area, he noticed that the left corner of the shelf buckled outward from the wall. He moved forward for a closer look, old grit crumbling under the soles of his house slippers.

There was a gap of a few inches between the back of the shelf and what should have been the stone wall. He shone the light in the aperture.

There was a concrete floor on the other side.

He set the flashlight down beside him. Then he gripped the warped edge of the shelf, and pulled.

It swung outward with little resistance, some hinge mechanism squeaking with the movement. Like a door.

I'll be damned.

He really needed to get ready for work. He had a busy day ahead full of meetings and project work. Taking off last Friday had already put him behind.

But he *had* to look at this. His curiosity had hit a fever pitch.

With the shelf pulled back far enough to give him room to pass through, he picked up the flashlight again and slowly brushed it across the exposed area.

The dimensions were about six by eight, like a small bathroom. A free-standing set of wooden shelving stood opposite the hidden doorway. There were four shelves, and they held an assortment of objects. Intricately carved wooden artifacts like the one he'd found in the garage yesterday. Mason jars full of mysterious fluids. Small cloth sacks that contained who knew what. Candles inside glass containers, the containers painted with what appeared to be representations of Catholic saints. A butcher's knife. A bottle of dark rum. A human skull.

What was this place? Laveaux's storage closet for his vodou paraphernalia?

But Len found his biggest discovery when he angled the light across the floor.

A trapdoor was set in the middle of the room. It was square-shaped, maybe four feet by four feet, with a weathered steel lid and a thick handle. A bulky, rusted padlock and hasp secured the hatch to the floor.

Len couldn't believe it. These rooms, and whatever area existed below, sure as hell were not included in the house's floor plans. No one had told them anything about this.

But Dr. Laveaux had known about it.

Len bent on one knee. He grabbed the lid's handle. Pulled.

No luck. The padlock was rusted, but it held firm. He hammered the bottom edge of the flashlight against the lock a few times, to no avail.

He pushed back to his feet, blew out a deep breath. He searched the dusty shelves, seeking a key to the lock, but found nothing.

In absence of the key, a good bolt cutter would do the trick. During his sophomore year in college, he'd worked a part-time job at a public storage facility. Whenever a customer let the lease on a storage unit expire, it was his responsibility to snap off the padlocks so management could auction off the contents left inside.

Unfortunately, he didn't own a bolt cutter large enough to handle the lock. He'd have to pick up one from a hardware store.

Work or not, he would do that today.

He swept the flashlight beam across the trapdoor again.

What was hidden under there?

19

Olivia arrived at the office at eight-thirty sharp.

She was a partner at Wolfe & Kramer, an employment and labor law firm located on the tenth floor of an office tower in Buckhead. The firm practiced in a wide range of areas: sexual harassment, employment discrimination, overtime violations, retaliation, worker's compensation claims, and more. Olivia practiced primarily in the areas of sexual harassment, employment discrimination, severance agreements, and contract claims. The United States was a litigious country, which guaranteed that her work day was always packed with activity.

That Monday would be no exception. She had a long list of meetings and conference calls on her agenda, and she had to go downtown later that morning, too, for a deposition in a gender discrimination case.

Coffee in hand, she settled behind her big mahogany desk. Achieving partner had been difficult, a goal she had labored for many years to attain, but it definitely had its perks: besides the hefty salary, she had a spacious corner office with floor-to-ceiling windows that granted a panoramic view of downtown Atlanta's skyline. Bright spring sunshine made the skyscrapers appear to be gilded in gold.

Normally, the postcard-quality vista soothed her. Made her feel secure in her hard-earned success. She didn't come from a wealthy family. No trust fund or familial connections had given her a head start. She'd had to pave her own way, and in the end, that made her accomplishments all the sweeter.

But two things spoiled the view that morning. The frightening incident she'd experienced on her morning run, that she still couldn't explain logically; and this Laveaux character with whom she still needed to deal.

She couldn't do anything about the hallucination, except pray that nothing like that happened to her again. But she could get some answers on Laveaux's claim on her house.

Her realtor, Kim, had suggested contacting the real estate attorneys who had handled the closing. The more Olivia had thought about it, the more useless that approach seemed to her. She was a lawyer, too, and could anticipate their canned response: *we executed all of the steps necessary to complete the transaction in accordance with all applicable laws. We can assure you that the prior owner has no legal right to the property.* They wouldn't respond positively to her suggestion that they had failed in any way whatsoever to perform their due diligence. Before she could get legal counsel involved, she needed to have tangible evidence of an error, not unsubstantiated proclamations from a pissed off old man.

Instead, she was going to call the company that had sold them the house: King Realty Associates. The real estate investors who had originally snatched up the Victorian in foreclosure.

She had brought from home the long black folder that contained all of the documentation on the house sale. Opening the folder in the middle of her desk, she thumbed through the papers, found the details on the realty company.

Her executive assistant, Bernice Jackson, often placed phone calls for her, the assumption being that a partner was too important to play phone tag and leave voice mail messages. But this was one call that Olivia was making herself.

She grabbed a legal pad and a pen, and punched in the number on her desk phone. The line rang three times before a young woman answered.

"Good morning, King Realty Associates." She had a syrupy southern drawl, but her voice was soft, as if she'd just gotten out of bed.

"Hi, this is Olivia Bowden. May I speak with Reggie King, please? This concerns a property for which he was listing agent."

Silence on the line.

"Hello?" Olivia said.

"Umm . . ." The woman released a deep breath. When she finally spoke again, her voice sounded fragile as glass. "Umm . . . I'm sorry . . . Mr. King is umm . . . no longer with us."

Olivia placed her pen on the desk. Her intuition buzzed. Something was wrong.

"He no longer works there?" Olivia asked.

"Umm . . . no." The woman sighed again. Cleared her throat. "I'm sorry . . . can you call back some other time?"

"Wait, please. What happened to Reggie King?"

"Umm." The receptionist hesitated. "I'm not sure . . . I don't know if I'm supposed to tell anyone."

"Please, tell me. We purchased a house from Reggie. I met him personally on two occasions."

"Okay." Another heavy sigh. "Mr. King is . . . he's deceased, ma'am."

Olivia felt as if she'd been kicked in the stomach.

"Deceased?" Olivia said.

The woman murmured a barely intelligible, "yes."

"When?" Olivia was shaking her head. "I last saw him a month ago."

"Saturday night. It was a car accident . . ."

Oh, my God.

"Everyone here in the office is stunned," she continued, "the rest of the staff is just here sitting around and we can't believe it, you know, we're like in a daze . . ."

"I'm very sorry," Olivia said. "I can call back at some other time."

"Okay, ummm . . . maybe I can have another agent help you? Virgil worked closely with Reggie . . . he might get in soon."

"Have Virgil call me whenever he gets a chance," Olivia said. She gave her office and cell phone numbers.

When she hung up, she felt numb.

The listing agent for their house died in a car accident, the night before Dr. Laveaux showed up at their front door with his three-day deadline for them to get out. Was that a coincidence?

She desperately wanted to believe that it was.

But you don't really believe that, do you?

Drumming her fingers on the desktop, she glanced at her clock. She needed to be on a conference call in ten minutes. An important discussion with a client for which she had to be focused.

Nevertheless, she opened Google in her laptop's web browser and typed in a search term designed to extract anything that existed online about King's accident.

The search engine returned a dozen hits from various news

sites, all of them from Sunday. She quickly scanned a couple of them.

Evidently, King had been driving in East Atlanta, around ten o'clock at night on Saturday, when he'd plowed his Mercedes into a large oak tree at a high rate of speed. Another driver had come upon the wreck and called an ambulance. King was dead by the time the paramedics arrived.

One of the stories featured a photo of the wreck. The sedan was as crumpled as a smashed soda can.

What had happened? Had he lost control of the car? Decided to commit suicide? Been intoxicated?

She found no mention of alcohol, or other passengers or drivers involved, though she figured that pending a toxicology test, it was too early to know whether King had been drinking. More details would possibly be revealed later, unless King's family put a lid on it.

She glanced at her watch. Her meeting was set to commence in three minutes. She had to prepare.

It was just as well. Her plan to speak to Reggie King about the Laveaux situation had, literally, hit a dead end.

20

Len barely made it to work in time for a standing Monday morning meeting.

Pulling himself away from the secret room and trapdoor had been tough. He felt as if he teetered on the edge of a major breakthrough: the real reason why Dr. Laveaux was so determined to get the house back. The door in the floor had to conceal something of immense value. Why else would it have been hidden and locked?

He couldn't wait to get back home and find out.

The video game company for which he worked, Three Sixty Interactive, was headquartered in Midtown, in an office suite within walking distance of Piedmont Park and the High Museum. Sometimes, for a change of pace, his team held meetings at the park. That Monday morning, however, they gathered in their regular conference room.

A round, granite-topped table stood in the center of the space. In keeping with the company's open access policy, all four walls were paneled with floor-to-ceiling windows, allowing everyone outside the room to see what was occurring within, and vice versa. A couple of bean bag chairs stood in the corner, and two enormous flat-screen TVs hung suspended from the ceiling on opposing sides of the room, like sets in a sports bar. When college basketball's March Madness season was in high gear, colleagues would hang out in there catching the games and checking their tournament brackets.

Their Monday meeting was all business. His six-member group of team leads in their respective departments huddled at the table, everyone armed with their iPads and beverages, ready to march through the weekly project agenda. They were a motley crew of programmers, developers, designers, visual artists, writers, and analysts; jeans, sneakers, and t-shirts were *de rigueur*. In his blue oxford shirt, khakis, and Rockport loafers, Len was the most formally-dressed person at the table. It was appropriate, as part of his job as Game Director required handling the "suits"; the non-creative folks in other departments and the executive team. Showing up in the CFO's office wearing a *Star Trek* t-shirt and rumpled jeans would have failed to impress.

The team's current game-in-progress was scheduled for worldwide release at the start of the holiday season. It was the third installment in their multi-million-selling *In the Dark* franchise: an epic, survival horror series set in an apocalyptic world. Anticipation throughout the firm was high. As director, Len was ultimately responsible for delivering the game on time, and with the high quality expected from an AAA title.

The job brought loads of stress, but he loved it. He was living a childhood dream, staying immersed in video games all day and being well-paid to do it.

His coffee at his elbow, he walked through the meeting agenda with experienced ease, gathering updates from each team lead, inquiring about potential roadblocks, and confirming deadlines for the myriad set of tasks assigned out to each team. He was sipping coffee and listening to the lead writer's update when he happened to glance out the large window on his left.

April was walking past.

Len did a double-take.

She wore a Georgia Tech t-shirt that left her midriff exposed, high-cut yellow shorts that hugged her hips, and heeled sandals. Even by the company's liberal dress code standards, she was underdressed. Strutting past a row of cubicles, hips swaying, she looked over her shoulder, directly at him.

She ran her tongue across her lips.

Len swallowed.

Jesus, I've got to be imagining this.

She passed out of his field of view. He leaned sideways in his chair, trying to see where she'd gone—and noticed that everyone at the table was watching him.

"You here with us, chief?" asked Josh, the lead writer.

Len straightened. He pushed up his glasses on the bridge of his nose.

"Let's move on," Len said, and tapped his iPad with the stylus to expand the next item on the agenda.

He made it through the rest of the meeting only by going through the motions. His thoughts remained pinned on the impossible vision he had seen of his ex-girlfriend.

Maybe it's someone who only looks *like April,* he thought. *Someone who works there who happens to be a dead-ringer for her.*

It was a logical explanation. Perhaps the woman hadn't really been looking at him when she'd run her tongue across her lips, either.

When the meeting finally concluded a few minutes before ten o'clock, he left the conference room and strode down the same hallway that the April-lookalike had taken. He didn't see anyone who resembled her sitting in the rows of cubicles, but their company employed nearly five hundred people and leased three additional floors in the building. The woman could have worked on another floor. He didn't have time to track her down.

Shrugging, he turned and went to his own office.

His office, like all of the others, was paneled in glass. He had a nice view of Piedmont Park behind his back. Photos of Olivia and Kennedy occupied prominent spots on his desk, and posters of games he'd worked on hung from the walls.

It should have been a relaxing space, but his stomach was wound as tight as a coiled spring. His look-alike theory failed to reassure him. He couldn't get over the sense that he was overlooking an important detail.

Scratching the bite mark on his neck, he settled into his desk chair and clicked on his laptop to check e-mail.

Someone rapped on his door. It was Josh, the lead writer. Len beckoned him inside.

"Are you all right this morning?" Josh asked. "Talk to me, dude."

Len leaned back in his chair and tented his fingers. He and Josh had worked together for many years, and often socialized outside of the office, going to Tech football games together. Josh's wife and Olivia were friends, too.

Still, he had no intention of telling his friend what was going on. Mostly because he didn't think he could explain it without sounding totally bat shit crazy.

"Let me just say that I had a *very* long weekend," Len said.

"That's right." Josh snapped his fingers. "You guys were

moving into the new house. Crap, I hate moving. You seem as if you're totally out of it."

You have no idea, Len thought.

"It's Monday, and I'm already wiped out." Len shrugged. He scratched the welt on his neck again.

"Ouch." Josh winced. "What the heck happened there?"

"A horse fly had lunch on my neck."

"A fly did that? It's turning purple, dude."

Len was about to answer. Then he saw the woman again. She walked right past his doorway.

"What is it?" Josh asked. "You look like you've seen a ghost."

"Hang on." Len pushed out of his chair and went to the door, shouldering Josh aside.

The April twin was striding along the corridor, hips flexing in the too-tight shorts. She walked purposefully, as if she were in the office on important business. Reaching the end of the hall, she turned right, toward the restrooms. She disappeared inside the women's bathroom.

Either that woman is a dead-ringer for April, or I'm losing my mind.

One way to find out.

He went after her.

21

Len stopped outside the women's restroom.

He hadn't seen anyone go inside, or come out, since the April twin had disappeared within. A lifetime of learned discretion kept him from crossing the threshold. What if the woman simply looked like April and he walked in on her? What if there was another lady still inside who saw him come in? He could mumble an excuse, say he'd wandered into the wrong restroom by mistake, but given the visibility of his role at the company, he was reluctant to take the risk. He didn't want rumors circulating that he was some kind of pervert.

But something was bugging him. Getting a second look at the April doppelganger had launched a new line of worries. He was convinced he'd seen a tattoo of the Greek letter *pi* on the small of the woman's back, peeking above the waistline of her skin-tight shorts.

What were the chances that a woman who looked exactly like April would have the same tattoo as well?

So that means I must be losing my mind. April has been dead for fifteen years.

Finally, a female colleague of his approached. It was Tiffany, one of the level design artists on his team. She was dressed in her usual Goth chick fashion—all black—that accentuated her milk-pale complexion. Len dug his hand into his front pocket and pulled out three quarters.

"Hey, Tiff," he said. "Since you're heading in there, can you do me a quick favor, please?"

"What's up?" she asked.

"A young lady who went in there a second ago dropped these

quarters on the floor," he said, and showed her the coins. "Can you give them to her please?"

"Aren't you the good Samaritan?" Tiffany said. "Sure, man. No problemo."

"Thanks." He dropped the quarters into her palm. "I'll wait here."

"Oh, okay." Her jet-black eyebrows arched in a quizzical expression. "Be right back."

She entered the restroom, and came back only ten seconds later.

"There's no one in there," she said.

"Are you sure?"

"Wanna look for yourself?" She gestured to the door. "I won't tell."

Len shook his head. "She must've left before I could catch her. Thanks anyway."

He turned to leave, but Tiffany stopped him with a touch on his arm.

"Don't forget your quarters, man." She had extended her hand.

"Yeah. Thanks."

He accepted the coins. Dumped them into his pocket and wandered into the men's restroom, feeling as lost as if he'd awakened from a dream.

It's true. I totally imagined seeing April. What the hell is happening to me?

It was a standard office suite washroom: tile floor, fluorescent track lights, two sinks, two urinals, and two toilet enclosures with privacy doors. He was the only occupant.

He shuffled to one of the sinks and flipped on the tap.

I've got to get my shit together. Like, now.

He removed his glasses, ran cold water into his cupped palms, and thoroughly rinsed his face. The cold water was bracing, exactly the effect he wanted. He exhaled. Face dripping, he glanced up into the big mirror.

Dr. Laveaux was reflected in the glass, standing right behind him.

Len uttered a soft cry of shock. He spun around.

Behind him, there was only a paper towel dispenser and a stainless steel wastebasket.

Heart thudding, he wiped water from his eyes with the back of his hand. Swallowed. Turned back to face the mirror.

Dr. Laveaux was still there. But only in the mirror. An amused smile creased his ageless countenance.

Another hallucination? Jesus.

Hands shaking, Len picked up his glasses off the counter and slid them onto his still-wet face.

Laveaux raised his spindly index finger and pointed at Len.

"Two days and you be gone out Dr. Laveaux's house, boy," Laveaux said, and his nasal voice came to Len as clearly as if he stood right beside him. "Clock ticking down, uh huh . . . two days and you be out . . ."

Len hurried out of the restroom, shoving the door hard with his shoulder. Someone on the other side of the door yelped in surprise. Len crashed into the guy—it was a programmer on his team—and they both went sprawling to the floor outside the washroom.

"Dude." The guy sat up, readjusted his bifocals. "Tackle me like we're playing *Madden*, will ya?"

"I'm sorry, my mistake," Len said. He got up, took the man by the arm and helped him stand.

"Are you okay?" his colleague asked. "You look totally freaked out."

"I'm fine. Sorry again about running into you."

Head down because he didn't want anyone else to see the terror in his eyes, Len rushed back to his office. He closed his door and almost collapsed into his chair.

His hands were still trembling. So were his knees. He felt as if he might just shatter into a thousand fragments like a fragile piece of pottery.

Yesterday, Laveaux had warned him to be out of the house in three days. There were two days left until they hit the deadline . . . according to the vision of Laveaux in the mirror.

A *vision* had warned him, for crying out loud.

It's official, he thought. *I'm going nuts.*

22

Olivia had to be downtown for a deposition at the court reporter's office by eleven-thirty. She hated rushing, so with an hour to spare, she grabbed her leather satchel, strolled out of her office, and took the elevator down to the building's parking garage.

She was still trying to process what had happened to Reggie King. Wrapping his car around a tree, only two nights ago. Was it coincidence? Or had Dr. Laveaux paid King a visit, too, and promised revenge?

She struggled to shove the thoughts away and focus on work. Later, she would think about these things in detail, draw a sensible conclusion, and come up with next steps.

One of the many perks of partnership was that she had a reserved parking spot near the bank of elevators. When she exited the elevator and left the glass-walled vestibule to enter the garage, she had to walk only twenty paces to reach her Audi sedan. Most evenings, at the end of a long day spent in four-inch heels, she appreciated the short trek.

As soon as she emerged in the garage, she noticed that someone was sitting on the hood of her car.

She halted in her tracks.

It was the same man she'd seen while jogging that morning. The gray Georgetown hoodie. Rumpled, torn jeans. Bare, dusty feet. Head bowed and buried within the shadows of the hood, he swung his feet against the car's side panel, rocking to a silent beat.

She curled her fingers around the set of keys in her palm.

"My brother is dead," she whispered. "He is not sitting on my car. He is not real."

The brave thing to do was to banish this twisted hallucination by confronting it head-on. She *knew* it was all in her head. She didn't believe in ghosts, not really. And even if this were a ghost, spirits were formed of ethereal matter, like smoke, and couldn't physically harm her.

Go on, girl. Take charge. Like you always do.

But she couldn't make her feet move forward. Her shoes might as well have been concrete blocks.

The figure's head snapped up, the hood slipping away. Michael glared at her, his chin wreathed in vomit.

"Big sister bitch!" he said.

He leaped off the car and onto the pavement. He scrambled after her.

Olivia let out a strangled scream. She swung back toward the vestibule doors so frantically that she felt her right heel snap. She swayed, almost lost her balance and hit the concrete, but managed to correct herself just before she fell.

Dragging her foot, she stumbled inside the vestibule. She mashed the button to summon the elevator.

"You bitch!" her brother shouted. He was racing to the doors, feet slapping against concrete. Vomit dribbled from his chin and spattered his sweatshirt.

Oh, Jesus, this can't really be happening.

The elevator was taking an eternity. Leaning against a wall, she took off both of her high heeled shoes and jammed them into her satchel, allowing herself to run like hell if she needed to do so.

It's impossible but I can't deal with this, it's too much.

Michael reached the vestibule's glass double-doors just as the elevator chimed its arrival. She plunged inside the car, her bag swinging wildly from her shoulder. Punched the lobby level button and cowered against the back wall.

The elevator doors slowly began to close.

"Get back here, you fucking bitch!"

Michael ran to the elevator. He had a syringe in his hand. The needle was so huge it might have been used to inject a whale.

"Let me show you how it feels, sis," he said.

He thrust his arms between the doors, forcing them back open.

Olivia screamed. She swung her satchel at him. The bag connected with his head. Grunting, he stumbled backward and fell onto the vestibule floor, syringe clattering out of his fingers. His limbs trembled, as if he were gripped by a seizure.

God, I'm so sorry, Michael. I didn't mean to hurt you.

Tears spilled out of her eyes as the doors closed. She put her hand to her mouth to choke back a sob.

None of this actually happened, she told herself, in a mantra. *It's all in my mind.*

She wiped the tears out of her eyes, almost angrily. She had to get a hold of herself. She was at work. She didn't dare to allow anyone there to see her in this distraught state.

From the lobby, she took another elevator, back to her office on the tenth floor. She opened a lower desk drawer that she kept locked, and found the bottle of anti-anxiety medication.

The prescription meds were her secret. Len didn't know anything about them. In her opinion, your spouse didn't need to know every nook and cranny of your life.

She took a dose and chased it with a long sip of water. Then she slid on the spare set of pumps that she kept on hand, fixed her make-up, and returned downstairs.

The security guard on duty at the front desk was a lanky black man who looked old enough to have personally witnessed the Emancipation, but she decided to seek his help anyway.

"Someone hanging around your car, sweetheart?" He gave her a slow once-over, and couldn't suppress a flirtatious smile, exposing at least two gold teeth. "Well, I guess I need to go check it out, don't I?"

"If it's not too much trouble." She had to resist rolling her eyes.

The guard—his name tag read "Willie"—spoke to someone on a two-way radio. His colleague offered to escort Olivia, but Willie insisted on doing it himself and having the other guy relieve him at the front desk.

"Young buck don't know nothing," Willie said, holstering his radio. He winked.

Give me a break, she thought. He was old enough to be her grandfather.

The other guard, a much younger man, arrived about a minute later. Olivia was tempted to ask him to go with her instead, but didn't want to be offensive. She just wanted someone else at her side for back-up.

Willie ambled from behind the desk. In her heels, she was about five-eight, and he was at least a half foot shorter than she was.

But his diminutive stature didn't keep him from sizing her up, again, and grinning.

"I see you here every morning," he said as they walked to the elevators.

"Yes, I work at Wolfe and Kramer," she said.

"That right? You a secretary, sweetheart?"

Why did a young black woman working in an office automatically have to be a secretary? This wasn't nineteen seventy. Hell, they weren't even called secretaries any more.

"No," she said, and left it at that.

They boarded the elevator and rode down to the first level of the parking deck. Old Willie couldn't take his eyes off her. She kept her gaze on the wall. The last thing on her mind was entertaining the clumsy advances of some lecherous old player.

The elevator finally beeped. Before leaving, she swept her gaze around the vestibule.

There was no sign of her brother.

"After you, sugar," Willie said, and beckoned for her to exit.

She exited the car, feeling Willie's gaze pinned like a magnet to her rear end. She pointed through the glass doors.

"The black Audi parked over there," she said. "See it? That's my car."

"Ain't that something?" Willie let out a low whistle. "Some fella sure is taking good care of you, ain't he?"

Olivia let the comment pass. She didn't Michael lurking around her car. She should have been relieved, but she was not. She had wanted someone else to witness what she'd seen earlier. A thirty-party confirmation would have set her mind at ease.

They approached the car. Willie shuffled around the sedan, squinting, clearly with no idea whatsoever what he was supposed to be doing, while Olivia unlocked and opened the driver's side door.

She found no evidence that anyone had been inside. Everything was as she'd left it that morning. The interior smelled of leather, and faintly of the perfume she regularly wore and the apple juice that Kennedy had probably spilled on the car seat that morning.

"Anything else you need, brown sugar?" He glanced around. "You might have yourself a stalker, could be sneaking around in here."

"I'm fine, thanks for your time."

He started to turn, paused. "What you doing for lunch, cutie pie?"

"Excuse me?"

"They got some good sandwiches in the café in there, figured you and me could grab a bite and get to know each other." He licked his lips.

"No, thanks. Have a good day." She turned to get in the car.

"You get outta Dr. Laveaux's house, you know what good for you and that family," he said behind her. "Got two days now, uh huh, clock ticking down."

Olivia froze. Willie's voice sounded . . . different. Still his own voice, but with a strong nasal inflection shot through with a Haitian accent. Like Dr. Laveaux.

Willie stood beside the car. His eyes shone. He was grinning. It was as if Laveaux had climbed inside his body and taken over.

No, he can't do that.

"*Apre bal, tanbou lou.*" He snickered. "*Mache chèche pa janm dòmi san soupe.*"

Her mind slowly processed a translation of the Haitian Creole: There are consequences to your actions. You'll get what you deserve.

She raised the tiny can of pepper spray attached to her key chain, and aimed in his direction. The attached keys jingled as her hand trembled.

"Stay away from me," she said, in a thin voice. "Stay away from my family."

"Huh?" Willie blinked. "I asked you to grab a bite with me sometime, young thang."

Olivia stared at him. Whatever evil presence had possessed him—or that she had imagined had possessed him—had vanished. He looked like nothing more than the harmless, flirtatious old man that he was.

She lowered the pepper spray. "Sorry . . . I . . . I thought you said something else."

"Well, all right then." Willie chuckled, but he was scratching his head. "Then you have a good day, peaches. Drop by and see me sometime when you ain't too busy."

He ambled away, whistling a song. Olivia slid behind the wheel and dragged the door shut.

I'm losing it. I really am.

And as much as she was afraid to admit it, her worst suspicions about the old doctor were proving to be true.

23

Len spent the next couple of hours going through the motions.

For about a half hour, he supposedly examined a quality assurance issues report from their game testing team, but was unable to focus on the words on his computer screen. Attended a budget meeting in which he stared out of the window and didn't speak a word. Got on a conference call with the marketing team, and paid no attention to the competing voices that filled his office.

He probably should have gone home. He wasn't getting any work done, and he had plenty of vacation time banked away.

But he was afraid. The old Victorian was Dr. Laveaux's domain. Len had no idea how these things were happening to him, but he sure as hell knew why.

Two days and you be gone out Dr. Laveaux's house . . .

He called Olivia from his office. Tried her work Blackberry, got no answer, and then tried her personal cell phone. She didn't answer that line, either. Probably, she was in a meeting. He didn't know what he would have said to her anyway, but he craved to hear the voice of someone who could assure him that he hadn't lost his mind.

Around noon, by sheer force of habit, he shuffled down to the cafeteria on the lower level. It was a cavernous space, full of round tables and serving areas, and at that hour, the room was packed with people who worked in the various companies located in the office building.

Len got in line. Tempting aromas filled the air, but he didn't have an appetite. He grabbed a plastic tray and pushed it along the metal track, selecting the food items he might have wanted if he could bear to eat: a turkey-and-Swiss sandwich, a bowl of vegetable soup, a garden salad, a glass of iced tea.

He took his tray to a vacant table in the corner of the dining room. Along the way, he'd passed by several groups of colleagues and ignored them. He was in no mood for chit-chat.

But a few minutes after Len sat, Josh came over and dropped into the seat across the table. Slices of pepperoni pizza were piled high on his plate.

"Mind if I join you, man?" Josh said, and promptly started devouring pizza like a human garbage disposal.

Len didn't reply. His lunch untouched, he stirred his iced tea with a straw.

Chewing, Josh wiped his lips with a napkin. "What happened this morning?"

Len blinked. "This morning?"

"You don't remember?" Josh said.

"A lot has happened this morning, Josh."

"We were in your office chatting, and then you looked like you saw a ghost and ran out."

Len finally lifted his glass and took a sip of tea. It was unsweetened, but the bitterness seemed to blow the fog out of his brain.

Munching pizza, Josh watched him, expectant.

"Do you consider yourself an open-minded person?" Len asked.

"Open-minded? I've always been a free spirit. Look at the weird crap that I write. You know that about me."

"What do you think about the supernatural?"

"The supernatural?" Josh swallowed, sipped his soda. "Such as?"

"Ghosts. Spirits or whatever. Hauntings. That kind of stuff."

"Did you move into a haunted house, man?" Josh asked.

Len straightened in his chair. "What?"

"So I'm right," Josh said.

"How did you guess?"

"You told me before the house is over a hundred years old." Josh shrugged and bit into another slice of pizza. "That's a lot of history, a lot of shit going on. Haunted places are always full of awful incidents over a long period of time."

"You've studied this subject," Len said.

"I have a layman's knowledge. I read a lot of books. I write game scripts for survival horror, dude, and I'm damned good at it. That means I gotta know my shit."

"Right." Len felt his appetite surfacing. He picked up his turkey sandwich and took a huge bite. "What do you know about vodou?"

"Not a subject I've studied in much detail, but I know a little bit. Why?"

"I'll get to that. So the house we moved into this past weekend? The former owner dropped by yesterday, told us he was basically scammed out of his house. He gave us three days to move out."

"No shit?" Josh's eyes widened. "Is he telling the truth? Was he scammed?"

"Don't know," Len said. "But *he* believes it, and that's what's important."

"You can't talk a crazy man out of his delusion."

"Exactly." Len was nodding. "I think this guy is some kind of vodou priest, from Haiti. A *bokor* is what he would be called, a sorcerer. I've found several strange things in the house: statues, pictures, candles, jars of weird stuff. Like ritual objects."

"But that's not what has you freaked out, is it? You saw something after the meeting this morning, didn't you?"

Len hesitated, wiped his hands on a napkin. "This stays between us."

"Of course." Josh frowned. "Come on, dude, we've known each other for years. I've always respected what you tell me in private."

"I saw someone walk through the office that couldn't be here," Len said.

"Who?"

Len lowered his voice to a whisper. "My ex-girlfriend. She's been dead for fifteen years, Josh."

Josh had been in the process of picking up another slice of pizza. It slipped out of his fingers and dropped back onto the plate.

"I heard her in the house last night," Len said. "I've seen her at the office today, twice. The second time is when you and I were talking. I saw her walk down the hallway and go into the ladies' room. I asked someone to go in there, and the restroom was empty."

"Shit," Josh said.

"Then when I go into the bathroom to try to get my bearings,

I see him in there. The former owner. In the mirror."

"Then what happened?" Josh was leaning forward so far in his chair that it looked as if it might tip over.

"He told me we've got two days to get out of the house, and the clock is ticking." Len grabbed his glass of iced tea, drained the rest of it in a couple of long gulps. "I know, this whole story sounds totally ridiculous, but I swear, I didn't make up any of this."

"I believe you," Josh said, flatly.

"You do?"

"You're a cool customer, Mr. Easygoing. You wouldn't make up something this crazy."

"Thanks," Len said. He laughed, uneasily. "I needed to hear someone tell me I wasn't nuts."

"Hey, you're nuts if you stay in that house. You need to get your family out of there, man. Today."

"It's not that simple."

"It's simple, all right. Here's how you do it: pack a suitcase. Book a room at a hotel. Hire movers to take the rest of your stuff out of there." Josh was shaking his head. "This guy has tapped into your mind and has you seeing things. What happens when you reach his deadline? It's going to get a lot worse if you don't give him what he wants."

"I can't get Olivia to talk to me about it," Len said. "I think she's scared, too, but she shuts down when I bring up the subject. I think she knows something isn't right."

"You've got to protect what's yours," Josh said. "By any means necessary."

It was a quote lifted from the first installment of their franchise series, *In the Dark*, and had been used in the marketing materials, as well. *Protect what's yours.* Len agreed with the principle, but how did it apply to his situation? What could he do?

In a flash, he realized the next step was obvious. He pushed away his lunch tray and rose from the chair.

"Where are you going?" Josh said.

"Thanks for the chat," Len said. "I've got to get out of here and take care of some business."

24

Len took the rest of the day off, claiming to his boss that a family emergency had arisen. He didn't have to lie. He had an urgent need to leave the office, and it was all for the sake of his family.

The first thing he did was buy a gun.

At a gun & ammo shop in Midtown, he asked the guy behind the counter to recommend a reliable weapon for home protection. The clerk suggested a Beretta nine millimeter compact pistol. The Beretta had a three-inch-long barrel and a magazine capacity of fifteen rounds.

It was the first time he'd purchased a firearm, but not the first gun he'd handled. His dad had been an avid collector of rifles, shotguns, and handguns, and when Len was a teenager, his dad had demonstrated their proper use. Len had never felt the need to personally own such a weapon. Until then.

He also bought a couple of extra magazines of ammo, a leather holster designed for concealed carry, and a portable gun safe that could fit into a standard-size drawer.

Thus far, Dr. Laveaux's assault upon his life had been entirely psychological, the old man somehow plumbing painful memories that Len had never shared with anyone. He didn't know how Laveaux knew of his troubled past with April, didn't know how he was apparently triggering these visions of her. But he wanted to be prepared for anything.

Of course, he had to be careful to use the pistol only in the right situation. He wasn't going to open fire on a man in a mirror. His life, or the lives of his family members, would need to be on the line.

Next, he visited The Home Depot. He purchased a list of items: a bolt cutter with blades large enough to dismantle a padlock, duct tape, a set of dust masks, two heavy-duty flashlights, a utility pouch that could attach to his belt, two battery operated lanterns, and plenty of batteries. He bought another padlock, too.

It was three o'clock in the afternoon when he pulled into the driveway at home. He had a little over two hours at his disposal before he'd need to pick up Kennedy from preschool.

From the exterior, the rambling Victorian looked utterly normal, like a cutout from a Norman Rockwell painting. Sunshine glinted on the front windows, and a breeze stirred the hedges and the rose bush flanking the veranda. There was no hint of a house that concealed dangerous secrets and hidden lairs.

Jacob was outside weeding his lawn. Getting out of his SUV, Len waved at him, decided to have a word.

"How's it going, today?" Len said after they shook hands. "Getting ready for the next woman in your rotation to come through?"

Jacob laughed and mopped sweat from his forehead with a handkerchief.

"Yes, sir." Jacob chuckled again. "Tonight, it's Sheree. I met her at an art gallery in the West End. She was the most stunning piece in the whole gallery, brother, let me assure you."

"No doubt," Len said. "Hey, you enjoy researching the history of homes, right?"

"Indeed I do." Jacob tucked his handkerchief into his back pocket, the humor fading from his eyes as his demeanor turned serious. "You have a project for me?"

"Can you find out what stood on our property before the house was built? Or possibly, who first owned the house?"

"Shouldn't be too difficult, no sir, not at all." Jacob stroked his goatee. "Is there some aspect in particular you want to learn about?"

Len hesitated. "I'm curious about the basement."

"What did you find in the basement?"

"There's a hidden room down there," Len said. "I think there's a concealed area even farther below."

"Is that so?" Jacob's eyes danced with interest. "You've seen this?"

"I have a good hunch." Len made a show of checking his wristwatch. "I've gotta run, man. If you can find out something, I'd really appreciate it."

"I'm all over it, yes sir," Jacob said. "Happy to help. I'll drop by when I get something."

It was obvious that Jacob wanted to know more, and possibly wanted Len to invite him inside to inspect the discovery with his own eyes. Len was reluctant to involve him on that level, didn't want to risk bringing his neighbor under Laveaux's radar. It was safer for Jacob to remain on the periphery of the situation.

Crossing the street to return to his vehicle, Len noticed his wheelchair-bound neighbor sitting on the veranda. What was his name again? Bill something. The guy watched Len closely; Len waved at him, and predictably, got no response except a blank stare. Poor guy.

Len brought his purchases inside via the side door. The Victorian was as quiet as a mortuary. Sunlight filtered through the blinds, dust motes swirling in the shafts of light.

In the kitchen, he stood at the counter and made his preparations. Then, he delved into the basement.

25

The antechamber behind the false wall was exactly as Len had left it that morning. He switched on one of the new, battery-powered lanterns. It filled the space with a cool white glow.

After placing the lamp in the corner, he turned his attention to the trapdoor. He picked up his brand-new bolt cutters, tightened his grip on the rubber-coated handles.

Here goes nothing.

It took three attempts to cut through the padlock. The first two times, he didn't position the tool quite right, but on the third attempt, with the blades held at the proper angle, he was able to cut through the lock as easily as if it were a ribbon. It fell away from the hasp with a soft click.

Kneeling, he grabbed the defeated lock, slid it aside. He flipped away the hasp and got a firm grasp on the door handle.

He pulled.

Damn, but it was heavy. The lid must have weighed fifty pounds. He rose to his feet, steadied himself, and wrapped both hands around the handle. Again, he pulled.

He felt his back muscles, already sore from an exhausting weekend of moving, clench painfully with the effort.

How did Laveaux manage to open this? He must be stronger than he looks.

The hinges squeaked as he lifted the lid. A heavy, fetid odor drifted from the widening portal, swallowed him like a fog. It was the stench of mildew, rot, and God knew what else. He coughed, but kept lifting.

The hinges allowed the door to rotate a full hundred and

eighty degrees, until the top of the lid was parallel to the floor. Len dropped the hatch with a clang and moved back a couple of feet to catch his breath, his forehead dripping with sweat.

The miasma rising from the depths below was unbearable. He slipped on one of the dust masks he'd purchased, was finally able to breathe without gagging.

Flashlight in hand, he inspected the access portal.

It was a staircase. The stairway was narrow, the steps formed of old, crumbling stone, the walls festooned with dusty cobwebs. The walls were constructed of bricks, huge blocks lying atop one another, held together with crusted mortar.

He counted twenty steps before they appeared to end at a broad concrete slab that served as a floor. The flashlight's limited range didn't allow him to see much else.

What else was down there? Most important, what exactly was its purpose?

He could not fathom the answers to those questions. The existence of this passage was so far outside the realm of his experience that he had no solid foundation upon which to base his assumptions.

What was that?

Len paused, flashlight beam fixed on the staircase. He had heard something below. The echo of what had sounded like a scuttle. Something scraping against concrete.

It was probably just the old house making noises, loose stones tumbling away, displaced by his opening the hatch.

But it hadn't sounded like that, had it?

Slowly, he traced the light down to the bottom of the steps again, to the floor.

And saw a face out of a nightmare. Glowing yellow eyes, a mottled face striped with red streaks, a wide mouth like a shark's, rows of razor teeth glinting.

Len screamed, the flashlight dropping out of his hand. It clattered onto the steps and rolled down, the light bouncing crazily off the walls.

He grabbed the edge of the hatch and lifted it, a surge of frantic strength allowing him to easily hoist the door. He slammed the lid back onto the floor with a boom that shook the walls.

Fingers trembling, he slipped the new padlock over the hasp, locked it. Double-checked it to ensure it would hold.

Heart knocking so hard that his rib cage ached, he backed

away from the hatch. He snatched off the dust mask and sucked in deep gulps of cool, fresh air.

He half-expected the hatch door to buckle upward as whatever he'd seen down there tried to force its way out. But nothing happened. He didn't hear any noises issue from beneath, and the door remained still.

A door guardian, he thought, and wondered where the insight came from. *That's what I saw. Something Laveaux summoned or created to guard whatever he's hiding down there.*

He had the Beretta secured in his holster, and the gun was loaded. But he didn't have the nerve to open the hatch again. Call him a coward, but that devilish face reminded him of his worst childhood night terrors.

He collected his things and left the room, ensuring that the false wall was securely in place. He returned upstairs. Closed and locked the basement door. Then he swung a chair from the dining room table and jammed it underneath the doorknob.

Exploration time was over. He and Olivia had to have a serious, no-more-secrets discussion, and he wasn't going to accept anything less. No more stonewalling. No more bullshitting.

They had to talk about getting the hell out of there.

26

Later that afternoon, Olivia had an unexpected visitor at her office.

Since her experience in the parking garage, her work day had slid back on track. The deposition went as planned. Other meetings, calls, and work activities proceeded without a hitch. It was as if the incidents from earlier that day had never happened.

The anti-anxiety medicine was working exactly as she'd hoped it would.

There were undeniable side effects to ingesting a drug that slowed down the functioning of the central nervous system. She wasn't as mentally sharp as she liked to be, needed a bit more time to process information. And addiction was always a concern. She was cautious in her use of the prescription, never took more than the recommended amount, and only when she felt she had no other viable option and needed quick relief. It was, ultimately, a short-term solution.

But her primary goal, at that point, was simply to survive the day without suffering another "psychological event," as she'd come to think of it. Later—she didn't know exactly when, merely *later*—she could define a real action plan for dealing with the root cause of her issue.

When her internal phone line rang at four-thirty, however, she was sucked right back into the very topic she'd been trying to avoid.

"I have a visitor for you, Olivia," Bernice said, her voice amplified on the speakerphone. "He doesn't have an appointment. But he says it's urgent."

Olivia glanced away from her laptop display, where she'd

been composing an-email. She frowned. She wasn't a physician; she didn't get walk-ins.

"Who is he?" she asked.

"He says he's from the real estate company that sold your house to you," Bernice said. "Mr. Virgil Benoit?"

Her stomach plummeted. She didn't know the man's name, but she knew what this was all about. She'd called his firm that morning, learned about Reggie King's car accident—*was it really an accident?*—and had asked someone from there to get back in touch with her.

Tell him to go away, she almost told Bernice. *I've had enough drama for today.*

But if the man had visited her office to see her, then what he needed to tell her had to be important. In her predicament, she couldn't afford to turn him away.

"Take him to Stone Mountain, please," Olivia said, using the name of one of their conference rooms, so labeled because its window faced the eponymous mountain that loomed east of the city. "I'll be there in a minute."

"Is everything okay?" Bernice asked.

Olivia understood the concern behind the question. She rarely had anyone outside of her business circle visit her at the office, with the exception of Len and sometimes her mother. Bernice was fishing for information.

"No worries," she said, in her most assuring tone. "I've got some business details to wrap up with the house."

She flipped out her compact and checked her makeup—purely by force of habit—and approved of the professional, put-together woman she saw reflected in the small mirror. The woman gazing back at her could handle anything; that was what she told herself. Whatever the visitor's purpose, she was going to keep things under control.

She left her office and headed to the conference room.

When she entered, Virgil Benoit was standing at the floor-to-ceiling window, taking in the view. He was a younger guy with that baby-faced, fresh out of college look. She pegged his age as mid-twenties. He was short, perhaps five-four, but broad-shouldered, and wore a blue dress shirt, dark slacks, loafers. He had a thinly-defined goatee that made him look like a teenager struggling to cultivate facial hair.

"Hey, that's a sweet view y'all got," he said. She heard a

Louisiana bayou accent breeze through his soft voice. "Don't realize how big that mountain is until you take a step back and look at it, uh huh."

They shook hands. His palm was as damp as a wet napkin, which she found off-putting, but she chalked it up to nerves on his part.

"What can I do for you, Mr. Benoit? You didn't contact me in advance." She remained standing beside the conference table, arms crossed over her chest, gaze steady on his as she intentionally projected a demeanor that declared: *I'm at work, you'd better not be here to waste my time with nonsense.*

He broke eye contact and chuckled self-consciously. He stroked his goatee. "Ma'am, I'm sorry I didn't call to make an appointment. But you called us this morning about your house."

"I heard about what had happened to Reggie, I'm sorry."

"Pardon me for saying, but the truth is, Reggie brought it on himself." He looked at her. She noticed his hazel eyes were outlined in red, from either fatigue, or tears.

"I thought he had a car accident," she said. "What are you telling me?"

"You mind if I take a seat, ma'am?" He touched his faint goatee again, a nervous tic apparently.

"Help yourself." She indicated a chair, and then eased into the seat located cater-corner from his.

Sitting, Benoit steepled his fingers. He drew in several deep breaths, calming himself.

"You were saying," she said.

He cleared his throat. "It was shady, all right? Nobody wanted to listen to me, I said doing this stuff was gonna catch up to us sooner or later. Reggie was like, whatever. It all caught up to him when he did it to the wrong person. Like my mama says, God don't like ugly."

Olivia felt as if she had dropped into a conversation in mid-stream.

"Mr. Benoit, let's start from the beginning, please," she said. "What was shady? Explain that to me, please."

"Umm." He fiddled with his goatee again, looking around the conference room as if he were suddenly unsure he wanted to be there. "What kind of lawyer are you, ma'am? Are you a . . . prosecutor or something like that?"

"I practice employment law, not criminal law. You can speak

to me freely. I only want to know the full background of the home we purchased."

"All right, all right." He spread his palms on the table. He had fingers like sausages, his nails gnawed almost to the quick. But when he spoke again, the steadiness had returned to his voice. "So the foreclosure, it was shady, okay? Reggie went to Morehouse with this guy who knew Dr. Laveaux's business, they were in the same frat, and kept in touch over the years and worked on deals together sometimes. So like six months ago, they decided to pull the money outta the house, yeah."

Olivia felt a flutter in her stomach. She didn't like where this was headed.

"How did they accomplish that?" she asked.

"The house was paid off, free and clear, right? So Reggie's friend, Jamal, like I said, he knew Dr. Laveaux's business. He did some investing for him here and there, was promising the doctor that he was going to pull some of the equity out of the house to finance some things Dr. Laveaux wanted to do. And get this: Jamal knew the man was going to be out of the country for like six months. So right after the doctor left town, Jamal stole his identity."

Tension clamped Olivia's stomach. "Go on."

"Jamal and Reggie used that to apply for a home equity loan, did it all online. Reggie had this other guy we use do the appraisal. Reggie set up a special bank account for the transaction, and soon as the loan got approved, boom. He sucked out all of the available balance. Dr. Laveaux had no clue, he wasn't even home. They walked away with a *lot* of cash, everybody got a nice cut."

My God, Olivia thought. *It's exactly what I was afraid of finding out.*

"How much?" she asked.

"A hundred and eighty gees," Benoit said.

She noticed that Benoit wore a platinum Rolex, an outrageously expensive watch, and wondered if he'd purchased the time piece with his ill-gotten profits from deals like the one he described.

"I think I can fill out the blanks of what happened next," Olivia said. "Clearly, no one in your enterprising crew was going to repay the maxed out home equity loan. Dr. Laveaux knew nothing of it as he was out of pocket. Therefore, the lender commenced foreclosure proceedings."

Benoit was nodding. "Dr. Laveaux was never notified of

nothing until he came back and found out his house had been foreclosed on."

Olivia was shaking her head. "That's cold-blooded."

"The kicker is, when the foreclosure went through, Reggie swooped in and picked up the house cheap at auction on the courthouse steps." Benoit chuckled, but it was a grim sound, devoid of humor. "He was a smooth operator, you know?"

"And he turned around and sold it to us for *another* handsome profit," she said.

"That's how it went down," Benoit said, bobbing his head. "Wasn't the first time he'd pulled that off, either, yeah."

Olivia touched her abdomen. She felt nauseous.

"Why?" she asked. "Why did they target Dr. Laveaux for this scam?"

Benoit tickled his goatee, shrugged. "Money. Nothing else. They saw a chance to get paid and they took it."

"It always comes down to plain, old-fashioned greed," Olivia said.

"But they did it to the wrong guy." He shifted in the chair. "Dr. Laveaux, uh . . . he stopped by our office last week. Guess he'd just gotten back from Haiti."

"I've met him before," she said. "He visited us yesterday."

"He did?" Benoit audibly gulped.

She nodded. "But go on."

"Dr. Laveaux called Reggie out for what he did and demanded his house back. Sounded like Jamal had confessed everything to Dr. Laveaux. Man, I mean, Jamal was *driving* for him."

Olivia remembered the man that Len had told her about, Dr. Laveaux's "chauffeur." She doubted his new driver had willingly volunteered for the job.

"Reggie actually laughed at Dr. Laveaux, right there in the office," Benoit said. "Then he showed him the door. Where I come from, you don't disrespect a man like him like that."

She didn't ask what he meant by his statement. She could guess.

"They said Reggie died in the car accident, but let me tell you, ma'am . . ." Benoit's voice trailed off. "Dr. Laveaux made it happen. He'd *said* it would happen."

His eyes pleaded with her to believe him. She merely pressed her lips together tightly. She didn't want to believe him. But she knew better.

"My family is from Haiti," she said. "I understand some things about a man like him."

Benoit smiled with obvious relief. "So you get it, too. It ain't a joke. Reggie thought he was just some weird old dude that dressed funny. I tried to tell him, my nana told me stories about men like him. He brushed it off, said it was ignorant black folks talking superstitious."

"Why did you come here to tell me this?" she asked. "You could have shared this information over the phone. Or you could've kept your mouth shut."

Benoit stared down at his fingers splayed across the tabletop. "I was afraid you'd hang up on me. I needed you to understand how important this is. Reggie got what he had coming, and so did Jamal, I guess, but you folks didn't do nothing wrong."

"I don't think that's the issue any more," she said. "Laveaux was scammed out of his home. He wants it back. Can you blame him?"

Benoit was shaking his head. "I wish I'd spoke up sooner at work about this."

"Your sudden acquisition of a conscience isn't going to matter anymore either, is it?" she said. "It's too late. You kept your head down and allowed these things to happen."

"I know." His lips trembled. "I'm sorry."

She pushed away from the table and stood, hands balled into fists on her waist. She felt like putting one of her two-hundred dollar pumps up his ass. But what was the use? The damage was done.

"Laveaux has already given us a deadline to move out of the house," she said. "He said to be out in three days. We're on day number two."

Benoit stared at her. His eyes were as large as coffee saucers.

"Ma'am, you've gotta get outta that house," he said. "He gave Reggie three days, too. Three days to make it right, he said." Tears spilled from his eyes. He sniffled, and his next sentence came in a tremulous voice.

"His time was up Saturday night."

27

Olivia tried to resume working after Benoit left the office, but she couldn't focus sufficiently to even write an e-email. She sat at her desk, staring blankly at her computer screen, her mind looping through what she'd learned.

Everything Laveaux had claimed was true. He had been defrauded out of his home. He was justifiably furious, and she could understand—while not condone—the threats he'd initially made to them.

But the facts of the matter didn't make the road ahead any smoother. They still had a mortgage on the property, and someone still had to pay it. They couldn't simply move out and hand over the keys.

She needed to talk to Len about this turn of events. But it wasn't a conversation that she wanted to have over the phone. The gravity of the situation demanded a face-to-face discussion about their future in the Victorian; they would talk about it that evening and figure out what they needed to do.

A knock came at her office door. Bernice stepped inside. She was wearing her jacket.

"I'm about to head home," Bernice said. "Do you need anything before I go?"

Olivia glanced at her digital desk clock. It was a quarter to six. Lost in her thoughts, she had completely lost track of time, too.

"I'm fine, thanks. I'm leaving shortly, myself."

"Did everything work out okay with your house?" Bernice asked.

Bernice had been her executive assistant for several months, but Olivia had never shared any truly personal details with her. The woman was a sweetheart, extremely competent at her job, and a fellow soror, but from Olivia's observations, she was a bit of a gossip. The last thing Olivia needed was to have this shady business about her house circulating around the office water cooler.

"We're getting to the bottom of things," Olivia said, in a tone that sounded more confident than she felt. "It'll all work out."

"Good, good," Bernice said, yet she obviously craved a juicier response. "Cliff and I do some real-estate investing, on the side. We have a *lot* of experience dealing with properties all over the city, I could tell you some stories, girl."

"No doubt you could," Olivia said, and didn't add anything else. She wasn't falling for the bait.

Bernice smiled, a wistful expression. "Well, let go and let God, as my pastor says. You have a good evening."

Olivia waved, and turned back to face the computer. Her inbox bulged with unread e-mails that had arrived within the past hour. She wasn't really in the mood to deal with any of them, but the brief interaction with Bernice had snapped her out of her daze. She began to work through the messages, replying, deleting, and filing in folders as needed. If she worked only when she was in an ideal mood, she'd never accomplish much of anything.

Her Blackberry chirped. Caller ID displayed her home telephone number. Perhaps Len wanted her to pick up something on her way home.

She answered the call. "Hey, babe."

"Always on the job, huh, sister?" It was an unfamiliar woman's voice. She sounded Olivia's age or slightly younger. "Like Lenny says."

"Excuse me?" Olivia said. At the mention of "Lenny," her voice lost its polished edge. "Who is this?"

The caller let out a throaty laugh. "Oh, Lenny hasn't told you about me yet? His numero uno girl, April, from back in the day at Tech? The redbone sister with the cute face, small waist, and big behind?"

Rising from her chair, Olivia kept the phone pressed against her ear. She paced in front of her desk. The packet of risqué photos she'd discovered in Len's office that morning immediately came to mind.

"Lenny's always *loved* to snap pictures of me." April snickered. "Can you blame him?"

Olivia checked the caller's phone number again, convinced she had misread it the first time. But another look confirmed it. Was this for real?

"What the hell are you doing in my house?" Olivia asked.

The woman purred like a well-fed cat. "Mmmm. I've been here all day, girl. With Lenny. I've been taking him back down memory lane."

Olivia had to stop pacing and lean against her desk. She put her fingers to her temple. Her pulse throbbed. She felt tears pushing at her eyes.

This was too much stress for her to handle in one day. The visions of Michael. The revelation about the house. Now this.

I'm going to kill him.

"How long . . ." Olivia's voice cracked, and she had to start over. "How long has this been going on?"

"Lenny's out picking up your precious little girl," April said. "I'm going to skedaddle on my way in a few. I don't want to be a home wrecker, 'specially when kids are involved . . . but after I laid it on Lenny today, he's talking about leaving you. I wanted you to know that."

"You wanted me to know that you fucked my husband in our bed," Olivia said.

April laughed. "You should thank me. He was damn near 'bout to lose his mind. I cleaned out his pipes, girl. He'll be nice and calm for a while now."

Olivia felt dizzy. Nearly stumbling, she made her way back to her desk chair, dropped into it.

A framed family portrait stood on her desk, angled toward her. The three of them grinning on what had seemed like a perfect day. She blinked back a wave of tears, but they kept on coming.

She'd worked so hard, and had sacrificed so much, to build a stable, happy life. Aggressively pursued higher education and a lucrative profession. Married a soft-spoken man who'd appeared completely devoted to his family. Waited years to have her first child, putting off motherhood until her career had hit its stride.

In the end, none of it had mattered.

April was still talking, her voice seeming to come from far away. "I thought you deserved to know the truth. I'd want to know the truth if I were in your shoes . . . don't want some man dogging me out behind my back and giving me sloppy seconds . . ."

"Listen, you better be out of my house by the time I get there, bitch," Olivia said. "You hear me? Or I will fuck up both you and Len."

Olivia was speaking to a dial tone. The woman had hung up.

Sniffling, she pulled a box of Kleenex toward her. She blew her nose, dried her eyes.

I cleaned out his pipes, girl . . .

She grabbed her purse and headed for the door.

She couldn't wait to get home.

28

Len had picked up Kennedy from preschool and brought her back home. It took a supreme act of willpower for him to return to the house. But he was not allowing his family to spend another night under that roof.

He'd packed a suitcase with clothes and other necessities for himself, Olivia, and Kennedy. He left the luggage standing beside the front door. When Olivia got home, he was going to tell her what happened, and they were going to get out of there. They could check into a hotel that night and figure out their next steps.

He prayed only that Olivia believed him. She could be so damned stubborn that she might insist on seeing first-hand evidence of his experience. He had no intention of going into the basement ever again, so if she wanted to satisfy her curiosity . . . well, she was on her own.

He sat on the sofa in the family room while Kennedy watched TV: an episode of *Doc McStuffins*, one of her favorite characters. As she watched the show, she munched on a cup of cheese crackers. She was happily unaware of anything amiss, and he wanted to keep it that way.

When he heard Olivia parking her car in the garage, his heart leapt. He went to meet her at the mud room entrance off the kitchen.

"Hey, we need to . . ." he started to say, and his next words faltered on his lips as he saw the expression on her face.

Her face was a mask of pure rage. He'd seen that look only once before, during the worst argument of their marriage a couple of years ago, and he'd hoped never to see it again.

What did I do? Nothing, I can't think of anything. She can't be pissed at me.

She gave him a withering look. Brushing past him, she stomped inside and slammed her purse onto the kitchen counter.

"What happened?" he asked.

Her eyes were bloodshot, as if she'd been crying. Her hair, normally perfectly coiffed, was in disarray, strands sticking out in random directions.

"Where's Kennedy?" she asked, in a wire-tight whisper.

"She's watching TV in the family room. What's going on?"

Olivia stormed out of the kitchen, heels clocking against the floor. He followed her.

She was heading upstairs. Feet banging against the old steps. Len glanced in the family room, saw Kennedy was still happily engrossed in the cartoon. He hurried after Olivia.

He caught up to her as she was kicking open the door to their bedroom.

"Olivia, dammit. Will you *please* tell me what's going on?"

She stopped beside the queen-size bed. Fists bunched on her waist, she stared at the mattress like a detective searching for evidence of a crime.

"What the heck are you looking for?" he asked.

Slowly, she swiveled to face him. Her nostrils flared.

"Did you fuck that bitch on our bed?" she asked, still in that deadly whisper.

No, not this again. More false accusations of bad behavior. Where was this coming from?

"I don't know what you're talking about," he said. "I haven't done anything."

"Her name is April," she said, continuing to whisper. "She's your old college girlfriend. The bitch in those pictures I found this morning."

Oh, no. No, no, no.

Involuntarily, he took a step back. Olivia advanced toward him. Her eyes burned.

"Sounding familiar now?" she said.

"Olivia, listen—"

"You brought here over here today, *Lenny*," she said. "Into our home. Into our bed."

"You've got this all—"

"You fucked her in our bed!" She slammed both her fists onto the mattress, pounded it once, twice, three times. The accent pillows tumbled off the bed and bounced onto the floor. *"Our bed!"*

"Listen to me carefully." He struggled to keep his voice calm. Matching Olivia's volume would only cause things to spiral further out of control. "None of what you're saying is possible. April Howard is dead."

He watched her flinch as if he'd slapped her in the face. "What?"

"April has been dead for fifteen years." He removed his glasses and pinched the bridge of his nose. "I never told you about her. It's . . . complicated. But she killed herself, Olivia."

Olivia's expression flickered between shock, and anger. "But she called me."

He felt his stomach plummet as possible explanations spun through his mind. "She's gone. She couldn't have called you. There's something else going on here."

"Look." Olivia handed him her Blackberry. "She called me from here, our house, at five fifty-seven this evening. Look at the call history."

Len navigated to the call history menu, selected incoming calls. He found the call from their home landline, at the exact time Olivia had stated.

"I wasn't even here then," he said. "I was picking up Kennedy from preschool."

"So the house called me on its own?" She laughed hoarsely. "Do you know how ridiculous that sounds?"

Len sat on the bed. He dragged his hand down his face.

"It doesn't sound ridiculous at all, considering what I've seen lately," he said.

Something in Olivia's gaze shifted. He had touched a nerve.

"You've seen things, too, haven't you?" he asked. "Things that can't possibly be real. Haven't you?"

She chewed her bottom lip, tears hanging in her eyes. Finally, she wiped her eyes, nodded.

"I've seen April," he said. "I heard her walking through the house late last night. Then I saw her at work, roaming down the hallways."

"Are you serious?" she said.

"I wish it were a joke. I tried to rationalize it, thought I was seeing someone who only looked like her. But that's not it. It's an illusion, I guess."

"I've seen Michael," Olivia said, her voice hushed, as if speaking such words in a normal tone would be an admittance of something she dared not consider. "Twice today."

Len knew all about the guilt that Olivia bore over her younger brother's death. He'd tried to explain that it wasn't her fault, that Michael was a grown man who'd made his own decisions, but she still blamed herself. You couldn't reason your way out of guilt, and no one could talk you out of it, either. You had to discover some deeper insight or epiphany—and if he'd known how to do that, he wouldn't have walked around feeling ashamed of what had happened to April.

"I'm so sorry," Len said.

Sighing heavily, Olivia sat next to him on the bed. She kicked off her pumps and drew her legs up onto the mattress.

After a moment's hesitation, Len reached for her hand. She let him take it. Her palm was damp. Probably, his was sweaty as well. But he needed the grounding effect of their hands connected, and he suspected she did, too.

For perhaps a minute, neither of them spoke. The Victorian creaked and groaned as a breeze sifted past. Len thought of what Olivia had revealed—*the house called me on its own*—and flashed back on what he'd seen in the cellar. This place they'd dared to call their home was full of lives already—and Dr. Laveaux was the director of the cast, calling the shots from the shadows.

"The next question is: how is all this happening?" Len said. "I have a good idea."

"It's Laveaux," Olivia said.

"Oh?" He glanced at her. "You're finally willing to speak his name?"

"I'm sorry, Len. I didn't want to open that door. But it's too dangerous for us to avoid any longer. There's a lot that we need to discuss."

"Agreed. And you know what? Why don't we have this conversation outside the house? On neutral ground. We can grab dinner somewhere and lay everything on the table."

"Not a bad idea." Olivia nodded, pushed off the bed. "Let's go get Kennedy."

They returned downstairs. Len trailed Olivia into the family room.

The TV was on, but Kennedy was gone.

29

"Kennedy?" Olivia said. "Where are you, baby? It's time to go eat dinner."

There was no answer. Len remembered that Kennedy had recently learned how to play hide-and-seek. She loved to creep inside closets and cabinets, pull the door shut, and quietly wait for someone to find her. It was cute, but when they were in a hurry to go somewhere, it could be maddening.

He had another lurking suspicion, however, that made the flesh tighten at the nape of his neck.

"The basement," he said.

"What?" Olivia used the remote control to switch off the television, and gave him a skeptical look. "How could she get down there? We keep the door locked."

Len didn't stop to explain. He raced down the hallway and into the kitchen. Olivia followed close on his heels.

Earlier, he had used a chair to barricade the cellar door. That chair had been slid away. The door had been locked, too. It hung wide open.

Under ordinary circumstances, he would have stared in disbelief. Not then. There were forces at work inside the house. Powers beyond his comprehension bent toward tearing his family apart.

Were they too late?

He flipped on the light above the staircase. "Kennedy!"

No reply. He looked to the bottom. No sign of his daughter. He'd been terrified by the idea that she had come down there and fallen down on the stairs.

"There's a flashlight on the counter," he said to Olivia. "Grab it."

Olivia picked up the light, handed it to him. He flicked it on, directed the beam into the layers of darkness untouched by the overhead bulb.

He didn't see Kennedy.

Olivia's fingers dug almost painfully into his shoulder. "You really think she's down there? I can look through other parts of the house."

"I'd barricaded the door, Olivia. They opened it to lure her downstairs."

"Who is 'they'?" she asked.

As fast as he dared, Len picked his way down the narrow, steep staircase, flashlight angled ahead of him. Olivia followed close behind.

"We aren't the only ones living in this house," he said.

He reached the bottom of the staircase. Hurrying toward the secret room, he panned the light around. He called out for Kennedy, and so did Olivia, but they received no answer.

Please, God. Don't let them hurt our baby.

The section of shelf that concealed the hidden antechamber was partially open. Silvery light shone from within.

"What the hell is that?" Olivia said, beside him.

"Later," Len said. "I'll tell you everything."

He found Kennedy inside the antechamber, her face revealed in the glow of the lamp he'd placed in the room earlier. The trapdoor was wide open, foul vapors steaming from the depths. Kennedy knelt on the floor above the lip of the staircase. Her eyes were rapt with curiosity.

I closed the hatch, Len thought. *I closed it and locked it.*

The brand new padlock lay in the corner, snapped in half as if worked over by his own bolt cutters.

Kennedy turned at their arrival. Pointing below, she wrinkled her nose.

"Mommy, Daddy . . . something's stinky down there."

Olivia hooked her hands underneath Kenney's armpits and dragged her away from the portal. Kennedy yelled and squirmed in protest. Olivia hauled her out of the room, but when Len met his wife's gaze, he saw the same fear that had his own heart pumping about two hundred beats a minute.

He approached the edge of the shaft. He saw only formless darkness below. No door guardian.

But he remembered a comment Laveaux had made at the park yesterday.

Dr. Laveaux could use a child like her. She's perfect for the house, he thinks, most suitable.

If they had arrived only a minute later, would Laveaux's minions have lured Kennedy down there? The thought made his knees weak.

He slammed the trapdoor shut.

30

They went to a restaurant on nearby McClendon Avenue called La Fonda Latina. Located in what was once a service station, the cantina served up a reliable menu of reasonably priced, Latin-themed fare. Len and Olivia had eaten there once after concluding one of their many pre move-in visits to the Victorian, and marked the place as somewhere to frequent when they eventually settled into their new home.

Now, they were in the restaurant to talk about moving out.

The small dining room was decorated in festive colors that reminded Len of a carnival. Business was brisk on a Monday evening, the happy hour crowd ordering pitchers of margaritas and bowls of *queso* dip. On a large flat-screen TV above the bar, the Atlanta Hawks were getting ready for tip-off.

A server brought chips and salsa as soon as they were seated at a corner booth. Kennedy dove right in, balancing on her knees on the seat and leaning over the table. She was a picky eater, but she loved tortilla chips.

Getting out of the house had soothed Len's nerves. Being inside the Victorian had felt like waiting at the dentist's office while a cavity throbbed in your molar; you knew something unpleasant was coming your way. He ordered a pint of Dos Equis and crunched on a couple of chips.

Olivia looked calmer, too. After requesting a margarita, she had let her hair down and unbuttoned her blouse a notch. Len noted that she kept her hand on Kennedy's back, however, as if determined their daughter would never wander into harm's way again.

"Now," he said, "let's talk."

"You go first," she said. "I'm still gathering my thoughts."

He told her everything. About his research last night into Dr. Laveaux and his belief that the guy was a powerful vodou sorcerer, a *bokor*. The late-night vision of April walking through the house and attempting to lure him into the cellar. The appearance of both April and Laveaux at his job. His purchase of a gun. His discovery of the hidden room and staircase in the cellar—and the terrifying glimpse of the door guardian . . .

Sipping occasionally from her margarita, Olivia listened without interrupting or scoffing at any of the details he shared. Before they could jump to interpretations, she said, "Now, it's my turn."

She told him about her investigation into the house and talking to King Realty. The death of Reggie King in a car accident on Saturday night. Her chilling visions of her brother, Michael. The building security guard who'd reminded her of the deadline, in Laveaux's unmistakable voice. The agent from the real estate group who revealed the details of his company's scam of Laveaux. The phone call from someone claiming to be April.

"Wow," Len said, when she concluded. "I thought I was the only one who'd had a crazy day."

"Unfortunately not." Olivia smiled weakly.

Their entrees had arrived several minutes ago—fish tacos for Len, a veggie burrito for Olivia, and cheese quesadillas for Kennedy—but Kennedy was the only one eating. Len had been so engrossed in their conversation that he'd forgotten all about the food, and Olivia hadn't touched anything, either.

He finally picked up one of his tacos. "You didn't want to talk about Laveaux before. I got the impression you knew something about him that scared you."

"I suspected he was a *vodouisant* when we met him at the park yesterday," she said.

Len sipped beer. "A what?"

"*Vodouisant*. A practitioner of vodou."

Len bit back the sharp retort that came to mind. He was still annoyed that she had knowledge of these things but had refused to divulge them. "Okay, and how did you know that?"

"When I noted his style of dress, and then, when he began speaking Creole, it was apparent to me." She stirred her margarita with a straw, her gaze clouded. "But I didn't want to admit it. That's not the sort of thing that a rational, educated person likes to discuss."

"What did he say to us in Creole? Could you understand him?"

"He was repeating old Haitian proverbs. Threats, basically."

"That's a surprise. I thought he was telling us to live long and prosper."

Olivia blurted a laugh into her hand. It felt good to see her smile. He wasn't intentionally trying to be funny, but humor was one of the few ways of coping with a situation, that, in all honestly, was utterly terrifying.

She said, "From what I remember, he said something about our marriage, and how it was not going to be happy. Then that we'd get what we deserved, and justice was on his side, because he was stronger. That's the rough meaning behind what he said."

"Charming." Len folded his arms on the table. "Be straight with me. How much do you *really* know about this stuff, Liv? Your folks are from Haiti."

"Len, please. I'm supposed to be a vodou expert because my family is from Haiti? That's the equivalent of someone assuming that since you're from Georgia, you must be a peach farmer."

"Point taken," he said.

"But I know a fair amount. The lay of the land, so to speak."

He took another bite of his taco, waited for her to continue.

"First of all, it's a religion," she said. "It's not about blood sacrifices and zombies and sticking dolls with pins, like you see in the movies. It's about the *loa*, who essentially are spirits that have jurisdiction in certain areas of life. They aren't gods, per se, but lesser spirits that people can call on for assistance."

"I read a little about that yesterday," he said.

"Those initiated to practice vodou, the priests and priestesses, are called houngans and mambos. You've also got the *bokor*, who aren't priests necessarily, but they perform both beneficial and harmful services."

"Like Laveaux," he said.

"I'd heard whispered stories in my family over the years about certain people affected by the magical aspects of vodou. Aunt Viola had a love spell put on that man and finally got him to marry her . . . or Cousin Philip landed that job because he beseeched the *loa* for help. And I've heard other things." She hesitated, lips pressed together. "But I've never had any direct, personal experience with that side of vodou, until now."

"I don't know what Laveaux did to us, but he's dug deep into both of our heads," he said. "We're being tortured by visions of people from our past."

"With whom we have unresolved issues, evidently." Olivia's gaze sharpened. "What's the story between you and your old ex-girlfriend? You said she committed suicide?"

"After we broke up, yeah. It pushed her over the edge. She had a lot of other issues, though, already. I guess our break-up was the last straw."

Her eyes were kind. "That's not your fault, Len."

"Your brother overdosing wasn't your fault, either."

She winced. "Well. We're both carrying unresolved issues, like I said. Laveaux is using our own weaknesses against us. The question is: how? That sort of thing is far outside the scope of my limited knowledge."

Neither of them spoke for a moment, the unanswered question hanging over them. Communicating openly with each another had cleared the air in many ways, but there was still so much they didn't know.

Kennedy continued to nibble on her quesadilla. In between bites, she flicked her fingers across the screen of her LeapPad, a tablet designed for children. They never would have allowed Kennedy to play with the device at dinner, under normal circumstances, but needed to keep her engaged for an extended meal.

Len said, "Is there anything in vodou that talks about basements that lead deep underground, and what purpose that would serve?"

Olivia shook her head. "We need to learn more about the history of the house. Laveaux hasn't always owned the Victorian. Maybe it's some kind of bootlegger's storehouse or some such area that Laveaux had employed as a ritual space."

"I did ask Jacob a favor this afternoon," he said. "He's a house history buff, remember? I asked him to check out the history of the place. Didn't tell him why I wanted to know, though."

"I agree, keep him out of it. No reason to endanger him."

"Whatever is down there is interested in her." Len nodded toward Kennedy. "Remember what Laveaux said to us at the park? That she was perfect for the house, whatever the hell that meant."

"Nothing's getting to her." Olivia put her arm protectively around their child, drawing a strange look from Kennedy. "Keeping her safe is my top priority."

"Keeping *both* of you safe is my top priority." He set down his drink. "Which is why we've got to give up the house."

She stared at him. "It's not that simple."

"I get it, you love the house, but there are other authentic Victorians around, Olivia." He shrugged. "We'll just have to find another one. Preferably one that isn't haunted."

"Do you honestly think our course of action is that straightforward?"

"Of course it is. We know Laveaux was the victim of fraud. It's his property. As far as I'm concerned, he can take it. I'm never spending another night in that place, not after what's happened."

"What about our mortgage? How do you propose we handle that?"

"There has to be some kind of legal alternative. You're a lawyer. You tell me."

"First of all, Laveaux would have to seek redress through the courts. Does he strike you as the sort of man who's going to depend upon the legal system to get what he believes belongs to him?"

Len said nothing. He knew the answer.

She continued: "Was he the victim of fraud? Yes. It happens every day. Realistically, the best that he could get, if he goes to the courts, is a judgment against King Realty. Perhaps a payout for the appraised value of the property, and if he has a good lawyer, some extra cash thrown in for his emotional distress. The judge would *not* give him back this house because we have a valid mortgage."

"What if we move out?" he said.

"Then we'd default on a loan for three hundred and fifty thousand dollars. We're on the hook for that unpaid balance. We do quite well financially, but we don't have that kind of money lying around. It would be a catastrophe."

"I wasn't talking about abandoning the property," he said. "We could move out, rent a place, and sell the house. Put it back on the market and get the best deal we can."

Her lips twisted, as if she'd bitten into a bitter apple. "I don't like that."

"Come on, Liv." He bent forward, arms pressed on the table. "You remember how we had to fight off other bidders to get that house, right? If we put it back on the market, buyers would be salivating to get their hands on it."

"We might not break even, Len. We had to invest a significant amount in order to move in, if you recall."

"We can absorb a loss. I don't give a damn about the balance sheet."

"Then we pass on the Laveaux problem to someone else?" She gave him a pointed look. "Ethically speaking, do you think that's the right course of action? Would you want someone to do that to us?"

"I want to keep our family safe."

"That's a top priority for me, too." She bent forward and took his hand in hers. "But we have to consider the downstream consequences of our actions. *Someone* has to deal with this man."

"Does it have to be us? Call me a self-centered ass if you want. We have no way of countering him. Maybe the next folks who move in will."

"Are you really going to punk out like that?" she asked. "If we were back in the Civil Rights era, I suppose MLK couldn't have counted on *you* to march with him, could he? Far be it from you to take responsibility for anyone outside your precious little circle."

Len grimaced, exhaled through clenched teeth. He should have anticipated this response from her. Olivia had never been one to bury her head in the sand and ignore the problems facing the world beyond their four walls. She ran races for charitable causes, gave money and time to foundations that fed and clothed the needy, and provided pro bono legal services for those with modest means. It was a trait of hers that he admired; she inspired him to look outside his own insular lifestyle and participate in the greater village of society, and she was setting a wonderful example for their daughter to emulate.

But at that moment, it only frustrated him.

"You can't possibly feel safe staying there," he said. "Not after what just happened with Kennedy. Not after everything we've discussed."

"Who said we would stay there? I'm not an idiot. I know it's unsafe. We need to check into a hotel."

"Good. We're on the same page."

"Tonight, we check into a hotel," she said. "Tomorrow, we talk to someone who might be able to help us deal with Laveaux."

"Who?"

"A family friend," she said. "You met her at our wedding and she came to Kennedy's christening, too. She told you to call her Marie, even though you felt uncomfortable with that since she's so much older than you."

Len thought for a moment. "You mean your godmother? But she's like ninety-something years old, isn't she?"

"And she's still sharper than the two of us put together." Olivia flashed a smile of pride. "I can tell you that for a very long time, Marie has made her living 'helping' people stuck in various situations, using certain . . . methods."

"She's a *vodouisant*?"

"She gets things done. So people say." Olivia offered what Len took as a hopeful smile. "We're long overdue to pay her a visit."

31

They checked into a Marriott Suites in Midtown. To Len, it felt surreal to stay in a hotel room in his own city. The last time he'd done so, it had been the night of their wedding, where after the reception at the hotel, he and Olivia, both of them tipsy after too much champagne, had staggered into the honeymoon suite and hastily set about the business of consummating their marriage. He barely remembered it.

He was a lot more alert this time around. Although they had removed themselves from ground zero, the Victorian, Laveaux had repeatedly proven earlier that he could tap into their heads from anywhere. They had to stay on guard.

But Kennedy was cheerfully curious, as if they were embarking on an exciting adventure. Len remembered his daughter had never been in a hotel before, and wished he could have offered her such an experience under a different set of circumstances. She was pointing at objects and wanting to run around in the lobby, and neither he nor Olivia was in the frame of mind to allow her to explore, or to answer her endless questions.

They received a suite with a king-size bed, and a sofa bed. The room was on the fifteenth floor and granted them a stunning view of the night-swept skyline. Kennedy stood at the window, gawking at the light-studded skyscrapers, while Len and Olivia unpacked.

They had brought mostly the essentials: a couple days' worth of clothes, their computers, snacks for Kennedy, and some of her favorite books, movies, and toys.

Len brought the Beretta he had purchased, too, sealing it in his back pack with an extra magazine of ammo.

During the drive from the restaurant to the hotel, Olivia had called her godmother and spoken to the woman's granddaughter. Marie had already taken to bed, but her granddaughter assured Olivia that she would be thrilled to see them and asked them to visit tomorrow morning. They planned to drop Kennedy off at the daycare center, to keep her routine as normal as possible, and then pay Marie a visit at her home in Social Circle.

While Olivia gave Kennedy a bath, Len sprawled across the bed on his back. He scratched the bug bite on his neck—the damn thing still itched like mad—and let his hand drop like a dead weight to the mattress.

All he wanted to do was crash. That day felt like the longest day he'd ever lived.

The sounds of Kennedy splashing in bath water soothed him. As he closed his eyes, he could easily imagine that he was lying in his own bed at home, slowly drifting off to sleep while wrapped in the warm cocoon of his family.

A nearby section of the mattress groaned under someone's weight. He swung his head around, wakefulness snapping like electricity through his muscles.

It was April. She sat on the edge of the bed, only a foot or so away from him. Legs crossed, she wore a candy-red thong and not much else. Her skin glistened in the lamplight, as if oiled, and the scent of her perfume surrounded her like a halo.

This was the closest yet that he'd ever been to this illusion of her. Although Len told himself that she was only a figment of his imagination, the level of detail made his heart clench. From the tiny beauty mark on her smooth cheek to the silver tennis bracelet that glimmered on her left wrist, the vision looked as real as she ever had.

He bolted upright and got off the bed.

"Hey, Lenny," she said, her voice as sweet as syrup. "Been missing me?"

It took him a few seconds to gather enough air to speak.

"You aren't real," he said. "You're only in my mind."

"Is that what you think?" She pouted. Her lips were painted a shade of red that matched her thong. "I'm back 'cause we've got unfinished business."

Len pressed his hands to his throbbing temples, as if he could rip her out of his thoughts. He closed his eyes for a moment, opened them. She was still there.

This is insane. How do I stop this?

"What unfinished business?" he asked. "What the hell do you want?"

"Oh, you know." She ran her tongue across her lips. "I want what I've always wanted, Lenny. I want to fuck you until your cock turns blue and then I want to slit your throat with a razor and watch you bleed out."

For a heartbeat, lurid images whipped through Len's thoughts of how her words might play out. He saw her straddling him and grinding relentlessly on top of him, until he was raw and aching. Saw her swipe a razor across his carotid artery. Could see dark blood pumping out of his neck as he gasped and moaned . . .

"No." Len was shaking his head. "No. Get out of here."

April rose from the bed, her sinuous body uncoiling like a snake's. She advanced toward him.

He moved away. Soon, his back met the wall.

This is not real, she can't hurt me, he repeated to himself.

"This is what you've always wanted, too," she said. "You've always wanted it to end this way."

She closed her fingers over his belt buckle. He grabbed her wrist.

He didn't know what he expected—perhaps he'd through his hands would pass through her body as if she were only smoke. But her flesh was solid, and as cold as meat left sitting in the refrigerator.

She laughed, and flicked her tongue toward him. A razor glistened on the tip.

Shouting, he pushed her away. He scrambled across the room, his foot getting hooked on a chair leg and causing him to lose his balance. He spilled to the carpet.

The April-thing pounced on him like a spider attacking a stunned insect. She was petite, but inhumanly strong.

Ice-cold hands roughly flipped him onto his back. She climbed on top of him, her knees pinning his arms to the floor. He squirmed, tried to throw her off, but it was like trying to wrestle from underneath a three-hundred pound man.

"I've been dying to kiss you, Lenny."

She bent down and mashed her lips against his. Her lips were like cold rubber. She forced her tongue into his mouth, and he felt that razor on the tip slice across the roof of his mouth with a hot, tearing sensation. Warm blood flooded his throat.

Gagging, thrashing frantically, he finally managed to free an arm. He swung his elbow and connected with the side of her head.

She tumbled off of him.

Regaining his balance, he stumbled across the carpet and banged open the bathroom door, praying the presence of his family would save him.

Kennedy was splashing happily in the bathtub as Olivia soaped her back. Both of them turned at his abrupt entrance.

"What happened?" Olivia said. "Is everything okay?"

"Whas wrong, Daddy?" Kennedy asked, looking as concerned as her mother in spite of her mispronounced words.

Bent over on the tile floor, panting, Len ran his finger inside his mouth, pulled it out. There was no blood, no wound. But the memory of the razor cut made his mouth tingle.

"What is it, baby?" Olivia came to him and put her hand on his shoulder.

Len swallowed. He turned and looked through the doorway, into the room.

The suite was empty.

April was gone.

32

Olivia put down Kennedy for bed. Kennedy didn't whine, as she usually did. She seemed pleasantly exhausted by all of the day's activities. Clutching the Kitty-san toy that Len had given her last night, Kennedy burrowed under her blanket they had brought from home, and sighed with contentment.

Olivia kissed her on the cheek and switched off the bedside lamp. The television was the only light source in the room.

Kennedy may have been at peace, but in the silver glow issuing from the TV, Len looked like hell. He wouldn't divulge exactly what had happened while she'd been giving their daughter a bath, but she assumed he'd experienced another frightening "event." Slumped in the recliner next to the bed, he flipped through channels, but his haunted eyes were fixed on a location beyond the screen.

Olivia didn't feel much better. It had been a terribly long day, and she had a dull, aggravating headache. She searched through their luggage and found they didn't have any ibuprofen.

"I'm going to the gift shop," she said. "I've got to pick up something for this headache if I hope to get any sleep."

Len grunted. "We'll be here."

After checking herself in the bathroom mirror—when they'd arrived, she'd changed into a pink t-shirt and jeans—Olivia slipped on her flip-flops, and quietly eased out of room.

As she took the elevator down to the lobby, she scratched the back of her leg. The insect bite continued to annoy her. She couldn't recall if they'd brought any anti-itch ointment from home, and decided she'd pick up some of that in the shop, too.

She was browsing in the store when she glanced up and saw Michael crossing the lobby.

Her gut contracted into a knot.

Please, God. Not this. Not now.

Michael wore the same grey Georgetown hoodie, ripped jeans, and no shoes. Hood drawn over his head, hands gathered in his pockets, he shuffled past the front desk. He didn't look in her direction, and of course, no one noticed him passing by. Turning at an intersection of corridors, he vanished from view.

Olivia felt a panic attack coming on. She put her hand to her chest and forced herself to draw slow, deep breaths.

"Are you okay, ma'am?" asked the store clerk, a young Latina woman. She came from behind the counter, eyebrows arched with concern.

I'm a long way from okay. I'm tormented by visions of my dead brother and I'm about to lose my shit for real.

Olivia pushed out a deep breath and wiped the beads of perspiration from her forehead. "I'm fine, thanks. Hot flash, I suppose."

"Oh. My mom gets those. She says a cold pack helps a lot. I don't think we have any in here, though."

"I'll be fine. Thanks for your concern."

Olivia paid for her purchases and left the gift shop, the plastic shopping bag clenched in her fist.

If I can get back to the room without incident, I'll be okay.

She hurried to the bank of elevators. With each step, she looked around, but she didn't see Michael anywhere.

Perhaps the event was already over. Regardless, when she got back to the room, she was going to take another dose of her anti-anxiety medication. She didn't know how much more of this madness she could handle without cracking up.

Fortunately, she didn't have to ride the elevator alone. When the next car arrived that was bound for the upper floors, she boarded with a trio of Chinese men dressed in suits and speaking Mandarin.

She had taken Chinese language courses in undergrad and spent a week in Beijing, visiting with a friend from school whose family lived there. Her Mandarin was rusty from disuse, but she distracted herself by attempting to follow the group's conversation.

Unfortunately, the men disembarked on the tenth floor. She was left alone in the elevator.

Just let me get to the room, please.

157

The bell chimed. She had reached the fifteenth floor.

She stepped into the corridor. The hallway was quiet, and dimly lit.

There was no sign of Michael.

She slid the key card out of her pocket and hurried in the direction of their room, following the posted signs. A left turn at the end of the hall, and she should have been only ten feet away—

But when she made the turn, she found Michael sitting on the floor, right next to the door of their room. Back propped against the wall. Head bowed, the hood concealing his face. Hands buried in the hoodie pocket. Dusty, bare feet splayed across the carpet.

She put her fist to her mouth, choking back a scream.

He can't hurt me. He's only a figment of my imagination.

She had given herself the same reassurances before, but the vision of her brother was no less frightening. Every aspect of him appeared to be utterly genuine.

She could even smell him: he reeked of body odor and the rancid stench of vomit.

Her headache intensified from a dull ache, to a savage pounding that felt as if someone were striking the back of her skull with a sledgehammer.

"Let me pass," she said softly. "I don't want us to fight anymore. Please."

Michael didn't respond. His head drooped nearly between his knees, as if he were asleep.

Or dead. Maybe that's the next phase of this insanity. I'm supposed to discover him dead with his throat clogged shut with vomit.

She whispered a prayer. Keeping to the opposite wall, she edged past him, ready to make a mad dash down the hallway at any second.

He didn't move.

Once past him, she took a long step to the other side of the corridor. Slowly, she approached the door. Inserted the key card in the slot.

As the tiny light on the door panel flashed green, Michael snapped to attention.

"Hey, sis," he said.

He snatched a syringe out of his pocket and rammed the needle through the top of her foot.

Olivia was so terrified that she couldn't draw the breath

necessary to scream. Wheezing, she staggered through the doorway and crashed to the floor.

The syringe jutted from her foot like an exclamation point, the glass barrel full of a toxic-looking, greenish-brown fluid. Her foot burned. It felt as if a corrosive acid were sizzling through her bloodstream.

Oh, sweet Jesus, please . . .

Outside the doorway, Michael crouched on his knees. He'd pulled away the hood. A beard of vomit wreathed his chin.

"See how it feels, sis?" he said. "You selfish fuckin' bitch."

Olivia's stomach buckled. She gasped, sour bile surging up her throat. Gagging, she rolled over, onto all fours. Dizziness swam through her, and she felt a rising tide of nausea that seemed as if it would consume her.

I deserve it, I let my brother die . . .

"Sweetheart, what's wrong?"

It was Len's voice, coming to her as if from the end of a long tube. A light clicked on in the room. She felt strong hands grasp her arms and lift her upright.

She tried to speak, but her stomach continued to twist through painful spasms. Len dragged her into the bathroom. Dropping to her knees, she crouched over the toilet and vomited into the bowl.

Nothing came up. She was dry-heaving.

"You saw him again, didn't you?" Len asked.

Her eyes watering, Olivia nodded.

"Waited for me outside the room," she said. Her voice was hoarse, her throat aching from the scalding digestive acids.

Len gave her a hand towel. She accepted it gratefully, turned and rested against the bathtub with the towel pressed to her face. Her skin was flushed, filmed with cold sweat.

She lifted her foot in the air. There was no syringe, no mark of that needle plunging through her skin. All in her mind. God.

Len left the bathroom and returned a few seconds later with a bottle of water. He offered it to her. She unscrewed the cap and drank half of it, savoring the coolness rushing down her throat. Finally, her stomach began to settle, too.

"Did I wake Kennedy?" she asked.

"She's knocked out." Len flipped down the toilet lid and sat on it. "Slept through it all."

"I would've hated for her to see me behaving like that. I would've scared her to death."

"It's not your fault, Olivia."

"But it *is*," she said. "That's the significance. That I believe what happened to Michael was my fault. That you believe what happened to your ex-girlfriend was your fault."

"Yeah." Len removed his glasses and pinched the bridge of his nose. "I need to let it go."

"That's Laveaux's power over us," she said. "Our skeletons in the closet."

"Do you really think your godmother will be able to help us?"

"At this point," Olivia said, "I think she's our only hope."

33

Len figured he must've been totally wiped out from the events of the day, because when he lay down to sleep, he drifted away so quickly it was as if he'd been administered a dose of a powerful anesthetic. When he finally opened his eyes, yawning, he frowned at the unfamiliar clock on the nightstand.

We're in a hotel, he remembered. *Evacuated from our house like a family fleeing a hurricane.*

He squinted at the clock's fuzzy digits. It was 6:27 in the morning.

They had left the light burning in the bathroom, the door cracked open a few inches. In case either of them awoke and needed to move quickly, they didn't want to fumble around in an unfamiliar, pitch-black room. Shifting on the bed, he saw Kennedy was still asleep, tangled in blankets. Olivia lay on her back, hands laced behind her head.

"I'm awake," she said.

He picked up his glasses from the nightstand, slipped them on. "How long have you been up?"

"Since a few minutes before six. On a normal day, I'd be deep into my run by now."

"I don't think this is going to be a normal day, in any sense of the phrase."

She turned to face him, her head a dark oval in the shadows.

"Any dreams?" she asked.

"Nothing that I can remember. You?"

"Slept like the dead. Perhaps our minds were too overworked to withstand more torture."

"We should be grateful for the rest. It's day three of his deadline."

Olivia reached across the bed, over Kennedy, and took his hand. She squeezed. Her skin was warm and soft, and he felt a tingle of pleasure.

Whatever this day holds, we can handle it, he thought. *As long as we're together.*

"We should start getting ready," he said, but as he spoke the words, Olivia already was rising out of the bed.

They were scheduled to visit Marie at ten o'clock in the morning. According to Olivia, her godmother took appointments seriously, and they didn't dare arrive late if they expected her assistance. Len jumped into the shower after Olivia finished, and while he got ready, she awoke Kennedy.

After some discussion over a quick, room-service breakfast, they decided their initial plan to drop off Kennedy at school was still a good idea. They wanted to avoid disrupting her weekday routine, and believed she would be safe at the facility, which had numerous safeguards such as pin-only entry, closed circuit cameras monitoring every area, and a security guard on site. Besides, her safety had only been at risk in the Victorian. They would pick her up later, after they concluded their business with Marie.

Cold rain was pelting the city when Len nosed his Navigator out of the hotel's parking garage. The day's forecast included thunderstorms, and winds out of the northwest at up to forty miles per hour. They had a lot of driving ahead of them and could count on Atlanta drivers—notoriously terrible at navigating inclement weather—making the journey cumbersome.

Kennedy started to whine as they drew closer to their destination.

"Don't wanna go to school," she said.

Len looked away from the rain-swept road and glanced at Olivia. The look in her eyes reflected his thoughts. Kennedy was only three, but she wasn't fooled. In spite of their best efforts to simulate an ordinary day, she realized there was nothing typical about what was happening.

"But you like school." Len checked in the rearview mirror and saw Kennedy pouting. "You'll get to play with all your friends today and do fun stuff."

"No," Kennedy said. "I don't like that."

Len shrugged. Olivia turned around in her seat and smiled at Kennedy.

"Grandma's going to pick you up from school today," she said.

"She is?" Len said.

"I suspect we'll have plenty of things we'll need to do today," Olivia said. "I'll call Mom and ask her to get Kennedy later so we have more time to ourselves."

"Sounds good to me."

"No," Kennedy said.

She was still voicing her disapproval when Len swung into the Montessori school parking lot and parked underneath the sheltered entryway at the front of the building. She launched into full tantrum mode when Olivia unbuckled her from her car seat and started to pull her out of the truck. Olivia carried her inside as she flailed and shrieked. Len closed his eyes and laid his head against the headrest.

A few minutes later, Olivia climbed back into the truck. She was sniffling, too.

"I know it's tough to leave her behind," Len said. "But she'll be fine."

"I feel awful." Olivia found a tissue in her purse and used it to dab at her eyes. "She held onto my legs and wept like she'd never see me again. I had to pry her off of me."

"It's only for a few short hours. We need to be able to focus on our meeting with your godmother."

Sighing, Olivia gazed forlornly at the school. "Let's get out of here before I change my mind about leaving her."

Len wheeled out of the parking lot. The dashboard clock read twenty past eight; on a normal Tuesday morning he would have been on his way to the office. Both of them had called out of work, of course, taking sick days. Len didn't allow himself to dwell on the meetings, e-mails, and phone calls he was undoubtedly missing. Work would be there waiting for him whenever they finally settled this situation. He noticed that Olivia avoided checking e-mail and voice mail messages on her Blackberry, too, a remarkable achievement, considering that she typically checked the phone regularly, no matter what was going on.

Marie Toussaint lived in Social Circle, a small town located about fifty miles east of Atlanta. Len had never been there, so Olivia served as navigator, supported by the GPS on his iPhone. Cruising on Interstate 20 East, they put Atlanta's urban sprawl behind them, and cut through a countryside that steadily became more rural, with massive shopping malls giving way to strip malls, and eventually, free standing shops with signs that looked as if they hadn't changed in thirty years.

They didn't speak much during the drive, but that was fine with Len. Both of them were deep in their own thoughts, Olivia gazing reflectively out the rain-drizzled window, while Len kept his focus on the highway, his mind churning over what had happened to them in just two days to completely upend their lives. But he believed, strangely enough, that a long-standing blockage in their marriage was crumbling. For the first time in a while, they were absolutely on the same page with something critical to their lives. He was more clear-headed than he'd felt in years.

His phone beeped, prompting Olivia to straighten in her seat.

"The next exit is ours," she said. "State highway eleven."

"You sure you want to turn off? The way we're cruising, we'll be in South Carolina by lunchtime. I'm sure Charleston is nice this time of year."

"We can rent a beachside condo," Olivia said. "I can lie out in the sand and work on my tan. Bake me down from caramel to dark chocolate."

He grinned. "I can't remember the last time I saw you in a bikini."

"I can still rock a bikini, sweetheart. Trust me."

"I don't doubt that." A twinge of lust rippled down his spine. He reached across the seat and ran his fingers along her thigh.

"Down boy." Chuckling, she moved his hand away. "We'll have time for that later."

"Is that a date?"

"Men are unbelievable." She laughed. "Even in the midst of the most frightening situation we've ever dealt with, you've got sex on the brain."

"Don't blame me. It's the universal male hierarchy of needs. Food, sex, sleep."

"And in that precise order, too, huh?" She smiled.

The next exit neared. Len veered off the highway, windshield wipers ticking across the glass.

Social Circle had a population of about five thousand, one of those "blink and you miss it," towns spread throughout rural Georgia. The state highway took them through downtown. The heart of the city was lined with a quaint collection of shops and businesses: grocery stores, flea markets, banks, pawn shops, churches. He didn't see any building taller than two stories high, a marked change from the skyscrapers that clogged Atlanta's skyline.

Olivia called out a set of directions that took them away from the business district and deeper into the residential areas. They passed old, grand plantation-style houses standing on expansive plots of land. A trailer park packed with mobile homes and brown-faced men waiting to be hired for a day's work. A neighborhood of modest, ranch-style houses on a street framed with big oaks and maples.

Olivia asked him to park in front of a ranch house painted eggshell white, with green shutters. A magnolia tree stood in the small front yard, waxy leaves trembling in the rain. The carport attached to the house sheltered a white Cadillac STS sedan, and a red Mustang convertible with a black top.

"It's a quarter to ten," Len said. "She won't chew us out for being late, at least. Although I have to admit I expected a different looking home for an ordained *vodouisant*."

Olivia was checking her make-up in the sun visor mirror, but she suddenly shot him a heated look.

"Len, don't even think of using that term around her. Please."

"I thought that was what she does?"

"My godmother is very discreet about her affairs. She has to be. A lot of folks are superstitious and uninformed. If word leaked out, it would be a problem for her."

"Maybe I shouldn't say anything, then. I don't know what's safe to talk about."

"Smile a lot and be friendly. Answer her questions when she asks. But let *her* guide the conversation, please. You shouldn't let on that you know anything about vodou."

"That'll be easy." He opened his door and grabbed his back pack from the rear seat. "Because I really don't know a damned thing."

34

A striking young woman greeted them at the front door. She had dark, shoulder-length braids, a flawless cinnamon complexion, and grey eyes like a cat. She wore a white University of Georgia tank top that hugged her torso like a second skin and showed off her toned arms, and black Spandex that outlined her long, slender legs.

Len had to stop himself from gawking. Not only because he was with his wife, but also because the lady might be family, or close to it anyway. She looked vaguely familiar and he tried to remember where he'd seen her.

"Hey, Jade." Olivia gave the woman a warm embrace. "It's good to see you, girl. How've you been?"

"Good to see you too, Auntie Olivia," Jade said. "I've been great, staying busy in school and running around that track."

Olivia gestured to Len. "You've met my husband before, Len. At the wedding, I believe?"

"Oh yeah." Jade smiled, displaying perfect teeth. "The video game man."

"That's me," Len said.

Jade stepped forward and gave Len a friendly hug. Slipping back gracefully, she said, "Where's the little girl?"

"She went to school today," Olivia said.

"*Bonne-maman* and I were hoping to see her." Jade looked sad for a moment, shrugged. "She's out back. Can I get you something to drink? We put on a fresh pot of coffee right before you got here."

"Coffee sounds great," Len said, and Olivia agreed.

They followed Jade through the house. It was surprisingly

spacious, not nearly as small as it had appeared when viewed from the street. The rooms they passed through were fastidiously clean, decorated with plush furniture, family pictures, and lots of live, potted plants. Entering the tidy kitchen, Len inhaled the rich fragrance of freshly brewed coffee.

"Coffee from home, eh?" Olivia picked up an aluminum bag on the counter. The bag was blue, decorated with the silhouette of a rooster.

"It's her preference," Jade said. "Come along out back, guys, I'll bring the coffee."

"Where's that door go?" Len whispered to Olivia. He pointed to a scarlet-colored door on the far side of the kitchen. It was closed and secured with a keypad door lock, a detail that was utterly out of place in the quaint home.

Olivia shook her head sharply and took his hand, guiding him to follow Jade.

The back of the kitchen ended at French doors that led into an expansive, screened-in patio. An ornately carved metal cross hung above the doorway. Len had to bow his head slightly to enter, but the bottom of the cross still skipped across the back of his skull.

As he stepped into the warm space, a mélange of flora aromas touched his nostrils. The sunroom seemed to be a combination of a lounge, and a greenhouse. At the front of the chamber, four wicker chairs encircled a round glass table. Beyond the seating area, the room was crowded with several rows of plants. Len was no florist, but at a glance he could see that the collection represented a wide variety of species. Skylights paneled the ceiling, which would have admitted a generous dose of sunshine on clear days.

He spotted Marie near the back of the room, bifocals perched on her nose as she worked through the last row of plants, spraying them with a solution from a tiny plastic bottle she held in her gloved fingers. She waved at them.

"Good morning, *marenn!*" Olivia said.

"I'll be with you in a moment, my dears," Marie said. Len detected a trace of her Haitian accent. "Please, make yourselves at home."

"I'll bring the coffee," Jade said.

"The college girl." Len tilted his head toward the departing young woman. "Refresh my memory. She called you aunt . . ."

"Only a term of endearment," Olivia said. "We aren't related by blood but our families have been closely knit for a long time. We were neighbors in Port-au-Prince before we all fled Haiti forty or so years ago."

Nodding, Len indicated the plants. "Is your godmother also a florist or something?"

"Or something," Olivia said. "Remember what I told you?"

Len pantomimed zipping his lips shut and tossing away the key.

Marie emerged from the rows of plants. She was a petite woman, barely five feet tall, dressed in a yellow button-front blouse, khaki capris, and sandals. Olivia had told Len that she was ninety-two years old, but in Len's opinion, she easily could have passed for twenty years younger, and didn't appear to have aged a day since he'd seen her at their wedding six years ago. She had a thick mane of grey hair wrapped up in a brightly-colored scarf, a smooth, sun-bronzed complexion, and behind the bifocals, chestnut-brown eyes that danced with energy.

She hugged and kissed both of them, and they all settled into the chairs around the table. Jade brought a glass tray with a carafe of coffee, fresh cream, sugar, and cups. She disappeared from the sunroom, leaving the three of them to talk.

Rain ticked on the roof and windows. In the corner, a small heater hummed softly, warding away the morning's chill temperatures.

Olivia and Marie spent about five minutes on pleasantries, catching up the latest happenings with family and friends, and then Marie set down her coffee cup, adjusted her glasses, and studied Olivia carefully.

"What troubles you, *fiyel*?" she asked. "It's lovely to see you, but I know you're worried about something. Since your handsome husband is here and won't stop smiling at us, I do not think you're having marital issues."

Len blushed, but kept quiet.

"Never could fool you." Olivia put down her cup and knotted her fingers across her abdomen. "We have a situation with the house we recently moved into. It was a foreclosure. We got an excellent price."

"Yes, yes, occurring often in these times," Marie said. "So grateful we paid off this home many years ago."

"The former owner lost his property due to fraud," Olivia said. "There's nothing we can do about that, we didn't find out until yesterday. But he's angry and has demanded that we leave."

"Such a shame, but these things happen." Marie clucked her tongue. "What are you going to do?"

"*Marenn*, the man is one who serves the spirits," Olivia said.

Marie looked from Olivia, to Len. The skin had tightened around her eyes.

"How do you know this?" Marie asked. Her voice had lowered to a whisper.

Olivia nodded at Len. Len unzipped the back pack he'd brought inside and withdrew the framed photograph of Dr. Laveaux and Papa Doc. Before they'd left the Victorian last night, Olivia had asked him to bring the photo.

He slid it across the table to Marie.

She adjusted her bifocals and brought the photograph closer to eyes. A soft gasp escaped her.

Does she know Laveaux? Len wondered. Suddenly, she looked nervous as hell.

He started to ask Marie about her reaction, but Olivia silenced him with a hand on his arm.

Marie returned the photo to the table, face down. She pulled in a deep breath and closed her eyes for a few seconds, as if steeling herself to go on.

"*Fiyel*," she finally said, and looked from Olivia, to Len. "You should leave that house immediately and never return. It is not safe, especially with a child concerned."

"That's exactly what I've been saying," Len said.

"*Len*," Olivia said.

"I'm sorry, honey, but you know my stance on this," he said. "We've got to consider our daughter, above all else. Your godmother agrees with me."

Olivia glared at him. Then she turned to Marie, smiled sweetly—and began to speak in Creole, to which Marie replied, also in their shared tongue.

Len threw up his hands. "Oh, come on. You know that isn't fair, Liv."

But Olivia ignored him, and so did her godmother. The two women spoke for several minutes. Len had no idea of the specifics of the conversation, but from Olivia's impassioned tone and animated body language, he could guess that she was making her case to Marie for why they should confront Laveaux, and why they needed her assistance.

Finally, Marie shifted in her chair to face Len.

"You have seen things as well, yes?" Marie said. "Visions of someone from your past?"

"An ex-girlfriend from fifteen years ago. She committed suicide."

"That is unfortunate." Brow furrowed, Marie looked into the depths of her cup. "Did this man take something from each of you? Or give you something?"

"He hasn't been in the house, *marenn*," Olivia said, "not since we moved in."

"He hasn't given us anything, either," Len said.

Marie rose from her chair and came toward Len. Frowning, he reared back.

"What is this?" She grasped the collar of his polo shirt and peeled it away, revealing the insect bite. She prodded the lesion with her index finger.

Len winced. "Careful. That hurts."

"How did this happen?" Marie continued to study the wound.

"I was bitten by a fly," he said.

"A fly. I should have guessed." Marie made a spitting sound. "When?"

"Yesterday," he said. "Olivia was bitten, too."

"My bite is on the back of my leg," Olivia said.

Marie moved away from him. She picked up her coffee cup and took a small sip. Len noticed her hands trembled slightly.

"Both of you have been poisoned," she said.

"What do you mean?" Len asked.

"For you to see these terrible things, he would need to take something from you," Marie said. "Or, he would need to feed you something."

"He used a fly to poison us?" Olivia said.

"These things can be done by those who have the knowledge," she said. "This is a special one. I believe I've heard of him."

"You actually know Laveaux?" Len asked.

Marie touched Olivia's shoulder. "For what you've requested, your husband must agree as well. Leave us, please, *fiyel*."

Olivia smiled tightly, rose from the table, and left the sunroom, but not without casting an anxious glance at Len, as if to say, *don't screw this up.* He felt like sticking his tongue out at her, but knew that would have been silly—and their hostess had taken on such a solemn demeanor that he didn't dare make light of their situation.

Marie extended her hand toward Len. "Come with me, dear."

35

Marie guided Len to her collection of plants near the back of the sunroom.

"I have a lot of questions," he said. "But Olivia warned me to only speak when spoken to."

"She is protective." Marie offered a small smile. She indicated the garden with a wave of her delicate hand. "Now. Some of these plants I tend because I like to have them near. Others are herbs with healing properties."

Of course, he thought. *The woman's a root worker. I should have realized that from the start.*

She strolled along one of the rows. Len followed close behind, leaves brushing across his shoulders. The blend of fragrances swirling through the air gave him a slightly euphoric feeling.

From a small wooden table standing at the edge of the row, Marie picked up a tiny pruning snip and a red leather pouch. She slid her small fingers through the scissor handles and stepped back to the plants.

"What would you like to know?" she asked.

"I suppose we could start from the beginning," he said. "What exactly do you do, if I may ask?"

"Of course." She gently cradled a pink blossom and inhaled its scent. "I serve the *loa*. Do you know the *loa*?"

He stammered. "Well . . ."

She laughed, and her eyes twinkled as she regarded him. "You should. They know *you*."

He blinked. "I guess they're sort of like the spirits of vodou?"

"The *loa* are the ancestors," she said. "They have always been with us, over the many years, from Ife to Haiti, to the United States, and many other places. The *loa* assist us, and strengthen us, and come when we call. I serve the *loa* as a mambo."

"A priestess of vodou," he said.

Her eyebrows arched in surprise. Len blushed.

"I read that online," he said.

"I see." She used the scissors to cut a snippet from a flowering plant. She tucked the sample into the leather pouch.

"I read more, but I can't honestly say that I know what I'm talking about," he said. "Start with the basics, please."

"I don't know all that you've studied on the Internet," she said. "But vodou is not what you see in the movies. It isn't little dolls you stick with pins and curses and animal sacrifices. Those things are . . . entertainment. Not truth."

"Vodou is a religion," he said.

"Yes!" She favored him with a smile, and he felt like a student who had answered a question correctly in class. She said, "It is the religion of honoring our ancestors and inviting them into our lives to help us in our times of need. Yes, there is magic, too. But my work is not the same as the *bokor* who threatens your family."

"Dr. Laveaux," he said. "How can he do the things that he does?"

"As we say, the *bokor* work with both hands, the beneficial and the harmful. They know how to call the *loa* as well. Some *bokor* may call *loa* that are quite dangerous."

Len thought about the door guardian he'd glimpsed in the basement. In spite of the warmth in the room, a chill stepped down the ladder of his spine.

"Why is he interested in our daughter?" Len asked.

Marie shrugged, and snipped a portion from another plant, the leaf also going into her pouch. "Sometimes, the old envy the young. They covet their innocence, their energy."

"What do you think we should do?" he asked. "I mean, Olivia wants us to fight. Do you think that's a good idea?"

"My *fiyel* is a feisty one." Marie moved to another row of plants, turned and gave Len a stern look. "Know this. The road ahead for your family is dangerous. You will need courage, in abundance. *Men anpil, chay pa lou.* With unity between you and your wife, you can succeed."

"Can you help us?" he asked.

With a firm set to her jaw, Marie nodded.

"I will give both of you gris-gris." She tapped the side of her pouch. "As we've been speaking, I have been preparing the ingredients needed. The gris-gris will aid in your protection. But that doesn't mean you can behave like a fool. Use your good sense and if you must run, then run. You can return to fight another day."

"Understood," Len said.

"But the *bokor* has poisoned you," she said. "The gris-gris cannot take that away. To cure the poison and send him away, you must take something from him."

"Excuse me?" Len's heart thudded. "You mean, take something from Dr. Laveaux? Like what?"

"A piece of clothing. A hat. A handkerchief. It must be a personal item, close to him."

Are you out of your freakin mind? he thought. But he stopped himself, and said, "I don't know how we can do that."

"Eh?" Marie scowled and uttered something in her native tongue. "Did I promise you this would be easy?"

"So okay, we take something from him," Len said, trying hard to avoid a sarcastic quip. "And then what do we do?"

"Bring it to me."

"That's it? We bring his personal item to you, and you do your thing, and all this ends?"

"It won't be so simple," she said. "But yes, that is what we must do."

Len started to ask whether she was serious, but a fierceness that he hadn't seen before flashed in her eyes. It surprised him. Earlier, the notion that this small, gentle woman could have tangled with the fearsome doctor would have drawn a chuckle from him. But she had no fear in her eyes, and no doubt. Her resolve gave him an unexpected boost of confidence.

"All right," he said. "Then that's our plan."

And maybe, he thought, *just maybe, if this woman really knows her stuff . . . maybe we have a chance to get through this alive.*

36

It was half-past noon when they left Marie's house. For Len, stepping out of the warm cocoon of her home and back into the cold, stormy day was like awaking from a dream that he wished hadn't ended.

As he navigated the SUV back onto the town's main drag, he touched the gris-gris that hung around his neck, the small leather sack lying near his heart. The object pulsed with a subtle energy, but he wondered if his own imagination was responsible for that effect. He'd always been a sucker for good luck charms.

"Do you think these will really work?" he asked Olivia.

"I'm willing to give it a chance." She lifted her own gris-gris from its necklace and studied it. "Whether these truly possess magical properties to protect us, or merely influence us to make smarter decisions that keep us out of harm's way, the end result is the same, isn't it?"

"Laveaux's sorcery is real enough," Len said. "Why not your godmother's?"

"That's another way to look at it."

"It's like the timeless debate about the existence of God and the devil," he said. "You can't have one without the other."

"Heaven requires a hell. Good requires evil. None of them can exist without a contrasting extreme."

"Listen to us." Shaking his head, he could only chuckle. "A few days ago, did you ever imagine we'd be having a conversation like this? On some level, my mind is still refusing to accept that any of this is really happening."

She was nodding. "You keep telling yourself this is a long,

terrible nightmare, and you're waiting to wake up and breathe a sigh of relief. I know exactly how you feel. In spite of my basic knowledge of vodou and the things I'd heard over the years about Marie and others, I never actually *believed* any of it."

"Too educated to buy into superstitions," he said.

"Or too narrow-minded, as the case seems to be."

"If it's genuine, it will work whether we believe in it or not. It's like a gun. You don't need to have faith that firing a loaded nine millimeter at someone's head will kill them. Natural law guarantees it." He shrugged. "Are there laws of magic?"

"*Marenn* would say yes," she said, "as would the people who've come to her over the years for assistance. Just this once, I'm willing to shut out all of the rational arguments screaming in the back of my mind against everything we're doing, and simply follow her instructions."

Len steered onto the I-20 West entrance ramp. Vehicles blew past, ribbons of rain streaming from their tires. As was typical of Atlanta-area drivers, even in inclement weather, many insisted on driving as if they were on a racetrack.

"We need to go back to the house, you know," he said. "Just the two of us."

"It's inevitable. It's the final day of his deadline. If we're going to do this, now's the time."

They were quiet for most of the drive back to the city. Len kept the satellite radio tuned to a channel broadcasting old school R&B and hip-hop hits, while the windshield wipers thumped across the glass like a metronome. If they were driving to their doom, at least they enjoyed good cruising music on the way.

An hour later, he turned into the driveway of the old Victorian.

From the outside, everything about the house looked normal. Len had experienced so many troubling thoughts about the place that he wouldn't have been surprised to see it glowing with a supernatural hue. But it merely stood there in the clattering rain, windows dark, doors fastened shut, exactly as they'd left it the night before.

He parked in the garage next to Olivia's Audi and cut off the engine.

"Ready?" he asked.

She pulled her briefcase onto her lap. "As I'll ever be. Let's head in."

Len slipped his Beretta out of the back pack, and climbed out of the truck. He clipped the holster to the waistband of his jeans.

The gun's weight felt good, like a steadying hand at his side. It would be of no use against a tormenting hallucination, but if Laveaux made a cameo, as they were hoping, the pistol might come in handy.

Together, they hurried across the short stone walkway to the house's side entrance. Olivia used her key to unlock the door, and they went inside.

He switched on the light in the mud room, while Olivia went ahead to the main corridor.

"I'll check upstairs," she said.

"I'll finish looking around down here."

He flicked on lights as he entered each room: Parlor, family room, bathroom, dining room, library. He did not see any indication of a disturbance.

What was I expecting? For Laveaux to throw a party while we were out and trash the place?

With every light blazing, their furniture, photographs, and other knick-knacks were on full display in each room. The sight of all their stuff reminded him of how much effort they'd expended into moving into the house. The thought of having to pack up everything, again, and transport it somewhere else they could be safe, frankly pissed him off.

I'd love to put my foot up Laveaux's ass, I really would.

Lastly, he checked the kitchen. Nothing was out of place. The basement door was locked, as he'd left it, though he'd learned yesterday from their scare with Kennedy that locked doors meant nothing in this house.

Olivia entered the kitchen. "Everything's fine upstairs. I didn't hear you yell, so I assume we're copacetic here?"

"I've looked everywhere except the basement," he said.

She glanced at the door. He saw her face tighten.

She's no fool. She's not going down there, either.

"Want something to drink?" She crossed to the refrigerator. "Actually, I could eat something, too. We skipped lunch."

"You read my mind," he said. "I'm famished."

The doorbell rang.

37

Warily, Len peered out of the front window. He was expecting to see Dr. Laveaux, much like he had seen the guy standing at their door a couple of days ago, when this nightmare had begun.

But when he saw the figure waiting outdoors, the tension drained out of his muscles.

"It's only Jacob," he said.

"Thank God." The stress lines on Olivia's forehead receded, but her eyes remained sharp. "What do you think he wants?"

"Remember, I asked him to research the history of the house?" Len walked to the front door. "Maybe he's learned something useful."

After pulling down the edges of his shirt to conceal the gun riding on his hip, Len opened the door.

"Good afternoon, family!" Jacob said. He wore a red hoodie and jeans, his clothes spotted with rain. A black leather briefcase swung from his shoulder. "I've got breaking news for you fine folks: it's raining like a mother out here."

Len smiled. "Come on in, man."

"I saw you'd arrived home a short while ago." Jacob stepped over the threshold and slipped out of his sneakers, leaving them just inside the door. He grinned. "I thought you'd welcome an interruption to your day."

"Oh, it's no interruption," Olivia said, with a thin smile that didn't reach her eyes.

"I've got something top secret to share with you." Jacob tapped his briefcase. "Is there a table available where I can set up my computer, so we can all gather 'round and watch?"

"Sure thing," Len said. "Follow me."

He led Jacob into the dining room. Jacob placed his computer on the long oak table and settled onto a chair. He hit the button to power on the machine. The computer had an extra-large display, at least twenty inches, Len estimated.

"Are you watching movies on this thing?" Len eased into the chair beside Jacob. "The screen's huge."

"It's the equivalent of a large-print book." Jacob touched the frame of his glasses. "When you get to be my age, brother, you'll understand."

"Did you learn some information about our house?" Olivia asked. She stood in the doorway, arms crossed over her chest. "Is that what this visit is all about?"

"Yes, ma'am," Jacob said. "I promised your husband that I'd utilize my underworld connections to plumb the depths of your home's secret history."

Lines of worry bracketed Olivia's eyes. "I don't think this is a good idea."

Jacob's grin faltered. He glanced from Olivia, to Len. "I uh . . . I only offered to assist when Len told me he was curious about the property's background."

"It's not safe for you to be here," she said. "Maybe we can do this some other time."

"Wait, let's see what he found out, honey, okay?" Len said. He took Olivia's hand and tried to pull her toward him. She resisted for a beat, and then gave in with a tired shrug. He drew her onto his lap and wrapped his arms around her waist. He felt some of the tension seep out of her body as she allowed herself to recline against him.

"Okay," she said. "What did you find out?"

"Thanks to my membership in the Georgia Historical Society, I learned quite a bit of fascinating information, actually." Jacob opened a document on the computer. It looked like a scan of an age-tattered record. "This house was constructed on land that was formerly occupied by a school. Did you know that?"

"Never heard that before," Len said.

"What kind of school?" Olivia leaned closer to the screen.

"A medical school," Jacob said. "Specifically, the Evans College of Medical Science."

"Never heard of it," Len said, and Olivia was frowning and shaking her head.

Brandon Massey

Jacob opened another document. It was an artist's rendering of a Greek revival-style building, complete with elegant Doric columns in front.

"The medical college was opened in 1835," Jacob said. "It closed in 1893."

"This house was built in 1895," Olivia said. "It's one of the oldest homes in Candler Park, I know that much. It was here when the neighborhood used to be part of a city known as Edgewood."

"Very good," Jacob said. He winked at Len. "She's a keeper, brother."

Olivia smiled slightly, her initial frostiness at Jacob's visit thawing a bit.

"Tell us more about this school," Len said.

"The Victorian was built on this site shortly after the school closed," Jacob said. "The college enjoyed a good run. During the Civil War, injured and sick Confederate soldiers were treated there. But the war was merely a sidebar in the school's illustrious history."

He opened another document. A sepia-toned photograph of a mustached, stern-faced white man filled the screen.

"And he is?" Len asked.

"This is Dr. William Evans," Jacob said. "The school's founder. He also happened to be an intrepid researcher in the field of human and animal anatomy. This is most curious, considering that dissection was illegal in the state of Georgia until 1887."

All of them were quiet for a moment. The only sounds in the room were the soft hum of the laptop, and the rain plinking on the roof.

"Then he did his work in secret?" Len asked.

"He must have." Olivia drew in a sharp intake of breath. "Wait a minute. Damn."

"The basement." A chill cascaded down Len's spine. "The staircase under the hatch . . ."

"Has to lead to the school's old laboratory," Olivia said.

"Well, I didn't find any mention of a secret underground laboratory," Jacob said. "But it's evident that when the college was closed and the building was demolished, this house—*your* house— was built on the same foundation, and the original basement was left intact."

"The entrance to that original, deeper basement is hidden behind a false wall," Len said. "Then, you have to open a trapdoor

179

and go down a staircase." He paused. "I haven't gone down there yet."

"It makes a lot of sense, yes sir," Jacob said. "Due to the law, Evans and his faculty and students would have needed to conduct their studies away from prying eyes."

Olivia slipped off Len's lap. Hands on her hips, she stared at the laptop's display, but Len could see the gears spinning in her brain.

"So if human dissection was illegal," Olivia said, "where would this Dr. Evans have found the cadavers to use for his research?"

Jacob grinned. "Grave robbing, my dear."

"Grave robbing?" Olivia's lips curled with distaste.

"Oh, yes," Jacob said. "Throughout the South, black cemeteries were often plundered for such purposes. The men who procured the remains were known as resurrection men."

Len laughed. "Resurrection men?"

"Otherwise known as body snatchers," Jacob said. "It was a common practice, actually. Resurrection men were notorious for plying their trade amongst the members of the darker nation. Cemeteries were often unsecured in those days, particularly in the poorer communities. Also, in the South, resurrection men were usually black."

"Because a black man could travel unnoticed in the area," Olivia said. "Conversely, a white doctor visiting a poor black cemetery would have attracted far too much attention."

"What a nice way to treat your own people," Len said.

"These resurrection men were well-compensated," Jacob said. "Paid for each corpse procured. In difficult economic times, people will resort to almost anything to feed their families."

"Understood," Len said. "But it's still despicable."

"Was there an old black cemetery in Candler Park?" Olivia asked.

Jacob sighed, shaking his head. "There were many through the metropolitan area, of course, but I haven't found record of one within the proximity of where we live. That doesn't mean one didn't exist, but the documentation of such things has always been laughable. People hungry for homes and land thought nothing of knocking down poor folks' headstones and building away."

"Didn't they ever watch *Poltergeist*?" Len said, and a laugh slipped out of Olivia.

"If all of us were aware of the history of the ground we walk on every day," Jacob said, "we would shudder. The earth is literally soaked with the blood of our ancestors."

Len pushed up his glasses on the bridge of his nose. "So to summarize, we think a resurrection man probably supplied this Evans guy. Evans and his students studied the stolen cadavers in the basement lab. Then the college was closed, torn down, and our house was built on the land."

"Yes, sir," Jacob said. "That's a rough outline of what likely took place. We don't have the evidence to support all aspects of that narrative, but given what we know about the historical period, and what you've found beneath, I believe it's a plausible assumption."

"Hold on," Olivia said. "Let's go back to the underground lab. We're forgetting the most obvious question of all."

"What's that?" Len said, but when he saw the gleam in Olivia's eyes, he thought he knew where she was headed.

"Did they ever clean out the laboratory?" Olivia asked. "That's what I would like to know. After Dr. Evans and his students completed their dissections . . . what did they do with the bodies?"

38

Len locked the door after Jacob departed. Jacob had expressed interest in seeing the hidden basement, but neither Len nor Olivia would entertain the idea in the slightest. Len knew they owed the guy, though, and resolved that he'd find a way to reward him for his assistance.

"We've got a clearer understanding of why Laveaux is attracted to this property," Olivia said. Standing in the wide entry hall, she sipped from a cup of hot green tea, and surveyed the house as if seeing it for the first time. "I think it's full of restless spirits."

"More like pissed-off spirits," Len said.

"I've no doubt that he thrives on that negative energy. On their anger. Imagine how many bodies were ripped from their graves, sliced and diced on a dissection table, and then discarded in a corner as if they were common household waste."

Len gazed at the hardwood floor as if it were transparent, giving him a view of what lay in the darkest reaches of the basement. "We don't know for sure that the remains were left down there."

"Where else would they have been taken? This was over a hundred years ago, baby. They didn't have a convenient process for the disposal of biological 'waste' if you will, certainly nothing approaching the systems we use today."

"Good point."

"Remember, too, they were breaking the law by engaging in those studies of theirs."

"Which makes it likely they would have concealed the evidence in an area they could control," he said. "So you think they heaped the bodies in a back room, and then what? Threw a bucket of lime on them or something?"

"Lime, or some other solvent that was readily available. Doesn't it make sense?"

He nodded. "We're speculating. But as speculation goes, it does make perfect sense."

"The house is teeming with bad juju." She sipped her tea, her eyes haunted. "Think of all the families whose deceased loved ones were laid to rest, and then violated by grave robbers and brought here to be 'studied.' It makes me sad."

"But somehow, Laveaux harnesses that bad juju, as you call it," Len said. "I think he can direct the spirits to follow out his orders, maybe. *Someone* has been moving around items in this house and opening doors, that's for damn sure. We didn't imagine those incidents."

"It's a workable theory," she said. "It can serve us until we learn otherwise."

Even floating around only a theory about why certain things had been possible in the Victorian helped Len to feel better. As if they had regained a measure of control over their fates. Fear blossomed best in the unknown.

"I feel as if we're making progress," he said, "but you don't look too pleased about it."

"If what we're discussing is true . . ." Olivia shook her head, lips pressed together tightly. "We need to make things right, Len."

"What can we do?" he asked.

She shrugged. "Excavate the basement to locate all the remains? Ask Marie to perform a purifying ritual, perhaps? I've no idea. We'll have to figure it out."

"We can't stay here. I hope you haven't changed your mind about that."

"We still need to take the proper steps, as decent human beings." She placed her cup on an end table, pulled her hair through her fingers. "All right. I'm going to go upstairs and check my e-mail, and after that, I'm going to fix something to eat. I'm starving."

He watched her ascend the staircase, his gaze riveted on the swaying of her hips in her form-fitting jeans. A familiar, warm tightness spread through his groin. He was starved, too, but not for lunch.

He followed her upstairs. She went into her office and began to set up her laptop on the desk, as he watched her from the doorway.

Perhaps all the discussion of death and old, buried secrets had given him a sudden appreciation for life, because he had never found his wife more desirable. Her jeans and simple blouse might as well have been a silk, two-piece teddy. The thought of touching her was almost unbearably thrilling.

Easing into her swivel chair, she glanced at him. "Need something?"

He approached her. Gently, he placed his fingertips on her shoulders. He began to slowly knead her muscles, working his fingers into the firm flesh.

"I only need you," he said.

"Mmm . . . that feels good." She released a deep sigh of contentment.

"We used to give each other massages all the time," he said. "Why'd we stop?"

"Life got in the way, I guess."

"We need to change that." He stroked the graceful curves of her neck and collarbone.

Instead of replying, she swiveled in the chair to face him. She unbuckled his belt and pulled down the zipper of his jeans. His bulge strained at the seams of his boxer shorts.

She slipped her fingers underneath, cupped him. He felt a delicious shiver at the contact.

"My old friend here has been neglected." She rolled down his boxers, releasing him. Gently, but possessively, she took him in her warm hands. "I think he misses his best friend."

"He does," Len said. "More than anything."

She rose out of the chair. She lifted her blouse over her head, tossed the clothing onto the desk. Len unhooked her bra, let it drop to the floor. She took his hands and placed them on her breasts. He squeezed gently.

"Interesting timing, we've got, huh?" he said.

"*Carpe diem*," she said.

She covered his mouth with hers, and from there, passion and instinct took over. They stripped out of their remaining clothes as if their garments were on fire, dropped them on the floor—and then they, too, wound up on the floor. Olivia wove a chain of warm kisses along the length of his body, and Len turned her over, and repaid the favor, marveling at the smoothness of her skin, wondering why he'd allowed this beautiful, sensuous woman, his wife, the mother of his child, to grow apart from him. He sucked her nipples, moved down her belly, and kissed the soft flesh of her inner thighs, Olivia murmuring in pleasure, her fingers tracing lazy circles through his hair.

I'm never going to let this woman get away from me again, he thought. *What we've got together . . . is too special to take for granted.*

She twined her legs around his waist. He rose on both arms, and she took him in her hand, and guided him deep into her. Her moist warmth enveloped him so completely that a chill coursed down his spine.

"Damn, I love you," he said.

Together, they rocked, and rocked.

39

Later, they showered together. They hadn't shared a shower in years, but that afternoon, it felt to Len like the most natural, appropriate way for them to bathe. They took turns soaping each other with a pouf sponge, rinsed off, and then held each other while the warm water cascaded over them.

He never wanted the moment to end. The feel of her body molded against his was so perfect that they might have been separated halves of the same object that finally had been fused together once again and made whole.

"I love you," she said, her head resting in the crook of his neck. "I've never stopped loving you, either."

"Love you, too." He kissed her wet forehead. "And I love you more now than I ever have."

"Hmm. Why is that?"

"Because we screwed on the floor like newlyweds." He rubbed her backside.

She laughed. "If you want adventure, babe, we can do a lot more than that. We can get back into some of the activities we used to enjoy, pre-Kennedy."

"I'll dust off my copy of the *Kama Sutra*." He kissed the tip of her nose.

They toweled dry, and dressed in the bedroom. They had both removed their gris-gris charms during their shower to protect them from getting wet, and now, slipped them back on.

Len strapped the holstered Beretta back on, too, feeling a bit like a gunslinger in an old spaghetti Western flick. But the presence of the weapon comforted him.

Thunder rumbled in the distance. Len glanced out the bedroom window and was surprised at the premature darkness that had taken over the afternoon. Wind skirled around the house, and the rain that had been falling all day increased in severity, marching across the roof like an advancing army.

"A storm is coming," he said.

"Good," she said. "The rain's been teasing us all day. Let it all blow out and get it over with."

Downstairs in the kitchen, Olivia rummaged through the refrigerator to find fixings for a late lunch, while Len checked in the pantry and found a large bag of potato chips. He tossed the bag onto the counter.

"Looks like we're having grilled cheese sandwiches," she said. "I could throw in an avocado, too."

"A meal fit for a king." He swung to the bank of cabinets. "Let me take out that Panini press your mom got us for Christmas. It's about time we used it."

"Mom would be happy to hear that her money wasn't wasted," Olivia said.

While Olivia worked on assembling the sandwiches, Len located the press—it was hidden away in a bottom cabinet—and set it up on the counter. He cleaned off the non-stick surface and plugged the cord into a nearby outlet. Slowly, the grill plates rose in temperature.

A burst of thunder rocked the afternoon, the loudest one yet. Lightning stabbed the sky, the ghostly incandescence flashing through the window above the sink. A gust of wind clouted the glass.

Overhead, the track lights flickered.

"I hope we don't lose —" Olivia said, and her words were drowned out by another explosive noise.

Len's first thought was that it was thunder, but the sound was much too immediate, had come from right there in their house and made the floor and walls tremble. He placed his hand on the gun.

Olivia watched him, veins standing in stark relief on her neck. She clutched the utility knife she'd been using to slice the avocado.

"Going to check it out," he whispered. "Wait here."

Tense, she nodded.

Len swallowed. Slowly, he entered the main hallway.

The front door hung wide open. Beyond the veranda, torrential rain and wind whipped the trees and shrubbery. A scrap of paper blew past, sucked away on the screeching gale.

But at the sight of the open door, fear had tightened Len's throat as if a noose had been pulled around his neck. The door had been securely locked. There was only one answer for how it had been blown open.

The chandelier swayed on its chain, rocked about by the breeze. Crystal tinkled, sounding like wind chimes.

Len drew the gun out of the holster and held it in both hands, muzzle pointed downward. He crept along the hallway, toward the door, intending to close it. Floorboards creaked underneath the soles of his sneakers.

He reached the threshold and was extending his hand to push the door shut, when something pushed *him*. It felt like a powerful gust of chilling air, blowing toward him from the open doorway, and the force was so strong that it lifted him off his feet, hurled him backward along the corridor at high speed, and slammed him against the mirror at the end of the hallway. The impact knocked the breath out of him as glass shattered at his back, and the gun flipped out of his hands. He collapsed to the floor, face-first, in a mess of mirror shards.

Distantly, he heard Olivia scream.

Gotta get up, he thought, faintly. He blinked, his cheek pressed against the cold floor. The world was as blurry as if viewed through a funhouse mirror. Blood filled his mouth, warm and salty.

He heard the front door slam with a boom that made the walls shudder, and then, footsteps clocking along the hardwoods.

With great effort, he raised his head, mirror splinters tinkling around him. His vision clarified.

Dr. Laveaux looked down upon him. The sunglasses concealed his eyes, but a sneer twisted his lips, as if he were regarding an annoying insect that just wouldn't go away.

"Time's up," he said, in that nasal voice of his. "Dr. Laveaux has come to reclaim what's his, *kochon*."

40

Len remembered the gris-gris, the charm lying next to his heart. *Protection*. He was as rattled as if he'd experienced a head-on wreck in a vehicle. But he was still alive, and perhaps that meant the magic had worked.

He struggled to his feet, pain rippling along his back muscles in hot bands. In the corner of his peripheral vision, he saw the gun. It lay at the base of the grandfather clock in the middle of the hallway. He needed to get his hands on it.

And somehow, as Marie had instructed, he needed to take something from Dr. Laveaux's person.

Laveaux glared down at him. He was more imposing than Len remembered. He might have been eight feet tall just then, but that was impossible, only a distortion borne of Len's fear.

Len dug under the collar of his shirt and withdrew the gris-gris. He clutched the amulet in front of him, like a Catholic priest in an old horror movie pressing a crucifix toward a vampire.

"Get back," Len said.

Laveaux snorted with derision. "You don't believe that foolish woman and her roots can trouble Dr. Laveaux, eh?"

The next thing Len knew, Laveaux's cold, long fingers had closed around his neck. Len gagged. Using one supernaturally powerful arm, Laveaux easily lifted him off the floor.

Len wheezed, his eyeballs feeling as if they were bulging in their sockets. His legs dangled in empty air. He tried to break the man's crushing grip, but it was like fighting the mechanical arm of a massive crane.

Laveaux snatched the gris-gris off Len's neck, the cord

snapping. He dropped the charm to the floor and ground it under his shoe.

"Your little girl," Laveaux said. "Give her to Dr. Laveaux, and perhaps he will allow you to stay on here."

Gasping, Len lashed out at the man with his feet. His shoes merely grazed the edge of Laveaux's jacket. Laveaux tossed him aside, and Len hurtled through the kitchen doorway and crashed against a chair.

Can't beat him, he thought dimly. He fought to breathe, his windpipe feeling as if it were full of pulverized glass. *He's too strong. Jesus.*

Suddenly, Olivia shrieked like a warrior princess. She rushed Laveaux, a chef's knife outstretched in her grip.

Laveaux whirled around with the agility of a young athlete. He backhanded Olivia across the face so hard that Len felt the smack in his own bones. Olivia staggered backward and fell on her butt on the floor.

Dr. Laveaux entered the kitchen, the top of his hat brushing against the edge of the doorway. His lips curled as he surveyed the room. "Eh, too modern. Dr. Laveaux prefers the old look."

Len grabbed the legs of the chair against which he'd fallen, and pulled himself upright. He lifted the chair in shaky arms.

Laveaux chuckled.

"Dr. Laveaux is blind," he said. "But he sees all that you do, in all its futility."

Grunting, Len swung the chair at Laveaux.

Laveaux blocked the furniture in mid-arc with his long arm, but the collision rocked him back on his heels and brought a brief wince of pain to his face. Len grabbed another chair. As he started to raise it, Laveaux surged forward. He knocked the chair out of Len's hands, causing it to tumble across the dinette table, dropping salt and pepper shakers to the floor. Len spun, to find something else to heave at the giant, and Laveaux seized him by the seat of his pants as if he were a child. He flung Len onto the counter.

Len grunted with pain as his shoulder slammed against the cabinets. Dishes and other items clanged to the floor. Len rolled off the counter and onto his feet, staggering. As he tried to regain his balance, one of his hands landed on the Panini machine. The hot grill plates seared his flesh, and he snatched away his hand with a howl.

Stupid, stupid, stupid. Tears flooded his eyes. He had to be smarter. Focus. Laveaux was vulnerable. Hitting him with the chair had weakened him. He could be hurt. He could be killed.

Get the damn gun.

As if she'd been struck by the same realization, maybe by marital telepathy, Olivia attacked Laveaux again. This time, he didn't whirl quickly enough to stop her. With a primal roar of rage, she drove a carving knife deep into the small of his back.

Dr. Laveaux went as rigid as if an electrical shock had snapped through him. He threw back his head and yelled hoarsely. His hat tumbled off his head and spun to the floor, revealing his lush grey mane.

Cradling his burnt hand against his chest, Len crept around the table and back into the hallway. He located the Beretta on the floor. Picked it up in his good hand. Steadied it with his wounded hand, wincing.

He swung back to the kitchen. Olivia had found another piece of cutlery, a paring knife, and was angling to carve up Laveaux with that one, too. She circled him, the table between them. A hatless Dr. Laveaux regarded her warily, a wounded but still formidable beast, the first knife sticking out of his back, bright blood dribbling onto the tiles in dime-sized drops.

"Stand back, honey," Len said, his voice ragged but full of iron. "I've got this."

Olivia glanced in his direction. Her hair hung in her face, and her eyes held a fierce resolve. But she noticed the gun he'd aimed at Laveaux.

She slowly backed away.

Laveaux watched her retreat and shifted to regard Len. He bared his teeth.

And vanished.

April was standing beside the table. She was naked, her smooth body glistening. She smiled and crooked a finger toward him in a come-hither gesture.

Len paused, the gun wavering in his grip.

Screwing with my head again. April isn't here.

"Lenny, my dear," the April-illusion said in a velvety voice that was such a perfect imitation that he felt his knees weaken. "Lenny benny, come over here and let me love on you. You know you want it."

Her eyes mesmerized him, promised a wild adventure of pleasure the likes of which he had never experienced—

"Shoot the bastard!" Olivia yelled.

By reflex, Len pulled the trigger, and the recoil and bang of the gun broke the hallucination. He saw Laveaux again, crouched ahead of him, a knowing grin playing across his wizened face.

He had fired, but had missed. The shot had blown a hole in a cabinet behind Laveaux and shattered a stack of dinner plates.

"Lenny . . . honey bear . . ."

April was back, her smile glowing.

Len gritted his teeth and squeezed the trigger, and once more Laveaux flickered back into view. The shot ripped through the top of his skull, crimson bits of blood, bone, and brains spattering the ceiling and walls. Laveaux's mouth widened into a rictus of pain. He staggered like a wino on a drinking binge. His sunglasses flipped to the floor.

His eyes were gone, Len realized with horror. Where Laveaux's eyes should have been, there were only mottled patches of flesh, as if the eyeballs had been extracted and the remaining flaps of skin crudely sewn together.

What in God's name had happened to him? Len thought.

And in the next breath: *It doesn't matter, I'm ending this.*

Taking a step forward, he fired again.

The next round tore out Laveaux's throat and spun him around, arms flailing.

Another shot, and the round plowed into Laveaux's back, between his shoulder blades. He collapsed to the tile floor, moaning softly. Unmoving.

Finally, Len lowered the gun.

41

As if emerging from a trance, Len became aware again of the storm lashing the afternoon: the rumbling thunder, pounding rain, and yowling wind. The noises would have muffled the gunshots and screams, for which he was grateful. He was in no state to explain this bloody tableau to the police.

He holstered the gun. His fingers felt numb from the weapon's recoil, and his wrists ached, too.

Olivia edged around the kitchen table. The side of her face was swollen and red from the vicious blow she'd taken from Laveaux. Righteous anger tightened Len's gut, but he reminded himself that at least she was alive.

She plucked Laveaux's hat off the floor. She held it away at arm's length as if it were contaminated.

"Do you think we still need his hat?" Len asked. "I think he's . . . gone."

"I don't know." She opened the pantry door. She dug into the Costco box full of white plastic trash bags, snapped one bag open, and dropped the hat into it. "Marie might still need it."

Len figured he should check whether the old man still had a pulse, too. But he didn't want to move any closer. There was so much blood; it spattered the floor, countertops, and cabinets. As he took it all in, a spell of nausea scrambled his stomach. He turned away with his fist pressed to his mouth.

I killed a man, I really did it, he thought. *This wasn't a game. This was real.*

Olivia touched his shoulder. "You okay, babe?"

He sucked in a deep breath. "I'll be fine. All this blood . . ."

"I can't look at it," she said. "And I can't think about what we did. We did what we had to do, Len."

"I know." He slipped off his glasses for a moment, pinched the bridge of his nose. "For someone who has a hand in designing brutal video games, I guess I'm a total wuss."

"Give yourself a break," she said. "We should check out your hand. Looks like you scalded it pretty bad."

Len had almost forgotten about the burn. "Your face is puffy, too. You'll need some ice on that."

"I'll live."

Steeling himself, he turned back to Dr. Laveaux. He thought he detected, barely perceptible, the slow rise and fall of the old man's shoulders.

"He's still breathing," Len said.

"No way." Olivia spun, eyes widening.

Len studied the fallen man for perhaps half a minute. He couldn't believe it. The pace of Laveaux's breathing steadily increased, as if someone was blowing life back into him.

"How?" Len asked. "In God's name. . ."

His voice trailed off as Laveaux yawned like a man awaking from a power nap. One big hand reached behind him and took hold of the knife that Olivia had buried to the hilt in the small of his back.

And pulled it out with an impatient yank.

"Sweet Jesus," Olivia said.

Dr. Laveaux's head rotated in their direction as if it spun on a swivel base instead of bone. Blood and bits of brain glistened in his long, thick hair like party glitter. His eyeless face regarded them, blood smearing his lips.

"*Dis ti piti tankou ou . . .*" Laveaux said in a wet voice. Frothy blood bubbled in his ruined throat. "Ten of you . . . couldn't do away with Dr. Laveaux."

Len and Olivia backed out of the kitchen.

"Wait, the hat," Olivia said. She had left the bag sitting on the table. She stepped forward quickly, grabbed it.

Using the counter to balance himself, Dr. Laveaux was getting to his feet.

Len had slipped the pistol into the holster. He didn't bother to draw it again. It was of no use against this man, or whatever he was.

Hand in hand, Len and Olivia backpedaled along the hallway. Her hand was clammy in his, her eyes wide with terror. They passed by a small mirror, and he caught a glimpse of himself. He looked just as shell-shocked as she did.

He threw open the front door. Outside, the storm raged, a jagged fork of lightning stabbing the sky.

Len looked behind them. Dr. Laveaux thundered into the hallway. He had put on his sunglasses again. He was moving faster, taking long, fluid strides, his hair flowing, shirt and suit jacket soaked with blood.

"Run!" Len said. "Get to the car!"

But Olivia was already plunging down the veranda steps. He followed her into the pounding rain. The downpour felt like icy spicules against his skin.

For one frantic moment, he thought he had forgotten his keys inside the house, that they would have to flee on foot. But he dug deep into his front pocket and found the ring.

The garage door was controlled by a fob attached to the set of keys. He mashed the button on the fob, and the sectional door began to rise, with infuriating slowness.

"You get behind the wheel." He thrust the keys into Olivia's hands. "I'll try to slow him down."

He risked a look over his shoulder. Dr. Laveaux was on the veranda and coming down the steps, his long, slender limbs giving him the appearance of a giant praying mantis.

"Still coming," Len said.

As the garage door clambered open, they darted inside, their heads brushing along the bottom of the door. Olivia raced to the Navigator and threw open the driver's side door, while Len squirmed between both of their vehicles, to the back wall, where glittering tools hung on hooks.

He found a suitable weapon: a digging shovel so new the price tag still wrapped the long handle. He lifted it off the wall and clutched it in both hands in spite of the pain in his scalded palm.

Olivia fired up the SUV's engine. The headlamps flared into life.

Len hustled out of the garage just as Laveaux was reaching the end of the stone walkway.

"Get away from us!" Len said.

Stepping forward, he drove the tip of the shovel blade into Laveaux's midsection as if he were spearing a beast.

Laveaux grunted and stumbled backward. He staggered to the soggy earth, mud splashing.

Roaring, Len swung the shovel at his head, the blade whistling through the air. Laveaux got an arm up in time to block the weapon from connecting with his skull, and with surprising quickness, extended his long arm and took hold of the tool's handle. He snatched it out of Len's grip so fast that Len's palms burned.

Behind him, Olivia hit the horn.

Laveaux tossed aside the shovel and got back to his feet. Electric-blue lightning lit up the sky behind him. Thunder crackled through the air, and a gust of wind whipped through his hair and suit.

Len found it was easy to believe, for one heart-stopping moment, that Laveaux himself had summoned the storm, that he could command the forces of nature to strike down Len where he stood, like some vindictive god from ancient legend.

Len whirled and ran to the SUV. He banged his knees against the doorframe in his haste to scramble inside.

"Go, go, go!" he said.

Olivia stomped on the accelerator. With a squeal of tires, the vehicle rocketed backward, out of the garage. An avalanche of rain fell onto the truck.

Len was straightening in his seat, reaching for the seat harness, when Olivia let out a cry and mashed the brakes so abruptly that he was thrown forward and nearly smacked his head against the dashboard.

"What?" They had cleared half the driveway. "What's wrong?"

"Back there," Olivia said softly, indicating the rearview mirror. Tears trickled down her cheeks.

Len turned in the seat. His heart stalled.

Kennedy stood at the end of the driveway. She wore a set of her favorite *Doc McStuffins* pajamas, and clutched a teddy bear to her chest. Her clothes and hair were soggy with rain.

"Mommy!" she cried. "Daddy!"

Impossible, Len thought.

But the vision was so real that his heart twisted.

"My baby . . ." Olivia said, and started to open her door.

"No." Len grabbed her arm. "It's not her. It's *him.*"

Sniffling, Olivia shook her head.

"Look around, he's disappeared," Len said, and gestured around them. "It's because that's Laveaux standing back there. It's another of his mind tricks."

"A trick." Chewing her bottom lip, Olivia removed her hand from the door. She stared at him with watery eyes. "Are you sure?"

"Baby, we've got to keep going," Len said. "Hit the gas."

"Mommy!" the Kennedy-thing wailed. The child began to shuffle toward them along the driveway, moving in a frighteningly accurate emulation of their daughter's movements, rain sloshing along its slippered feet.

It's not her, Len told himself sternly. *Don't fall for it.*

Olivia clutched the steering wheel, her tearful gaze riveted on the rearview mirror. But she didn't move.

"Go!" Len said.

"I can't," she said, shaking her head. "I . . . I can't . . . not my baby . . ."

"You have to go. Right now. Press the gas."

Olivia covered her face in her hands. Len snatched her hands away. He pressed his perspiration-filmed forehead against hers. Their noses touched.

He gazed deep into her eyes.

"Trust me," he said.

Slowly, she nodded. Wiped her eyes with the back of her hands. Clutched the steering wheel. Shifted her foot to the accelerator.

"Mommy, don't!" the illusion cried.

"I'm not your mommy, you bastard," Olivia said, and plunged her foot onto the pedal.

The vehicle shot backward with a screech of tires. Dr. Laveaux, back in his familiar form, moved to get out of the way, but the truck smacked him hard enough to knock him aside like a bowling pin. They rolled into the street.

Laveaux was sprawled face-down on the grass beside the driveway. But he was getting up again.

What the hell will it take to kill this guy? Len wondered. *Do we have to incinerate him, for God's sake?*

Olivia hit the gas pedal, and they roared away from the house.

42

When they had traveled a couple of miles without incident, Olivia pulled off the road and into the parking lot of a CVS Pharmacy. She cut off the engine. Rain pelted the truck, blurring the windows and obscuring the world beyond the glass. Len straightened in his seat and unbuckled the harness.

"Good stop," he said. As his adrenaline levels dropped, he was becoming more aware of the multitude of injuries he'd sustained in the battle at the house. "We both need to be patched up. I could take a mega dose of ibuprofen."

Quiet, Olivia laid her head against the headrest and closed her eyes. She reached for Len's hand, squeezed tightly.

"Fortunately, that's my uninjured hand," he said.

She was quiet for a moment longer, and then opened her eyes. She looked beaten, and it troubled him. Between the two of them, she'd always been the relentless force of nature that got things done, that motivated him to give the extra push when he felt like abandoning the effort.

"I don't know how much more of this I can endure, Len," she said.

"We gave a good fight," he said, but he knew what she meant. He was shaken by what they'd witnessed: the sight of the old man pushing to his feet after taking three rounds at point blank range was going to haunt his nightmares for years to come.

"He kept coming," she said. "He gets into our thoughts. I don't think I've ever faced anything more difficult than backing down that driveway."

"We're still alive."

"I know." She dragged her hand down her face. "But it certainly feels pointless to go on."

"We don't have a choice."

"There's always a choice."

"He's in the house now, Liv. Every material possession we value is there, things that can't be replaced. We can't simply walk away and never come back."

"We wouldn't be the first family to lose all of our possessions. Look at what happened in New Orleans with Katrina. You can lose it all, and still go on, so long as you're still breathing."

"So you want to quit while we're ahead," he said.

"I want to quit while we're still *alive*." She touched his arm. "Agree?"

"No. I'm not willing to give up. Fuck that."

She stared at him, redness outlining her eyes.

"Earlier, you were the one who wanted to hand him the keys to the front door and walk away," she said. "What's changed since then?"

Len gazed into the shifting walls of rain. He had about a dozen pain points spread throughout his body, each of them throbbing in sync with his heartbeat. His brain was stewed by the things he'd seen. And he had never in his life been so exhausted; fear sapped you of strength like no other emotion.

But quitting wasn't an option.

"We walk away, and he wins," he said. "Game over, throw down the controller and turn off the TV. I really *hate* losing, Liv."

She was shaking her head. "This isn't a video game."

"But it is a game, in a sense. It's a contest of wills. He may have won that fight at the house, but we didn't run away empty-handed." Reaching into the back seat, he picked up the white plastic bag. He dangled it between them. "We took his hat, a personal item, just like your godmother asked. We've got a chance."

"The gris-gris she gave us didn't work out so well."

"Those were for protection only," he said. "Given that both of us are still breathing, I'd say they performed as promised."

Lips pressed together tightly, Olivia stared at him for a silent, extended moment.

"So?" he asked. "Are you with me?"

"Well." A smile came over her, like sun breaking through clouds. "Don't take this the wrong way, but . . . I always thought I was the strong one."

"We're balancing each other now, I think.   You're strong when I'm weak, and vice versa.   That's how things ought to be."

"Sorry I was punking out for a minute there.   I'm just so damned tired and I'm scared for us."

"You're only human, Liv."   He grasped the door handle. "Ready?"

She nodded.   "Let's head inside and get what we need to fix ourselves up.   Then we can grab some food and go to mom's to regroup."

43

They swung by the drive-thru of a Chick-fil-A restaurant near where Olivia's mom lived in Decatur. They ordered chicken sandwiches, waffle fries, sweet tea, and the chicken nuggets kid's meal that Kennedy liked.

"I feel as if I haven't eaten in three days," Len said. With his newly-bandaged hand, he burrowed into the bag of food on his lap and tore open a sandwich wrapper.

"I'm usually not a fan of fast food, but this hits the spot for sure." Olivia was still driving, but she plucked fries out of the bag as she navigated to her mother's place.

It was a quarter past four o'clock in the afternoon. The thunderstorm had blown over, alleviating the false twilight from earlier, but the clouds continued to shed rain in a steady drizzle. Len had checked the weather forecast on his phone and found that the rainfall was expected to last throughout the evening.

Olivia's mom lived in a brick Colonial home on the edge of a cul-de-sac, wedged between a pair of immense live oaks. Olivia parked in the driveway.

"I just thought about something," Len said. "Your mom's going to take one look at us and think we've been in a fight. How do we explain our injuries?"

"We tell her the truth," Olivia said. "Or a slightly modified version of it. Someone broke into our house and we had an altercation."

"You don't want to tell her what really happened? I assumed she would believe us."

Olivia shook her head firmly. "She might, but the less she knows, the better. I don't want her involved."

"Marie won't tell her?"

"My godmother knows how to keep a secret. Let's go."

Her mother, Anabelle, met them at the front door. She was a slender woman in her early sixties, with salt-and-pepper hair and warm honey-brown eyes. Len had always thought that if he wanted to know how Olivia would appear in thirty or so years, he needed only to look at his mother-in-law. She was beautiful.

His own mom had died of cancer four years ago, and since then, he had grown closer to Anabelle. A retired school teacher, she was widowed, and he liked to drop by on the weekends and help her out with various tasks around the house. His handyman visits usually concluded with her offering him a big bowl of her delicious bouillon soup.

As Len had anticipated, she immediately noticed their wounds.

"My goodness," Anabelle said. She put her fingers under Olivia's chin and turned Olivia's face to the side, her eyes wide with worry. "What happened to your face, girl?"

"I'm okay, Mom." Olivia gently removed her mother's hand. "We had an incident at the house."

"Looks like you two had a *fight* at the house," Anabelle said. She glared at Len's bandaged hand. Her attention shifted from his wound, back to Olivia's face. Her eyes narrowed.

"It's not how it looks," Len said. He edged past Anabelle and into the kitchen. It was a small space, furnished with a wooden dinette table and matching chairs. He placed the bags of food on the table. "Someone broke into the house while we were there. We had a scuffle."

"Oh, Lord," Anabelle said, and put a hand to her mouth. "Did you call the police?"

"We did, and they came and made a report," Len said. He busied himself by removing items from the bags, taking care to avoid Anabelle's perceptive gaze. She had a bullshit detector that rivaled a police interrogator's, and he wasn't comfortable lying to her.

Anabelle began to fire questions at them, but Olivia stopped her with a question of her own.

"Mom, where is the baby?" Olivia asked. "Is she napping?"

"I put her down shortly after I picked her up from school," Anabelle said. "She might be awake by now."

"I'll go get her so she can eat," Olivia said. She left the kitchen and headed down the narrow hallway.

Len had sat at the table and was working through another sandwich. He offered food to Anabelle, but she declined with a sharp shake of her head. He'd forgotten that she was an organic food fan and fitness junkie like her daughter.

He was sipping from his cup of sweet tea when he heard Olivia scream.

He dropped his drink and raced down the hall, plunged into the bedroom.

Olivia stood in the middle of the room, fingers dug into her hair as if she wanted to pull it out, tears coursing down her face.

He started to ask her what was wrong, but noticed the bed was empty, sheets and blankets tousled. The room's only window faced the backyard, and it was wide open; a large, ragged piece of the screen flapped in the rain, the fiberglass wire sliced open by a sharp object.

Len's heart felt as if it had been ripped out of his chest.

No, he thought. *No, no, no.*

The bed wasn't completely empty. Something small lay on the mattress, half-concealed by a blanket. Len pulled it away, knowing what he would find.

It was the samurai kitty doll he had given his daughter, which he'd promised would keep away the monsters.

But the monsters had taken her.

Part Three

44

"I'm going back," Len said. He stood in the driveway next to his truck. Cold rain saturated his clothes and skin, but he barely felt it. Clenching his keys in his fist, he glared at Olivia. "Nothing's stopping me from going to our house and taking back our daughter. We *will* get her back."

Olivia said nothing, her tear-reddened eyes as grim as he'd ever seen them. Hair plastered to her forehead by the rain, she hugged herself, veins standing out on her hands and neck. She'd been hysterical after they'd discovered the empty bed, had turned the house upside down searching for Kennedy, refusing to accept what both of them knew to be true. Len had eventually pulled her into his arms and held her, whispering into her ear the mantra he had just spoken: *we will get her back, baby, we will get her back, we will get her back . . .*

In spite of his assurances, he was bewildered. They had left Laveaux behind at the Victorian, the man brandishing his fist at them. How had he gotten to their baby so quickly? Was someone else helping him? Could it have been the guy Len had spotted driving the old black Cadillac when Laveaux had first visited them?

Throughout the ordeal, Anabelle, had watched them, dazed. Unable to believe what had happened to her granddaughter, on her watch. She confided them that perhaps twenty minutes before they'd arrived, someone had rung her doorbell, but when she'd gone to the door, no one had been there, and she'd dismissed it, assuming it had been a door-to-door solicitor who'd wandered away. Len was certain it was Laveaux's helper. Ringing the bell was a distraction.

Anabelle wanted to call the police. Both Olivia and Len had

angrily forbid her from calling law enforcement. Firstly, the cops wouldn't believe the truth of what was going on. Secondly, the police would delay them up with endless questions, precious time that could be better spent handling this on their own. Thirdly, neither of them believed the cops could actually offer any assistance anyway. Dr. Laveaux, whoever he was, whatever he was, would not be talked down by a hostage negotiator, would not be defeated by guns and batons and handcuffs.

They had to fight magic, with magic, Len had realized.

"I have to go to the house alone," Len said. "Meanwhile, you need to take that damn hat we got from him, and go back to your godmother like she asked us to do. She can help us."

"I want to come with you," Olivia said softly. She expelled a breath through clenched teeth. "The very thought of my baby in the hands of that . . . *monster* makes me crazy."

Len didn't want to think about Kennedy in Dr. Laveaux's possession, either. Opening his mind to those fears would whisk him on a one-way trip to crazyville. He sealed off that pathway in his mind, and instead, focused on corrective action.

"Listen, we have to attack this on both fronts," he said. "I need to be there, at the house, to do whatever I can to get her back. But you need to be with Marie so we can end this once and for all. It wouldn't do any good for me to get Kennedy, but he's still after us."

"We won't have any peace until he's gone," Olivia said. She covered her face in her hands. "Oh God, I fucked this up, Len. I *chose* this house for us."

"No." He folded her into his arms. She shuddered against him. Pressing his head against hers, he said, "You're not going to blame yourself for what's happened. It's not your fault."

"Just like what happened to Michael, if I'd made a better decision, if I hadn't been so selfish—"

"Stop it, Liv."

"Now I've done it again, and my baby is the one who suffers—"

"No more." He put his finger against her mouth. Her lips trembled, tears mingled with rain streaming down her cheeks. "No more blaming yourself."

She sniffled. "You do it, too."

"Yeah," he said, voice shaky. "I'm going to deal with that. I'll have to. This guy knows how to keep pushing our buttons."

Olivia wiped her eyes, pushed out a deep breath. "All right. You need to go now. I'll borrow my mom's car."

"Take her with you," he said. "I hate that she's stuck in the middle of this and has no idea what's going on, but she deserves to know the truth."

"She knows more about the old stories than I do." Olivia gritted her teeth, her frustration so palpable that if Laveaux had appeared at that very moment, Len knew she would have pummeled the man to a pulp, sorcerer or not. "I'll call Marie and tell her we're on the way."

He kissed her lightly on the lips. She grabbed a fistful of his shirt and pulled him closer to her.

"Get our baby back," she said. "You hammer a stake into the heart of that bastard, set him on fire, you do whatever is necessary to fight him off, but you *get her back*, you hear me?"

Then she wrapped her arms around him. Len lowered his head and said into her ear, "*I promise*," and she finally let him go.

45

Len backed out of the driveway, windshield wipers sweeping across the glass. The dashboard clock read five o'clock. Sunset wouldn't officially arrive until about eight, but the mantle of storm clouds had kept the day submerged in a depressing, grayish gloom.

It was usually a fifteen-minute drive to their house in Candler Park, and he drove as fast as he could manage in rush-hour traffic exacerbated by rainfall. He slammed his fist against the horn several times, aggravating the pain in his burned palm, and executed a couple of hairpin turns, tires screeching, nearly flipping over the truck at one point when taking a corner too recklessly.

The chiming of his cell phone reeled him back in.

He'd stashed the phone in the holster mounted on the dashboard. Dropping his speed, he checked the display.

The incoming call originated from their house.

Len grabbed the phone. "Laveaux. You bastard, I'll—"

"Hi, Daddy," Kennedy said. "What're you doing?"

The sound of his daughter's voice was like a scalpel slicing his heart in half. She sounded cheerfully unaware of the danger into which she'd been thrust.

He pressed the phone so tightly to his ear that the casing would probably leave a red imprint on the side of his head.

"Hey . . . hey, pumpkin." His hand trembled on the steering wheel. "I'm on my way home to see you. What are you doing? Are you okay?"

"Yeah," Kennedy said. "Mommy says hi."

Len's blood ran cold. They had taught Kennedy to be careful around strangers. How else would Dr. Laveaux have cajoled and comforted a child? Who would have been more comforting to Kennedy than her own mother?

Len detected a voice in the background. The voice sounded uncannily like Olivia's, even matching the subtle nuances of the tone that Olivia usually took when speaking to their daughter, patient and kind.

Len was less than a mile away from their house, but he had to pull over, swinging into the parking lot of a gas station. He balled one hand into a fist, and bit a knuckle deeply enough to break the skin.

His grip on sanity had never felt so tenuous. What was happening here? Had he gone to work today, and was he now driving home to see his family? The utter normality in Kennedy's voice, and what sounded like Olivia, forced him to question if he had lost his mind and the past three days had been only some mad fantasy, a hyper-realistic hallucination from which he was just now emerging.

But his hand was bandaged. He had burned it during the fight; he clearly remembered the pain screaming through his palm. His back hurt like hell, and he had an assortment of other aches, too. His injuries were real. The nightmare was real.

"When will you be home, Daddy?" Kennedy asked.

"Very soon, pumpkin," Len said. "You be careful, okay?"

"Okay. Mommy wants to talk to you."

Len's heart boomed, his grip tightening on the phone.

"Hey, babe," a voice said that sounded uncannily like his wife's.

"Listen, you better not hurt my little girl," Len said. He hunched over the steering wheel, his free hand balled into a fist. "Not one hair on her head. Do you hear me?"

A snicker. "Dr. Laveaux told you he would have her, hmmm?"

"You just better remember what I said, you bastard. Not. One. Hair."

The line went dead. Cursing, Len slammed the phone against the dashboard.

He roared out of the parking lot, tires screeching.

46

Ten minutes later, Len lowered his speed and crawled past the Victorian.

Dr. Laveaux's black Cadillac was parked in the driveway, the sedan at an odd angle, front tires nearly on the grass, as if the driver had been under the influence. Otherwise, the place looked as ordinary as ever, with the exception of one detail: the porch lamp. The lamp glowed with a flickering, greenish hue that Len had never seen before, and in his fevered imagination, he could believe the lamp was like the throbbing heartbeat of the house itself.

He made a U-turn at the end of the block, doubled back, and parked on the street in front of the property.

He drummed his fingers on the steering wheel. After a moment's hesitation, he mashed the remote control clipped to the sun visor. He still had his pistol, but perhaps he could find another useful tool or weapon in the garage before he ventured inside.

Nothing happened. He pushed the button twice more, and the door didn't budge.

What was going on? Possibly they had lost electrical power in the storm, but if so, why was the porch light aglow? Something else had happened. He had the not-so crazy notion that Dr. Laveaux had assumed total control of the house, that no door would open unless he deemed it permissible.

He swept his gaze across the front yard, looking for the shovel he had attempted to use earlier to beat down Laveaux. It was gone.

The unresponsive garage door and the missing shovel stood in stark contrast to what Len had experienced there only a short while ago, and he was left worrying, again, that he was trapped in some sort of bad hallucinogenic trip, that nothing he'd seen earlier, or then, was truly real. That he was actually donning a strait jacket in a rubber-walled room.

He slipped off his glasses and rubbed his fingers into his grainy eyes.

Get it together, man. You've gotta hold on. Your family needs you.

He put on his glasses again, and re-assessed his situation.

He had the Beretta, for what it was worth, and an extra magazine of ammo. That and whatever he could find inside would have to be sufficient.

He grabbed his cell phone from the dashboard holster. He keyed a quick text message to Olivia: *@ house, going in, luv u.*

He waited a minute for a reply, didn't receive one. He thought of calling her, craved the comforting sound of her voice, but decided against it. He would have to assume that Olivia was in transit to her godmother's place in Social Circle. Waiting here and trying to get in touch with her was delaying the inevitable. His only objective was to get his ass in the house and retrieve his daughter safely.

He opened the door.

Outside, cold rain trickled underneath his collar. He surveyed the neighborhood, found the street empty, as if everyone had bunkered down in response to a tornado watch.

Jacob's Chrysler 300 was parked under the carport. Briefly, he considered asking him for assistance. But this wasn't Jacob's fight to wage.

He walked down the driveway, toward the Cadillac. Maybe he could find something inside the car that would help him.

He had never gotten a close look at the vehicle until then, and it was in worse condition than he had assumed. Corrosion spotted the tarnished black paint. The rear fender was dented in the center from a collision. The Cadillac badge on the trunk door hung askew. Whorls of hairline cracks marred the back window, a hubcap was missing, and the tires themselves looked almost bald.

The Georgia license plate was nine years out of date, too.

Placing one hand on the butt of his holstered pistol, like a cop making a traffic stop, Len approached the driver's side of the vehicle.

He peered inside the rain-beaded window, checking out the rear row of seats. Debris was everywhere: tattered clothes and food wrappers and other junk. It looked as though someone actually lived inside the car.

He moved to the driver's side window.

A face suddenly pressed against the glass. Len staggered backward with a short yelp of surprise, and almost fell down on the driveway.

Who the hell was that?

He drew the gun. He waited for a beat, expecting the stranger to attack. Nothing happened.

Slowly, he approached the door again.

The face—it was a man's—was mashed against the window, lips and nose flattened, eyes distorted crazily. It was the driver. The guy who had been in league with the shady real estate broker. A member of the crew who had stolen Laveaux's house.

"Help . . . me . . ." The man's voice was as hollow as the wind.

Len lowered the gun.

"Please . . ." The guy's eyes were red, crusted with dried tears. He looked severely sleep-deprived.

"Let . . . me . . . out . . ." He pressed his fingers against the glass.

Frowning, Len grasped the door handle. He tried to open it, but the door was locked.

The driver pounded his fist against the window, but it was a soft blow that barely shook the glass.

He's trapped in the car, Len thought. *Imprisoned by Laveaux's magic. Like a pet in a cage. Laveaux allows him out only when he needs him to perform a service.*

"Did you kidnap my daughter for him?" Len asked.

Tears coursed from the man's crusty eyes, and thick trails of greenish snot streamed from his nostrils.

"Help . . . me . . . man . . . trapped . . ."

"I can't," Len said. "I'm sorry."

"Please . . ."

Shaking his head, Len backed away.

The man beat weakly against the window a few more times, uttered a sob of resignation, and then sank into the shadows like a prisoner drawing back into the bleakness of his cell.

47

Putting the disturbing encounter with the trapped man behind him, Len hurried across the walkway. He approached the veranda steps.

And stopped in his tracks.

A raccoon crouched in front of the door; it was a huge specimen for its kind, weighing probably twenty pounds. The creature's obsidian eyes glinted in the eerie green porch light.

It glared at Len, daring him to come closer.

Len's heart lurched.

Out of all the animals on the planet that could have blocked the door, it had to be a raccoon. When he was a kid, a raccoon had once invaded their attic through a damaged eave. One of the biggest frights of his life had been when he'd climbed into that drafty attic on a Saturday afternoon to rummage through some old sci-fi novels, and the startled animal had dropped on top of him from the rafters. Its claws had left a scar on his forearm that he still bore.

Len slid backward a step.

The raccoon's lips parted to reveal pin-sharp teeth. It growled, muscles bunching underneath its fur.

"Easy now, buddy." Len moved another step backward.

Redness rimmed the animal's eyes, and a weepy discharge trickled from its nostrils. Rabies?

His mouth had gone bone-dry. He had a lurid vision of the animal launching off the veranda and tearing out his throat.

But was it real? Or was it another hallucination that Laveaux had fabricated to frighten him?

He had the pistol, but was reluctant to expend a bullet on a common species of local wildlife, and he didn't want the noise to draw the attention of the neighbors. There was another way into the house.

The raccoon watched him retreat. Fortunately, it didn't follow.

Slopping through puddles, Len reached the eastern side of the property. He searched for another rabid door guardian, and found the entry was clear.

A security door barred the way, forged from wrought iron. It opened smoothly. The interior door featured a pane of glass, venetian blinds covering the window. That door was locked. With trembling fingers, he slipped his key into the hole, twisted.

Although the key fit perfectly, the deadbolt resisted his turn, as if the cylinder were cemented in place.

Did he have the wrong key? He tried another one, with the same result.

"Shit."

It was unlikely that Laveaux had changed the locks. Impossible, actually. The lock resisted him just as the garage door had, enchanted by the madman inside.

He raised the butt end of the Beretta and hammered it against the corner of the windowpane. Glass tinkled. Another slam of the gun cleared a jagged hole large enough to accommodate his hand.

He disengaged the deadbolt lock from the inside, and twisted the knob. The door creaked open.

He slipped inside, allowed the door to shut behind him. Broken glass crunched underneath his shoes.

He was in the small vestibule called the mud room. Only a small amount of grey light filtered inside the chamber. He felt for the light switch. Nothing happened when he flicked it. Big shock there.

He waited on the threshold, letting his eyes adjust to the deep shadows.

The room contained nothing of interest. An umbrella leaned in the corner. One of Kennedy's jackets hung from a row of clothing hooks. They hadn't lived there long enough to fill the space with much of anything else.

He slipped his daughter's jacket off the hook and brought it to his nose like a bloodhound seeking a scent. It held the fragrance of the conditioner Olivia used in Kennedy's hair, which reminded Len of the light aroma of coconuts. Hot tears rolled into his eyes, and he had to return the jacket to the hanger to quell the sobs that wanted to burst out of his chest.

I'm going to get you out of here, pumpkin. I promise.

An interior door led from the mud room to the rest of the house. He turned the knob, nudged the door with his shoulder.

Somewhere beyond the doorway, claws scrambled across the hardwood floor. He heard a low, wet growl of feral rage.

His stomach flipped. Shadows flooded the area, but he spotted something as big as a tomcat scuttling across the hallway, and saw the flash of wild, rabid eyes.

He slammed the door.

It was another raccoon. Was it the same one he'd found guarding the front of the house, or a new one? Was there a nest of the damn things somewhere nearby? And a secret hole that allowed them inside? Or was all of it pure fantasy?

The animal's claws ticked across the floor, right past the closed door. He heard it breathing—wet, rumbling breaths that should have belonged to a bigger animal. Then it lowered its snout to the bottom of the door and sniffed.

"I'm in here, you sonofabitch," he said.

Shrieking, it clawed at the door. Len could imagine wood shavings peeling away. The creature was furious.

He picked up the umbrella that leaned in the corner. Leaving it collapsed, he ran his finger along the tip. It was coated in plastic, but still sharp enough to serve as a spear.

He waited a minute, until the raccoon finally stopped scratching the door and wandered away, claws scrabbling off into the distance. He drew in a deep breath, but it did little to calm his pounding heartbeat.

He opened the door. He clutched the umbrella handle in both hands, tip pointed outward, like a man levering a javelin.

The raccoon growled. He pivoted back and forth in the doorway, trying to see where it was coming from in the concealing shadows—and spotted the animal as it rounded a table and leaped at him, springing off the floor as if vaulting from a trampoline.

Yelling, he thrust the umbrella forward.

The makeshift weapon punctured the animal with a mushy sensation like driving a pole into a bog of mud. The raccoon screeched. Its bushy tail whipped across his face, the fur carrying an odor like rotted meat. The animal squirmed on the tip of the umbrella, impaled through the abdomen. Its claws swiped blindly, and thick ropes of saliva flew from its mouth as it howled.

Grimacing, Len swung the umbrella around, into the mudroom. He pinned the struggling animal to the floor and leaned all of his weight against the umbrella handle. The floorboards crackled. The raccoon roared, fury seething in its coal-black eyes, tail swishing, claws striking uselessly at the air. Blood welled from its pierced stomach in a dark river.

Finally, the animal's struggles ceased.

He had never killed a living creature any larger than a field mouse. Under normal circumstances, impaling a coon would have been an act of unthinkable cruelty. Under normal circumstances.

"Now I've got business to take care of," he said, voice hoarse and shaky. "Stay out of my damn way."

But the raccoon was gone. He was pushing the umbrella against the floorboards. There was no blood, no indication of what had happened seconds ago except for his slamming heart.

He stepped backward, letting the umbrella clatter to the floor. Bending over, he drew in cool breaths.

The bite mark on his neck itched. The *bokor's* poison. It still coursed in his blood, letting Laveaux manipulate his mind as easily as a puppeteer dancing a marionette across a stage.

But it wasn't going to stop him.

He wiped a band of sweat away from his forehead.

Then, he moved deeper into the house.

48

Upon entering the main hallway, Len heard footsteps. They came from upstairs.

He'd been heading toward the kitchen when the noises drew his attention. The weight behind the footfalls didn't sound as if they originated from another feral animal; it sounded like someone larger was up there.

Kennedy? Or was it another hallucination? He was reluctant to believe he could simply find his daughter wandering around upstairs, and he hesitated to change course. He'd been convinced that Laveaux would take her to the basement.

Although he and Olivia had waged a death match with Dr. Laveaux earlier, nothing in the house reflected what had happened. He remembered the mirror hanging at the end of the hallway had shattered when he'd crashed against it; now the mirror was intact. He moved through the kitchen doorway, and though shadows masked the room, he didn't see any of the destruction they had wrought a short while ago. It was as if the house had magically restored itself to its former state.

He flicked the light switch inside the doorway. Nothing happened. So much for everything being in full repair.

He crept deeper into the kitchen, pulled open a drawer, found the flashlight he was looking for, and thumbed it on. The cone of light sliced through the shadows.

A sweep of the light across the kitchen confirmed that the counters and cabinets were clean. The table and chairs were upright. Even the salt and pepper shakers had returned to their proper places. There was no blood, no broken dishes, no sign that anything whatsoever had occurred.

In the Dark

The cutlery block stood where he remembered it, knife handles glittering. He closed his fingers around the carving knife and slid the long, sharp blade out of its slot.

Now he had a blade, and a gun. Key video game fact: two good weapons were always better than one.

He panned the flashlight across the basement door. It was closed, and locked.

Overhead, footsteps creaked again. He heard the gurgle of water rushing through pipes. Someone was flushing a toilet, had flipped on a sink faucet, or was drawing a bath.

Light beam aimed ahead of him, knife gripped in his other hand, Len slipped out of the kitchen and back into the hallway. He reached the bottom of the staircase. The steps ascended into murky darkness.

"Kennedy?" He traced the light along the stairs. "Daddy's down here, sweetheart. Are you up there?"

No response.

He climbed the staircase, risers groaning underneath his weight. His leg muscles ached with each step. He was still sore from moving in all their stuff, though in light of the blur of incidents since Sunday, it felt as if they had moved in months ago.

He reached the top of the steps and shone the light around the hallway. It was empty. The only open door belonged to the bathroom at the end of the corridor. All of the other doors along the hall were shut.

"Kennedy?" he said. "It's Daddy. Where are you?"

Silence. No footsteps. No rushing water. The only noise was his racing heartbeat.

No, he heard something else, too. A soft dripping noise, from the bathroom, as if from a leaky faucet.

He approached the doorway, keeping the light angled ahead of him.

He was about to call for his daughter again—but when he saw what was inside the bathroom, her name withered on his lips.

The claw-foot tub was filled to the rim with water. April Howard was submerged within, eyes closed, head resting against her chest. Her left arm hung limply outside the tub. Blood trickled from her sliced wrist and dripped against the tile floor, pooled around her dead fingers.

Len felt as if the floor under his feet was tilting. The knife slipped out of his grasp. He sagged against the doorway to keep from falling to his knees.

An accusation had been scrawled on the wall above the tub, in a dark, runny ink that could have only been blood:

LENNY KILLED ME

Tears in his eyes, he was shaking his head. "No, no. I didn't do anything wrong. I couldn't . . . I couldn't help you."

The April-thing stirred. His hand shaking, he raised the flashlight. She had lifted her head out of the water, strands of long, wet hair matted against her face. Her eyes shone like onyx stones.

"I loved you, Lenny . . . and this is what you did to me," she whispered.

"You were sick. I tried to help you. You wouldn't let me."

She opened her mouth and pushed out her tongue. A razor blade smeared with blood glinted on the tip.

Len's knees quivered. His impulse was to turn and run like hell down the hallway. But that was the problem. Allowing Laveaux to use his past to frighten him. Part of the *bokor's* fearsome power lay in his talent to plumb the depths of the mind of another, discover the most dreadful buried secrets and terrors, and drag them back into the light.

Len decided that he wasn't going to run any more.

The April-thing flicked her tongue, and the razor clinked at Len's feet, like an offering. She began to climb out of the bathtub, water dripping from her naked body. Her flesh was marked with multiple cuts, all of them seeping crimson.

Len blinked back his tears. He kicked away the razor blade.

"I'll always regret what happened to you, April," he said. "But it wasn't my fault."

She stared at him. Then she opened her mouth wide and screamed, a blood-curdling cry that penetrated Len's brain like a steel spike. Wincing, he edged backward. She lurched toward him, her limbs flinging water and blood in almost equal measure, her face distorted in a mask of inhuman rage.

It took every ounce of courage in Len's soul to stop and stand his ground. "No. This is done. Go away and give me my daughter."

The April-thing froze. The dark eyes dimmed. Its entire body flickered unsteadily, as if it were no more real than an elaborate graphic cast by a film projector.

And that's all it ever was, he thought. *A vision created from the figments of my own imagination. It was never real. April has been dead for years.*

"Rest in peace," Len said.

He stepped out of the bathroom, and shut the door.

For a moment, he waited on the threshold, and listening. Half-expecting the April-thing to return to beat against the door, or shriek, or curse him. But none of those things happened. Blessed silence had returned to the house.

It was over.

A floorboard creaked behind him. He began to turn, but too late. He felt a heavy blow at the back of his head, and collapsed into darkness.

49

Olivia arrived in Social Circle without incident. The only thing that had followed her on her eastward drive was inclement weather. Although it was six-thirty in the evening, the thick storm clouds had plunged the day into a premature darkness, and a sharp rain battered the town.

Driving her mother's Honda Accord, she cruised along the town's quiet residential streets, following the directions on her phone's GPS. They had visited Marie only yesterday, but Olivia couldn't rely on memory to guide her to the house. It was tough to focus on anything except her daughter.

God, please let her be safe, oh please, Lord.

She had to believe that Len would get her back. Len had texted her earlier, stating that he'd arrived at the Victorian and was going inside, but she hadn't heard anything from him since. She was fearful of sending a return text or calling him: what if her reply came through just as he was trying to creep up on Laveaux? He had promised her would get their daughter back safely. She had to trust him.

She'd invited her mother to accompany her to visit Marie, but Mom opted to stay home. Olivia had explained to her, briefly, what was happening. Mom believed, as Olivia had known she would, but she wanted to stay behind at her house, in the unlikely event that Kennedy turned up. Probably, she was just afraid and didn't know what she could do to help. Olivia didn't push her. She understood.

She was scared, too.

She braked at a four-way intersection. Glancing away from the road, she reviewed the directions scrolling down her phone's display. She was only a quarter of a mile away from her destination.

When she returned her attention to the road, she saw someone standing in front of the car.

She sucked in a sharp intake of breath. The familiar figure wore the grey Georgetown hoodie, rumpled jeans. The hood was drawn over his head, but she didn't need to see his face to identify him.

Michael.

She clutched the steering wheel in a white-knuckled grip. Michael stood there in the rain, head lowered as if in prayer, his fingers splayed atop the car's hood.

He's not real. He's only a hallucination. Keep driving.

But she couldn't force her foot to move.

Michael left the front of the car and walked to the passenger side. Olivia mashed the button to engage the locks.

Nevertheless, he opened the door, and got in.

He reeked of body odor, and sour vomit. His bare feet were muddy. He dug his toes into the floor mat, leaving dark smudges.

"Hey, sis." He pulled away the hood and grinned at her, green vomit bearding his chin and staining his teeth. His eyes glistened. "*Vamanos.*"

"You aren't real," she said, but she'd be damned if every aspect of him was not perfectly detailed, down to the faint, dime-sized scar on his forehead. He'd acquired that scar when they were kids, playing tag in the den, and he'd smacked into the sharp edge of a dresser. Mom had taken him to the hospital and he'd gotten stitches.

"We've got some business to settle," Michael said. "Drive, bitch."

Olivia started to argue, but a car honked behind her. By reflex, she pressed the gas pedal and rolled through the intersection.

Michael dug his hand into the hoodie's front pocket. He withdrew a giant syringe filled with a black fluid that bubbled inside the tube like something from a witch's cauldron.

"Got a hot dose for you, sis." He flicked his finger against the needle's tip, testing its readiness.

"No." Olivia shook her head repeatedly. "No. You aren't real. *None of this is happening.*"

But Michael didn't vanish, didn't appear any less real. In a swift motion, he swung around in the seat and slammed the needle deep into her chest.

Olivia's mouth flew open in a silent scream. Her hands left the steering wheel as she tried to grasp the syringe to yank it out, but Michael was leaning over her, his vomit-smeared face inches from hers, one of his arms pressed against her throat, pinning her against the seat. His hot, foul breath washed over her as he said, "See how it feels to die, sis," and mashed the needle's plunger.

She gasped. It felt as if ice water was penetrating her heart. Dimly, she was aware of the car careening crazily across the road, the steering wheel twisting on its own. She stabbed her foot, but couldn't locate the brake.

The poison from the needle coursed through her blood in a cold river. Her stomach felt as if it were being turned inside-out. A suffocating column of vomit surged up her throat.

One way or another, she was going to die.

No, we've got to save my baby.

The thought of Kennedy pulled her back from the brink. Her little girl, kidnapped, abandoned without her family, needing them more than anything. *No.* She. Would. Not. Let. This. Happen.

The world wavered before her eyes, as if it was nothing more substantial than dream matter, and she saw the real world that lay underneath the illusions. The Stop sign at the four-way intersection. No one in front of her, and no one with her in the car.

She fastened onto that truth, below the superimposed, lurid images of her brother—and the world solidified with a sensation that made her ears pop, as if she were reaching a stabilizing altitude in an airplane.

Reality snapped back into place like a rubber band. The windshield wipers ticking back and forth. The engine humming. An R&B track playing at a muted volume on the radio, some Beyonce song. There was no syringe in her chest. She was alive and untouched.

She exhaled with a sob that rattled her entire body. Bending forward in the seat, shuddering, she rested her head against the steering wheel. She closed her eyes.

Please, God, she prayed, her pulse gradually slowing. *Please, don't let that happen to me again.*

The passenger door opened.

With a gasp, Olivia spun. Michael crouched in the doorframe.

"Hey, sis," he said. "Let's try this again, bitch."

He began to climb inside.

"No more." She pointed at him. Her finger trembled, but she held firm. "I'm done with this. I will mourn you for the rest of my life . . . but I will not blame myself for what happened. No more."

Michael hesitated. No, not Michael. Michael was dead. This vision of him was conjured from the depths of her unconscious, brewed from her guilt and sorrow and nightmares. The real Michael had been gone for years, his troubled spirit in a better place.

"I'm letting go," she said. "Good-bye."

She turned away, steadied her grip on the steering wheel, and drove to her godmother's house.

50

Olivia parked in the driveway behind her godmother's white Cadillac sedan.

She clicked off the GPS app on her phone and checked for a text message. With a mounting sense of dread, she found there was still no further word from Len on how things were going at the house. Surely, if all was well and he'd found their baby, she would have heard from him by then.

Stay positive, she thought. *This isn't over yet.*

She hurried through the rain to the front door, the plastic bag containing Dr. Laveaux's hat swinging from her grip. *I come bearing gifts*, she thought, and had to choke down a fit of nervous giggles.

Marie answered the door.

"God, I'm so glad to see you," Olivia said.

"Yes, child." Marie took Olivia's hand and pulled her into a tight embrace.

Her godmother smelled of rich, fragrant herbs and sweet cocoa. Her hair was pinned up in a black scarf, and she wore a flowing, satiny red dress, gold hoop earrings, a leather necklace studded with cowrie shells, and a matching set of bracelets. She looked ready to go to a party, but that was no surprise to Olivia. Vodou ceremonies often took on the air of celebrations.

Olivia looked around the house. "You're here alone?"

"Jade stays at the university some evenings." Marie shut the door. "I asked her to stay there tonight. Our work here may become quite . . . dangerous." The skin around her eyes tightened.

"I understand," Olivia said, though she had only a vague notion of what lay before them. She offered the plastic bag containing the hat to her godmother, but Marie declined with a stern shake of her head.

"Downstairs," Marie said. "Come."

Olivia tried to conceal her disappointment. She was hoping she could hand over the goods to her godmother, and then plop down on the sofa and chill out while Marie went away and performed her work. She hadn't expected to become a participant.

Her godmother led her into the kitchen. "Has your husband found your daughter yet?"

"I don't know." Olivia swallowed a lump of emotion. "He's trying."

"Then we will need to hurry."

Marie brought her to the red door in the back corner of the small kitchen. Olivia had visited her godmother at home many times over the years, but she'd never ventured through that door. It was kept locked at all times. She watched as Marie punched an access code into the keypad lock with her old but nimble fingers.

Opening the door, Marie smiled. "Finally, you get to see my *peristyle*."

Olivia followed her down the narrow staircase, wooden steps creaking under her feet. No electric light shone overhead, but a group of white votive candles stood on a small table at the bottom of the steps, their small, flickering flames relieving the darkness. A mixture of pleasing, earthy fragrances reached her nostrils as she descended deeper into the basement.

The temple was a large space, brightly lit by strings of small white lights twined around the rafters, and more votive candles. Glittering, sequined flags were pinned to the walls, alongside murals of dark-skinned figures adorned in bright clothing. A large table that Olivia recognized as the altar stood against the far wall, the surface crowded with candles, figurines of Catholic saints, a cornucopia of fruit, and glass bottles brimming with unknown liquids. The center of the ritual area was empty, the concrete floor bearing faint chalk marks from past ceremonies. A thick support beam stood in the middle, the surface painted with swirls of vivid colors.

Marie walked to the altar, dress swishing around her legs.

"We'll be alone for this?" Olivia asked. To her knowledge, most vodou was practiced with a group, every attendant channeling their energy toward summoning the spirits.

"In my more youthful days, I could call the *loa* alone—which is a rare gift." Marie offered a brief smile. "This time, I will need your help. You have his personal item?"

Olivia unraveled the knot of the plastic bag. She slid her hand inside—and stopped when she felt something shifting and squirming. She heard a loud, angry hiss.

With a startled scream, she let the bag drop to the floor.

A large black rat scampered out of the bag, a slimy pink tail trailing along its end. The rodent was as large as a cat, with beady, red-rimmed eyes and a bristly coat of fur. It scuttled across the floor, coming to a stop in the middle of the ritual space. Rising on its haunches, the rat opened its mouth, showing them its tiny but sharp teeth.

The largest rodent Olivia had ever dealt with was a field mouse, and it had been easy enough to sweep it out of the house with a brisk flick of a broom. The thing in front of her was like a sewer rat on steroids and probably would have torn a broom out of her hands.

Heart slamming, she moved to her godmother's side.

"Do you . . . do you see it?" Olivia asked her. "Do you see the rat?"

Marie nodded. Worry framed her delicate features.

Olivia had hoped that her godmother would say *no, you silly girl, it's a hat, see?* But if she saw it, that meant that Laveaux's magic had touched her, too, and Olivia understood her concerns. How could they fight Laveaux if they were both under his influence?

"It was his hat," Olivia said. "Just a plain black top hat."

"Away!" Marie said to the rodent.

She flicked a handful of water toward it, and the rat scurried away into the shadows in the far corner of the chamber. The creature blended so effectively into the darkened area that Olivia couldn't be sure exactly where it had gone. Hands knotted, she surveyed the shadows.

Sighing, her godmother returned her attention to the altar.

"I don't understand," Olivia said. "How can both of us see it?"

Marie glanced at her as if she'd asked the most foolish question possible.

"Because it's there," she said, with a tilt of her head toward the corner.

"His hat turned into a rat," Olivia said.

She almost laughed as she spoke the words. It sounded like a line out of a Dr. Seuss book. *His hat turned into a rat, and that, my dear friend, was that . . .*

"A clever defense, and not unexpected." Marie shrugged. "Without his personal item at our disposal, our work will be much more difficult. I will need you."

"Me? But what can I do?"

"Follow my instructions. We will have success if we work together."

"Well . . . okay." She saw the shadows shift as that damned rat lurked around them, and felt the hairs rise at the back of her neck.

Marie touched her cheek gently. "Forget about that abominable thing over there. You must focus, my dear. Your family needs you."

With effort, Olivia pulled her attention away from the creeping rodent. She could not wrap her rational mind around the literal metamorphosis of a plain hat into a living creature. But she'd had a lot of fantastic incidents thrown at her in the past three days that required her to suspend her disbelief.

And like Marie had said, her family needed her. Nothing mattered to her more than reuniting them safely. She would do whatever was needed

She faced her godmother.

"All right," Olivia said. "Tell me what I need to do."

51

Len awoke with the worst headache he'd ever had in his life.

Groggy, he blinked. His vision was blurry, and using his eyes made his head throb. As he continued to blink, wincing at the stabbing pain in his brain, the fuzzy world slowly clarified.

He lay on his side on a cold floor. The room was dimly lit, and familiar, but his mind was snagged on a low gear, and full understanding hovered at the edges of his thoughts.

"Good to see you're still with us, brother," a voice he recognized said. Jacob?

Len blinked again, pain shooting behind his eyeballs. Jacob knelt over him. Soft candlelight glimmered on his glasses.

In a rush of comprehension, Len recognized the location. They were in the cellar's anteroom. Votive candles flickered on the shelves. The hatch to the deeper basement hung open, pungent odors swirling from its depths.

How the heck did I wind up down here?

He tried to move, and discovered that his hands were bound in front of him. He lifted them and saw duct tape wrapped around his wrists.

"What the hell is going on?" Len said. His mouth felt full of marbles. "What're you . . . what're you doing here?"

"How's that insurance commercial go?" Jacob said. "Like a good neighbor, I'm there, or some such slogan. You know the one?"

Len decided that he didn't like the glint in Jacob's eyes. He sensed a sinister aspect in the man's intent that didn't bode well for the circumstances.

Groaning, Len pushed himself into an upright position.

Dizziness sloshed through him. The pulsing knot on the back of his head felt as large as an apple.

"Take it easy," Jacob said, and patted his shoulder.

"Who taped my hands?" Len asked, though he suspected he knew the answer. "And where's my daughter? Have you seen her?"

Jacob chuckled, started to speak, and then put his thick index finger to his lips, his gaze contemplative.

"It's complicated," Jacob said.

Len rested his head against the concrete wall. He could have taken about a dozen painkillers about then. His entire body pulsed painfully, as if he were one giant bruise.

As far as how Jacob fit into the picture, Len could think of only one explanation. His gun was gone; the holstered Beretta was clipped to the waist of Jacob's blue jeans. His cell phone was missing, too, was probably buried in the pocket of Jacob's red hoodie.

"You work for Laveaux," Len said.

"I owe him a tremendous debt." Jacob wiped sweat from his bald head with a folded handkerchief. "I labor willingly on his behalf. I'm not bound to him like one of his prisoners."

"What did he do for you? Work a few roots?"

"You ain't never lied." Jacob grinned. "Oh, my brother. Have you seen the delectable young women I've got coming over every night?"

Len only shrugged. But Jacob continued to babble.

"I've got *magnetism*, my man. I've got that mojo. You hear me?" Jacob snickered like a teenager and snapped his fingers. "Yes, sir. The ladies know it, and they can't get enough of it, jack."

"Are you serious?" Len said.

Jacob scowled. "Kiss my black ass. You're still a young buck, you don't know nothing about the road I've walked."

"Whatever, man."

"Listen. Every day at the college, I had to see these fine young ladies prancing around in their tight little skirts and shorts, showing all that lovely smooth skin, those pretty legs and plump behinds and nice, firm titties. Lord have mercy." He shook his head, anger seething in his eyes. "But they didn't want me. Some gap-tooted, fat old professor. They looked at me like I was their granddaddy, if they noticed me at all. You know what I'm saying?"

Len started to answer, *what the hell did you expect*—but Jacob continued on.

"Now not long after he moved in, I got some inkling of Dr. Laveaux's business," Jacob said. "Gentleman had a lot of visitors, and they came by at the oddest times—late at night, usually—as if they didn't want to be seen by others in the light of day. That was suspicious. But what *really* woke me up was what transpired with his next door neighbor, Mr. Knox."

"The man in the wheelchair?" Len asked. "You said he had an accident."

Nodding, Jacob said, "Oh, he had an accident all right, yes sir. When I related the story to you previously, I left out a few details. I told you that Knox chased his St. Bernard into the street and got hit by a truck, didn't I?"

"Something like that."

"But there's more, brother. See, before all that happened, Knox would walk his dog every morning, and it just so happens that his furry friend's favorite place to drop a deuce was right in the middle of Dr. Laveaux's front yard. Left a smelly pile so big you coulda lost your foot in it."

"He let his dog shit in someone else's yard?" Len said. "I'd have a problem with that, too."

"I saw this happen with my own eyes: One morning Knox was out walking the dog along the street, and Dr. Laveaux came onto his porch, dressed in his black suit as usual, and stood there and watched Knox come back his way. A pick-up truck was rolling down the street, too. Dr. Laveaux pointed from Knox, to the road, and I'll never forget what happened next for as long as I live. I'll be damned if Knox didn't drop that leash and walk right into the path of that truck. As if he were in a trance."

"He made the guy do it," Len said. "He can do that sort of thing."

"Uh huh, I saw the truth about the gentleman then." Jacob laughed. "I knew it was wise to give that brother a *wide* berth."

"But then he gave you mojo, or whatever the hell you want to call it," Len said.

"Oh, yeah." Jacob giggled. "Check this out. About a year ago, I was in a bad spot. I hadn't been with a woman since my wife passed, no one worth wanting anyway. I'd celebrated my sixtieth birthday. I was depressed. Had a cabinet full of Viagra but no reason to use it. Can you imagine how that feels?"

Len only stared at him.

"I got this wild hair up my ass that told me to ask my good

neighbor across the street if he could help me. I was scared to death to ask him, but I was at the end of my rope." He laughed again. "The gentleman agreed to perform services on my behalf."

"In exchange for you doing his dirty work," Len said.

"He said he'd call on me when he needed me. I got that call a week ago. Dr. Laveaux had been in Haiti for months and when he got home, he couldn't get into his own house. Why is that? Because you fools bought it from a bunch of con men."

"Hey, we didn't know anything about that," Len said. "We thought it was on the up-and-up."

Jacob scoffed. "I knew something shady was going on when I saw the sale sign posted in the front yard. I didn't have a way to get in touch with the doctor while he was abroad, or I would have told him he was being cheated out of his house."

"He's punished the men responsible," Len said, thinking about the man trapped in the car and the dead realtor. "We didn't rip off anyone. We're victims, too."

"He warned you and your family to leave." Jacob held up three thick fingers. "Gave you three days to clear out. Am I right? But you stayed on. Didn't you? Hard-headed. Well as my mama used to say, a hard head makes a soft behind."

"Where's my daughter, man?" Len asked. "Is she okay? Have you seen her?"

"Your little girl?" Smiling, Jacob cast a sideways glance at the hatch. "I told you and your wife the truth about what's down there."

"The basement of the old medical college? So she's down there? With Laveaux?"

"He says the spirits want her." Jacob slapped one big meat hook of a hand on Len's arm and squeezed, drawing a wince from Len. "Guess what? He says they want you, too."

52

Jacob hauled Len to his feet. Len wobbled, and Jacob tightened his grip on his arm.

"Get yourself straight," Jacob said. "We got ourselves some walking to do."

Len's heart lurched as Jacob forced him toward the access portal. His bound hands tingled with pinpricks, numbness settling in from the restricted blood circulation. He wriggled his fingers and tried to separate his wrists, but they were wrapped tight.

He reached the top of the staircase. Light flickered faintly at the bottom. But he didn't see the door guardian that he'd seen yesterday, and figured the thing, whatever it was, had been temporarily relieved from duty.

"Go on down." Jacob shoved him. "I'm right behind you."

Len carefully descended the stone steps, loose pebbles crumbling underneath his feet. He heard soft squeaking noises coming from somewhere below. Rats? His stomach did a slow flip-flop.

As he neared the bottom, he saw that the wavering light originated from a tall white candle nestled inside a wrought-iron wall sconce. It revealed a small vestibule-like area. A wide red door lay a few feet ahead, closed, and a multi-colored, sequined flag hung above the doorway. Len saw murals on the stone walls, too: colorful depictions of grinning human skeletons wearing top hats and smoking cigars, massive tombstones, and black coffins.

The air down there was thick as syrup, heavy with the odors of candle wax, and something else. Something that smelled like death.

Jacob stepped around him and opened the door, the door creaking on rusted hinges. A grey rat scrambled across the threshold, and Len let out a cry of surprise. Grumbling, Jacob got his boot on top of the rodent's skull. He crushed the animal's head, and then kicked it against the wall, where it lay quivering in a growing pool of blood.

"Looks like there's a rodent problem down here," Jacob said.

Len could think only of his little girl trapped in a subterranean hideaway infested with rats. His need to get her out of there had never felt more urgent.

Jacob brought him through the doorway and closed the door behind them. They were in a stone-walled corridor about eight feet high and ten feet wide. Two sconces were mounted to the walls on opposite sides, both containing lighted candles. The concrete floor was mostly clean, but cobwebs hung from the wooden rafters in sweeping arcs, like curtains.

More murals decorated the walls. Images of serpents. Skulls. Crossbones. Dark-skinned people dressed in colorful ceremonial clothing. Elaborate geometric symbols that Len couldn't begin to decipher.

The passageway extended for about ten paces, and terminated at a brick wall. Corridors branched to the left and right.

"It's hard to believe all of this was under your feet, isn't it?" Jacob asked.

"Where's my daughter?" Len asked. He shouted: "Kennedy!"

As his voice echoed down the tunnels, Jacob growled and thumped the back of Len's head. The pain brought tears to Len's eyes.

"Don't do that again," Jacob said. "The doctor is at work down here."

He pushed Len toward the right-branching tunnel. Another set of wall sconces illuminated the path. Two doorways stood on opposite sides of the corridor, both wooden doors closed. Faded nameplates were fastened to the wall beside each door, relics of the old college's secret lab.

Farther ahead, the tunnel intersected with another set of branching passageways.

"What's in these rooms?" Len asked as Jacob steered him past the doors.

Jacob grunted. "None of our damned business."

Len was tempted to shout his daughter's name again, to discover whether she was being kept inside one of those rooms, but the throbbing pain in his head reminded him to be careful. If Jacob hit him like that again, he might pass out.

At the next juncture, Jacob pushed him to the left. The putrid odors grew stronger. Two more doors stood along the corridor, both marked with old nameplates. Ahead, it branched again, right and left. Jacob pushed him to the right. Len counted two more marked doors. They shuffled to yet another intersection, and went left.

"Damn, it's like a maze down here," Len said.

Jacob only grunted.

There was only one candle lighting the way, leaving much of the tunnel concealed in shadows. After twenty feet or so, the passage ended at a brick wall; a closed door stood on the left. It was barred with a broad, rusted length of steel.

The stench of death was so thick in the air that Len's nostrils burned. Len studied the nameplate beside the door and could make out the faint letters: DISPOSAL.

"End of the line, brother," Jacob said. "Sorry it had to end this way, but like Kurtis Blow says, these are the breaks."

He pushed Len toward the doorway. Len stumbled, regained his balance, and turned to face Jacob.

"Hey, we have money," Len said. "Whatever it takes for you to help me find my daughter, we'll pay it. Name your price."

Jacob laughed. "You can't bribe me with money, man. Ain't interested. I got a good thing going here with the doctor. You can't top my deal with him."

"Then help me because *it's the right thing* to do. Because you have children of your own. You have to sympathize with how I feel as a father."

"You want me to betray Dr. Laveaux?" A frown furrowed Jacob's brow. "Fool, are you crazy?"

Jacob lifted the bar from across the door, the metal creaking as he moved it into a vertical position. He used a key to unlock the door, and pulled it open, the door opening outward.

The stench hit Len like an express train. Coughing, feeling dizzy, he peered inside. The interior was steeped in darkness, but he glimpsed, within the layered blackness, the wriggling forms of several rats swarming over something lying on the floor that resembled a decomposing human corpse.

In the Dark

He felt his gorge rising. It took all of his fortitude to keep from vomiting.

The feasting rodents ignored them, intent on their meal. In the shadows, Len noticed other, jumbled heaps of what appeared to be human remains, and he realized he was getting a glimpse of some of the dissected cadavers that the medical college had carelessly discarded, so many years ago.

"Go . . . go on in," Jacob said. He was coughing, too. He put his hand at the small of Len's back and pushed.

Len spread his legs and ground his heels on the floor, resisting. "Please, Jacob. I'll do anything you want. *Anything*. Just name it, I'll do it."

"Anything?" Jacob paused, stroked his goatee. His eyes sparkled. He coughed into his hand. "All right, I gotta say, your wife is one of the prettiest pieces of tail I've seen in a minute. Got an ass like an onion—makes me want to cry. How is she in the sack? Honestly?"

Len couldn't believe Jacob had turned the conversation in that direction. Was this dude a sex addict, or what?

"Well . . . what's your preference?" Len asked.

"Oh, Lord, my tastes run the gamut, brother." Jacob grinned. "What I like—"

The distraction gave Len the opening he needed. Stepping forward, he slammed his bound fists underneath Jacob's chin. Jacob's head snapped backward, teeth clapping together with an audible snap, his spectacles flying off his face. He staggered, eyes swimming with shock and pain, and crashed drunkenly into the wall.

Len charged him. He lifted his fists high and brought them down on the back of Jacob's bald head. A spasm rippled through Jacob. He spilled forward. But his bearish arms wrapped around Len's torso. Roaring, Jacob lifted Len in the air, swung him around, and flung him against the wall.

Len's head smacked against the bricks. The collision nearly knocked him out cold and spun his glasses off his face. But something, maybe the sheer will to survive, kept him from falling over the edge into blackness.

Jacob stumbled toward him, cursing and spitting out ribbons of blood. Len twisted around on the floor and did the only thing he could think of: he thrust his heel into Jacob's groin.

Jacob's eyes bulged, and a croak of pain slipped out of him. He went down like a felled oak tree and curled into the fetal position.

Brandon Massey

Len was panting. Cold sweat poured off him. His hands ached, the rest of his body pulsating with agony. But he could have screamed with satisfaction.

Across the corridor, the door had fallen shut.

Len picked up his glasses and carefully put them back on. Thankfully, the lenses were intact.

He slid across the floor and balanced himself against the wall. He listened for footsteps or voices, but silence filled the tunnels.

On the floor, Jacob continued to writhe and groan.

Len straightened his arms and pulled his right knee toward his chest, which allowed him to position his foot in the juncture of his taped wrists. He pressed his foot downward as if he were mashing a gas pedal.

His arms trembled from the effort, and his hamstring felt as it would snap like a rubber band, but the tape underneath his shoe slowly peeled away from his skin. Freed, he massaged his abraded wrists.

Jacob was still squirming on the floor, weeping and moaning.

"Oh . . . oh . . . brother . . . why . . . why you have to . . . do that man . . . shit . . ."

Bending over him, Len made a fist. "You move, and I'll knock your ass out. Hear me?"

Tears streaming down his face, Jacob nodded.

Len unclipped the holstered pistol from Jacob's waist, and secured the gun on his own waistband again. Then, he dug through the front pocket of Jacob's hoodie. He found the roll of duct tape, his cell phone, and a ring of keys.

He remembered that Jacob had used one of those keys to unlock the door to the cell across from them. Len slipped the ring into his pocket.

Jacob was showing signs of recovery before Len began his next step, so Len brandished his pistol.

"Stay on the floor," Len said. "Roll over, face down."

"Man, we can talk this out."

"Don't test me." Len cocked the trigger.

Jacob rolled over.

Len tore off several long strips of tape. He bound Jacob's arms behind his back. He secured his feet together at the ankles, too.

"Now roll over and face me," Len said.

Groaning, Jacob complied. Len shoved the muzzle of the gun against Jacob's beard-stubbled cheek. His eyes widened with terror.

239

"Where's my daughter?" Len asked.

Jacob's lips trembled. "I don't know . . . which . . . which room . . . exactly. Dr. Laveaux never . . . never told me. But . . ."

"But?" Len cocked the trigger.

Jacob squeezed his eyes shut, fat tears trickling down his face.

"But I think . . . it's a black . . . black door . . ."

"He's keeping her in a room with a black door?"

"Yes, sir." Jacob nodded vigorously. "Please, don't kill me. Oh, sweet Jesus . . ."

"If you tell me the truth, you don't have anything to worry about."

"I'm telling the truth, I swear on my dear wife's grave, please brother, you gotta believe me. Look for that black door."

Len believed him. There was no guile in his tearful gaze. The guy looked ready to shit his pants, if he hadn't already. He was a simple man who'd made a deal with the devil for easy sex and had clumsily attempted to hold up his end of the bargain. He was no cold-blooded killer.

But Len would have killed, eagerly and easily, to guarantee the safety of his daughter.

"Fine," Len said. He holstered the gun. "Then I'll have to find it."

53

Len abandoned Jacob on the floor of the dead-end corridor, bound hand and foot and with another strip of duct tape stretched across his mouth. Before Len had sealed his lips, Jacob pleaded with him that he was sorry and begged Len to let him leave, but Len ignored his entreaties. Jacob had no loyalty; he sold his services to the highest bidder. He would deal with Jacob after all of this sordid business was over, but for the time being, he needed to keep him out of the way and quiet.

Afterward, Len checked his cell phone. It couldn't find a signal; that was no surprise. He clipped the phone to his belt.

He would have to trust that Olivia had safely reached her godmother's house, and that they would assist him in some fashion. Meanwhile, he had to stay focused on finding his girl.

Pistol in hand, he crept along the tunnels. The basement was a labyrinth of stone passageways, and each of them contained one to many doors. He approached each door, identified its color—most of them an age-dulled brown—and moved on.

As he investigated each corridor, he tore a strip of duct tape away from the roll he carried and applied it to the wall. It was a crude sort of breadcrumb tactic to prevent him from wandering around in circles.

Nevertheless, worry began to cloud his thoughts. What if Jacob was wrong? What if there was no black door, but it was a different color and only looked darker due to a lack of light? Or what if Jacob flatly didn't know where Kennedy was being held? Hadn't he admitted that he wasn't exactly certain?

In the middle of a corridor, Len stopped. He pushed up his

glasses on the bridge of his nose.

"This is nuts," he said to himself.

He had by-passed several doors up to this point. Why wasn't he opening all of them and searching each room?

There was a door only five feet away from him. Like the others he'd seen, it was plain brown, not black. But he noticed one difference: a large drawing decorated the wall next to the doorframe, in red and black chalk; the design resembled a sort of compass. It was some kind of vodou sigil, he guessed. He had seen many such symbols on the corridor walls, but the proximity of this graphic to the doorway seemed significant.

Len turned the brass knob. Locked.

He rapped on the door. "Kennedy? Are you in there? It's Daddy, sweetheart."

He pressed his ear against the wood. He heard movement in the chamber on the other side. A shifting sound.

There was someone inside.

He dug the key ring out of his pocket. There were five keys, and the third one he tried matched the lock. He turned the knob and pushed the door open.

"Kennedy?" he said, and the last syllable of her name died on his lips.

He couldn't identify the thing coming to its feet, but it wasn't his daughter. In the shadows, it looked like a rotting human corpse. But it was moving, magically reanimated. Two glowing yellow eyes found him.

Len felt a cold flash of recognition: those luminous yellow eyes, that mottled face striped with crimson streaks, the wide mouth like a shark's, rows of razor teeth gleaming.

The door guardian, he thought.

He grabbed the knob and went to slam the door, but the guardian crossed the room with shocking speed, like a monster from a nightmare. Suddenly it was within the doorway, inches from his face. Teeth clicking. A mane of matted, dirty hair swinging like strands of rope. The stench of death oozing from every pore of its rotting skin.

Len spun and ran like hell.

He risked a look over his shoulder, and saw the thing was coming after him. It was hunched over, but leapt across the floor in quick bursts like some kind of grotesque ape. The creature growled with need, and it was *fast*, covering several feet with each leap.

242

Len's heart banged painfully against his ribcage. His feet slapped the floor, echoing through the corridors. He cut from one tunnel to the next. He didn't know where he was going, but saw the strips of duct tape he'd stuck on the walls blurring past, meaning he was back in familiar territory.

He had the Beretta in his hand, but the guardian moved so swiftly that in the time it would take him to aim and fire the weapon, the thing might have taken him down.

He fled around another corner. And ran into a wall.

Not a wall. A man who yelped in surprise and pain. Jacob. He must've managed to pull himself into a standing position and creep along the corridor. Len crashed into him at full speed, and both of them went sprawling to the concrete. Len rolled away quickly, saw the gun had popped out of his hand and lay against the wall. Jacob groaned, trying to speak behind the duct tape, but his eyes went wide when the guardian scrambled into the passageway.

It spotted Jacob lying in front of it, bound hand and foot, and Len couldn't help thinking: *dinner is served.*

With a snarl of pleasure, the guardian seized Jacob's feet in its hands. Len noticed the thing's hands were obscenely huge, and it had three fingers on each, all of them topped with claws as sharp as talons. Jacob's muffled screams filled the corridor, and he tried to squirm away, to no avail.

Len slipped back, as quietly as possible, and picked up his gun.

The creature had begun to drag Jacob across the floor. It was pulling him toward the disposal room in which Jacob had planned to imprison him.

Len raised the pistol. "Stop. Leave him there."

The guardian's head ratcheted in his direction, hair swinging across its face. Its eyes seethed.

The creature looked like a decomposing dead man, but its eyes were too bright to belong to a corpse that had crawled out of a grave. They gleamed with the sentience of something ancient, and terrible. Len tried to look away, but he was transfixed.

A man's stentorian voice penetrated his thoughts, as clear as a voice whispered into his ear: *I accept your offering, sèvitè. Leave us.*

The guardian turned its attention away from him. Len exhaled, unaware that he'd been holding his breath.

He lowered the gun.

The guardian—or whatever it was, Len wasn't sure any more—dragged a struggling Jacob into the darkness with the rats and human remains, and slammed the door.

Len wiped the back of his hand across his sweat-streaked face. On weak legs, he plodded away.

He followed the strips of duct tape back to where he'd left off in his search. The door to the chamber that had contained the guardian hung open. He pulled it closed.

Then he moved on.

Before he'd seen the secret basement with his own eyes, he'd guessed that the square footage of the old college's cellar would match the dimensions of the home that sat atop it. But his assumption had fallen far short of the reality. It was like discovering some new, subterranean world. There might have been ten thousand square feet of corridors and rooms down there. He understood why Laveaux had been so determined to regain his property: it was perfectly suited for a man who dealt in the darkest of the dark arts. He could keep prisoners, corpses, and other entities down there for years, conduct all sorts of blasphemous rituals . . . and no one living topside would ever suspect a thing.

Len crept into another passage, one that he'd not yet explored. The passage was weakly lit with a sputtering candle, but he could make out, at the end of the hallway, a single, dark-colored door.

He didn't trust his eyes. He lifted the candle out of the wall sconce and moved closer, shining the light ahead of him.

It was a black door.

54

The ceremony had begun.

Marie had given Olivia a lighted Sabbath candle, and asked her to move into the center of the *peristyle*, near the *poteau-mitan*, the brightly decorated support beam in the middle of the area. Marie proceeded to walk the large circle around them, trickling water from a small glass bottle onto the faded chalk lines. She uttered prayers as she purified the ritual space, using a blend of Catholic and Creole litanies.

Olivia had never imagined she would be here, in her godmother's temple, standing in the middle of a ceremonial vodou circle and hoping this would save her child. But the tools of science and logic had failed them. The fall back to her ancestral roots felt strangely reassuring.

As Marie finished her circuit, the black rat emerged from the shadows and approached the circle, crimson eyes glinting with a savage intelligence. Olivia shrank against the pole at her back, the candle shaking in her hands.

"Be still." Marie placed a gentle hand on Olivia's arm. "It cannot pass."

Indeed, the rodent paused a few inches away from the broad chalk curve. It rose on its haunches and hissed at them.

"What did you sprinkle on the floor?" Olivia asked. "Holy water?"

Marie nodded. The rat stalked the perimeter of the circle, pink tail glistening, but it maintained a distance of a couple of inches. The malice burning in its eyes had no place in the gaze of a lowly rodent; Olivia had the sense that she was gazing directly at Dr.

Laveaux, and that he was furious.

Next, Marie opened another decorative bottle.

"For Legba," she said. "An offering of cane syrup. Legba stands between this world, and the *loa*. He is the guardian of the gate."

Marie tipped the bottle, dribbling several drops of dark syrup onto the floor. In a loud, resonant voice, she said, "Legba, please open the door for us. You know me well and the offerings I regularly give you. Help us now."

The rat screeched. The sound raised the hairs at the nape of Olivia's neck. But the rodent still declined to violate the circle. After casting a final, hateful glare their way, it turned, tail swishing, and scuttled away into the darkened corner.

"Thank God," Olivia said.

"This is only the beginning," Marie said. From a small sack lying near the support beam, she withdrew another decorative bottle and twisted off the cap. "I must draw the *veve*."

"To create the doorway?" Olivia asked.

Marie grunted, intent on her work. She poured a powdery substance from the bottle into her cupped palm. The powder had the color and consistency of corn meal. She knelt, and letting the powder slowly trickle from her fingers, she drew a series of straight and curved lines, creating an intricate glyph at their feet.

Next, her godmother dribbled a liquid from another bottle—it smelled like rum—across the drawing at several points. Another offering, Olivia recognized. The *loa* would not come without a sacrifice of some sort.

But which *loa* was she going to summon? From Olivia's recollection, vodou had hundreds, perhaps thousands of spirits. The attorney in her who always wanted to understand all of the details of everything wanted to ask those questions, but her godmother had sank into a state of such intense concentration that Olivia kept her mouth shut.

"The candle, dear," Marie said. On her knees, she indicated a spot in the center of the *veve*. "Place it there."

After Olivia had positioned the glowing candle, Marie withdrew a rattle from her sack, and rose. She touched Olivia's shoulder.

"Stay against the poteau-mitan, now," her godmother said, "until I tell you to move. Do *not* step away, no matter what you see or hear."

246

"All right." Olivia swallowed the knot in her throat and tried to calm her racing pulse. "Understood. I won't budge."

"Focus your attention on the candle flame." Marie pointed. "Look at nothing else, until I tell you to look away. Yes?"

Olivia nodded. The instructions, though simple, conjured a thick ball of apprehension in her stomach. What was supposed to happen here?

"Think about your daughter, and nothing else," Marie said. "Think about her happy and safe in your arms, my dear."

Olivia had managed to keep thoughts of her baby out of her head since this ceremony had started, but the order to focus on Kennedy brought hot tears to her eyes. She let the tears flow down her cheeks and hit the floor; it felt good to cry, for the desire to save her daughter was as bright and pure as the candle flame that flickered in front of her.

Marie edged behind her, and began to shake the rattle in a rhythmic pattern. She chanted in Creole, but Olivia could not understand her: it was an incantation that had no meaning for her uninitiated ears.

Keep looking at the candle.

Then something happened. The candle flame grew larger. At first, Olivia thought it was an optical illusion created by her tear-clouded eyes, but as she continued to blink, her tears fell away, yet the flame increased in height, width, and depth. Strangely, she didn't feel any escalation in temperature in the room.

Behind her, the rattle shook, shook, shook, the sinuous rhythm matching her heartbeat. She felt her body swaying gently against the pole.

Ahead of her, the flame expanded until it was as large as a doorway—and she realized that was exactly what it had become. A fire-ringed portal that shimmered above the floor. Beyond the unearthly threshold lay a darkness deeper than night.

Keep your eyes on the flame, and don't move, Olivia reminded herself. *Don't move. Think about your baby.*

A low, whooshing sound was coming from deep within the portal. It sounded like an approaching jumbo jet. Her ear drums vibrated as the noise increased in volume and pitch. Her limbs shook. The fine hairs on her arms lifted and danced, and she felt the hair on her head rippling, too.

And then she was sucked inside.

55

Len examined the door.

It wasn't entirely black. Intricately-drawn sigils were carved into the wood along its entire length. The symbols emitted a soft, ruby glow. The effect could have been created by luminescent paint, but Len was pretty sure the carvings were evidence of Laveaux's powerful sorcery at work. This was the entrance to his place of power.

The door knob was gold-plated, and molded into an eerily realistic facsimile of a man's leering face.

He twisted the knob. Locked. But one of the keys on the ring he'd taken from Jacob fit the keyhole.

Len replaced the candle in the wall sconce beside the doorway. Whispering a prayer, he slowly opened the door.

It opened inward. Ahead, Len saw a short corridor illuminated by candles on opposite sides. The passage ended at a large chamber.

The heavy air smelled of melting candle wax, and something rotten, like rancid meat.

He heard a voice echoing from the room beyond. He recognized the speaker immediately: Dr. Laveaux. He was speaking in a foreign tongue, Creole, presumably, and in a commanding, resonant tone, as if he were conducting a ritual.

He's doing something with my little girl.

Anxiety knotted his gut. Len crept forward, clasping the gun in both hands. As he neared the end of the passageway, he lowered into a crouch.

The room looked like some sort of school auditorium. Len

reasoned that perhaps the college's professors would have used the area to demonstrate anatomical procedures on cadavers. A wide staircase descended about twenty feet, numerous aisles branching off from the stairs, which probably would have led to rows of desks.

The staircase ended at large, circular stage. Over a dozen burning candles outlined the perimeter of the elevated platform, their flames casting quivering shadows on the walls.

Dr. Laveaux towered within the circle, cane in hand, an altar of some kind standing behind him. He wore a new black suit and hat, and white powder coated his face. It gave him the freakish appearance of a circus devil.

A small bed stood within the circle, too. Kennedy lay on it, looking frightfully small and vulnerable. She appeared to be asleep.

Upon finally seeing his child, Len's heart almost imploded with emotion. It took enormous willpower for him to stay crouched and avoid running down the steps and scooping her up in his arms.

But with the distance between them, he couldn't be sure whether she was breathing, or not.

She's alive, he told himself. *She's only sleeping. Besides, a dead child would be no use to Laveaux or the spirits.*

That was when Len noticed the black candle that burned in the very center of the circle, situated within a large symbol that looked similar to the sigils he'd seen on the walls and doors of the tunnels. Tendrils of dark, toxic-looking smoke had begun to churn from the wick. The smoke gradually thickened, filling the ceremonial circle. That stench of rotted flesh that Len had detected before grew stronger.

Dr. Laveaux shouted what sounded like an expression of triumph, his voice rebounding throughout the chamber.

Len's muscles tensed. He was armed with the gun, but though that had slowed Laveaux before, it sure as hell hadn't killed him. He could perhaps fire a hail of bullets at him and stagger the guy enough to allow him to get Kennedy, but what would he do when Laveaux came after him?

What was Olivia up to with her godmother? They were supposed to be doing *something* to help him out here, weren't they?

Still crouching, Len edged forward onto the staircase.

That massive, churning cloud of black smoke troubled him. The smoke didn't disperse throughout the room as it should have; it was contained within the boundaries of the circle, where it continued to shift and writhe, as though something with sentient purpose were manifesting within it.

He was also peripherally aware of others gathered within the theater. Presences that he felt, but could not see. Perhaps the unhappy souls of those whose earthly bodies had been stolen from their graves and laid on dissection tables. He was no psychic, but damned if he didn't feel as if he were being *watched* by a curious audience.

He crept down another step.

A loose chunk of stone broke from underneath his shoe. The rock clattered down the staircase, all the way to the bottom, each hard bounce echoing through the chamber.

Len froze, clamping his teeth down on his tongue so hard that he tasted blood.

Dr. Laveaux spotted him. His powdered lips curved into a broad smile of pure malice.

If his daughter hadn't been in there, Len would have run for his life. But running was no longer an option.

Dr. Laveaux raised his cane and pointed in Len's direction. He uttered something that sounded like: *sacrifice* . . .

Len brought up the pistol just as a long tentacle of smoke peeled off from the shifting cloud. The smoky appendage slithered off the stage, to the bottom of the staircase—and rapidly climbed toward him. It moved with the sinuous speed of a giant serpent, and in the shifting layers of smoke, Len thought he saw rows of glinting teeth hanging in a mouth large enough to swallow a man whole. It hissed with unmistakable menace.

Terror clanged like a bell in his brain. He fired the gun, once, twice, three times, gunfire reverberating in the auditorium, but the rounds had no effect whatsoever on the ever-shifting creature. The bullets smashed into the steps and tore away chunks of stone, but the smoky snake-thing kept coming, wisps of cloud flickering.

Len turned to run, but the thing was already upon him.

Pain ripped into his right leg; it felt as if dozens of cold needles had punctured his flesh. He screamed.

Smaller tentacles peeled off from the ethereal creature and wrapped around his body. It was like being tied up within coils of rope. He shouted and thrashed.

A tendril darted into his mouth. It tasted like spoiled meat. The appendage wormed down his throat. He gagged as it plunged deeper into him, cutting off his airflow.

He couldn't believe it was going to end like this.

Game over . . . I failed . . . . sorry, sweetheart . . .

56

Olivia was zooming through a twisting tunnel of light, traveling with the velocity of a missile.

She remembered, as a child, experiencing dreams of flying, of zipping like Peter Pan through the air. Her propulsion along the glowing corridor had the distinct feeling of one of those childhood dreams. She felt buoyant with power and potential, every barrier stripped away from her, leaving only one overriding purpose: finding Kennedy.

The thought of her daughter was like a GPS signal guiding her across the void, and she didn't dare allow other worries to corrupt her focus and send her off course.

Yet in the back room of her mind, she also understood that her physical body had not truly exited Marie's basement via a fiery doorway. She understood this even though it *felt* as if she inhabited a body of some kind. She could feel her arms, fingers, legs. She could feel cold air rushing across her face. But her present figure felt lighter, as if she were formed from the material of the ether itself. A spiritual body, perhaps.

A portal loomed ahead, at the terminus of the luminous channel through which she traveled. She wasn't sure where it ended, but she was moving too fast to slow and reconsider. She plunged through the exit, and heard a loud *pop* as she left the tunnel.

Shooting out of the passage was like diving into an ocean. The atmosphere felt watery. There was no sound. She was in a darkened place, but there were dim points of light clustered throughout.

It was some sort of auditorium. Candles glowed, providing

the only illumination in the soundless area.

As she continued to look around, she noticed that she floated far above the floor.

Dr. Laveaux was directly beneath her. He stood within a ceremonial circle marked by burning candles. A large, toxic-looking cloud seethed near him. Not far away, Kennedy lay on a small bed.

My baby . . .

She started toward Kennedy, but stopped when she sensed distress. *Len.* Something was wrong with Len.

She located him on the staircase below. He was battling a python-like creature formed from shifting layers of smoke, its body trailing multiple writhing appendages. Intuitively, she understood that the cloud near Laveaux harbored a malevolent presence, and that it had sent forth that nightmarish thing to harm her husband.

She went to him.

Others were watching. She saw the faint, spectral figures of a gathered crowd lurking on the perimeter of the chamber. But none intervened to help, or hinder.

Traveling across the room was like power swimming, each stroke propelling her forward in great bursts. In a handful of heart beats, she was there.

The serpent was swallowing Len whole.

She acted swiftly, and without fear, for she somehow knew that nothing could harm her while she was there in her present form. She seized the snake by one of its smoky appendages, its wispy flesh strangely cold and slick in her fingers.

Malignant eyes found her. The creature hissed.

Undeterred, she flung it away with a heaving throw that sent it sprawling across the staircase.

The tumbling serpent's massive maw opened in an expression of fury, and it glared at her as if it would attack, but the larger cloud reeled the creature back into its churning mass. It melted away into the shifting orb of smoke.

Len was gasping, face wracked with pain. But he saw her, and his eyes were full of love and gratitude.

I'm here now, I'm with you, she said to him.

She touched his cheek. Her fingers tingled. He grasped her hand, kissed it, and while she didn't feel his lips, she felt a spark of something electric and sweet.

Let's do this, she said.

57

Len was teetering on the edge of death when Olivia appeared like an angel in the darkness. She ripped the snake-thing off him, and it didn't return to attack again, choosing to flee back to the mother cloud.

Olivia floated beside him, her body outlined with shimmering light. He could see every detail of her. But he could see *through* her, too, as if she were only a holographic image projected in front of him.

Let's do this, Olivia said, though he didn't see her spectral lips move. But he heard her voice in his mind.

He picked up the gun and got to his feet. Moving and even basic breathing hurt like hell. The unearthly serpent had nearly squeezed the life out of him. But no amount of pain was going to stop him from finishing this once and for all.

On the platform, Dr. Laveaux sneered at them. He directed the cloud toward Kennedy.

A tentacle peeled off from the entity and snaked toward their little girl.

Len plunged down the steps. But Olivia was faster. She streaked in a blur across the chamber and arrived at Kennedy's side. She huddled protectively over their unconscious child.

The appendage pulled back.

Laveaux uttered a sound of disgust. For the first time in Len's experience, the old *bokor* appeared indecisive.

But Len understood exactly what he needed to do next.

"Take Laveaux!" Len said. "He's the sacrifice!"

And he aimed at the doctor and squeezed the trigger.

The gun's report echoed off the walls. Struck, Dr. Laveaux

tumbled off the platform and dropped onto the stone floor, knocking over candles as he fell, their flames sputtering out.

The misty tentacle slithered across the stage, seeking the wounded man.

It demands something, Len thought. *An offering. It doesn't matter who or what it is—even the man who summoned it can serve as the sacrifice.*

Len advanced around the edge of the platform. Laveaux was sprawled on the concrete floor, blood seeping from the gunshot wound in his chest. He was struggling to get up, most of the white powder smeared away from his face, his hat askew. But the tentacle had found his leg.

Len pointed the gun at him.

"Don't hurt me, Lenny," April said.

The illusion was perfect. Len's finger twitched on the trigger.

"Stop it," Len said.

"Babe, I need you now," Olivia said.

In a blink, it was his wife, as beautiful as ever.

"Stop," Len said.

"Daddy, help!" Kennedy's innocent eyes pleaded with him.

"Enough!" Len said.

He shot Laveaux in the head.

Laveaux collapsed to the floor. The appendage coiled around his body, its various layers mummifying him. Slowly, it lifted him into the air.

Something was forming in the larger, sentient cloud. It looked like a gigantic mouth in an eyeless face. Rows upon rows of needlelike teeth glistened in that unearthly maw.

The tentacle carried Laveaux into the massive orifice. Laveaux was fighting, weakly, uttering commands in a faltering voice, but to no avail.

He was drawn deep inside the cloud, and consumed. His voice faded away into silence.

Len had expected the entity that Laveaux had conjured to vanish, too, but the dark cloud remained. It bulged and shifted, the mouth rippling.

Len looked at Olivia. She remained at Kennedy's side, shielding her. He met her gaze, and heard her words in his mind: *you have to send it away, Len.*

Len cleared his throat.

"Leave us," he said. "You have your offering."

The mouth shrank. A semblance of a face formed in the cloud: eyes, nose, and a smaller pair of lips than the monstrous maw that had consumed the old *bokor*. Len stared into the crude visage of the entity, and he had a sense that he was looking into the spirit of a conscious being that predated recorded history.

It left him breathless.

But the entity remained for only one reason. He had made an offering; it had been accepted. In return, he was expected to submit a request.

It was a simple transaction.

He was dealing with a seller that could have granted him anything in the world, or beyond. Perhaps that was how Dr. Laveaux had extended his lifespan and performed such miraculous feats. He'd struck a deal with the devil.

"I want peace for my family," Len said. He looked at Olivia. "Peace, and happiness for all of us. That is my request."

He wasn't sure what to expect, didn't know if the entity would reply *it will be done* or some such acknowledgement. But the wispy lips parted, and Len felt a gust of chilly air blow through him, rippling his clothes and almost knocking him off balance.

Then the features of the face melted away in the shifting cloud. Slowly, the cloud itself began to filter back into the candle wick as if being sucked down into a drain.

Soon, it had vanished.

The air changed, too. The atmosphere felt lighter, and the rancid odors that had filled the room had dispersed.

Len climbed onto the stage. He licked his fingers, ignoring the dust on them, and used his dampened fingers to snuff out the black candle.

The assembled audience of curious spirits had disappeared. Len felt their absence from the auditorium, but believed they still remained on the property, and would continue to dwell there, until someone freed their sounds to let them find peace.

He went to his family. Kennedy's eyelids fluttered open. She glanced from Len's face, to Olivia's glowing form.

"Mommy . . . Daddy?" She yawned. "Monter in here?"

"Not any more, pumpkin." Len picked her up. He kissed her forehead. "The monster is gone."

58

Len carried his daughter out of the house. He didn't stop moving until he had stepped off the veranda and into the front yard.

The rainfall had ceased. It was twilight, and the cloud cover had broken, revealing distant stars twinkling in the velvet sky.

"Whose car is that, Daddy?" Kennedy pointed at the black Cadillac. She tried to squirm out of his arms, but he held on tight.

"Hang on," he said. He moved across the driveway to get a closer look.

The driver's side door hung open. The Cadillac was vacant. All that remained was junk.

Len surveyed the street and the neighboring homes. He saw no sign of the escaped driver.

He gently placed his daughter on the ground, but kept one of her hands clasped in his. It was going to take him some time to feel comfortable letting her move out of reach, out of sight.

He slammed the car door. He started to touch his neck—scratching the insect bite had become a habit—but found the lesion had faded. His skin felt smooth and healthy.

Kennedy was still staring at the Cadillac, a scowl on her face.

"It's no one's car, not anymore," he said to her. "We're getting it towed away to a junk yard."

59

Olivia awoke with a gasp, and had no idea where she had wound up. Candles cast a dim light in an unknown room. She lay curled in fetal position on a leather settee. Perspiration drenched her clothes, her damp hair stuck to her face.

"Welcome back." Marie touched Olivia's shoulder. She settled next to Olivia on the sofa and offered her a steaming mug of a fragrant beverage that smelled like herbal tea.

Sitting up, Olivia accepted the drink. She was parched. She sipped deeply; the tea tasted of cane syrup and oranges.

As her sense of orientation returned, she saw they were still in her godmother's temple. But the *veve* had been swept off the floor, and most of the candles had been extinguished.

"What time is it?" Olivia asked, her voice scratchy.

"You've been asleep about an hour," Marie said. "It's nine o'clock. Do you remember what happened, my dear?"

"I'll remember it for the rest of my life. Every detail."

Marie nodded. Olivia took another sip of tea, and carefully rose off the sofa. It took her a moment to regain her sense of balance. She wasn't flying anymore, but was grounded in the real world. As exhilarating as the experience had been, she was glad to be back.

She walked to the corner of the basement.

"The rat?" Olivia asked.

"See the pile of ashes?" Marie said.

Olivia picked up a candle and panned it across the floor. She found, gathered in the corner, a small, dark mound.

Marie joined her. She gestured toward the floor.

258

"The *bokor* worked with the most dangerous and ancient of all the *loa*," she said. "Only the eldest of the *vodouisants* would even know their names and how to call them. This man we faced . . . he lived for hundreds of years, I believe, as impossible as that may sound."

"Nothing sounds impossible to me anymore," Olivia said.

"The *loa* assisted us," Marie said. "When one like him gains so much power, it tilts our world out of balance. Balance has now been restored."

Olivia nodded. "I saw it consume him."

"None of us are ever truly gone." Marie offered a small, enigmatic smile. "But he will not trouble us again."

It wasn't the answer she had expected, but it was the best she could hope for. She embraced her godmother tightly.

"Thank you, *marenn*," she said. "We owe you everything."

"You're welcome, *fiyel*. Now, go home to your family. Your husband called. He and your daughter are waiting for you."

60

Five months later . . .

At the end of the summer, Len, Olivia, and Kennedy moved into a new home.

While wrapping up the business with the Victorian, they had been living at their old townhouse in Midtown. They'd been getting by with only the barest of essentials. The rest of their belongings, they'd moved into storage. No one complained.

At the Victorian, Marie performed a purification ceremony, to free the trapped spirits and cleanse the home of other, more dangerous entities, a process that took an entire weekend. Afterward, Marie declared that the house was safe for them to inhabit. Neither Olivia nor Len had any interest in testing her assertion. They hired contractors to seal off the hatch to the lower basement. The workers filled up the portal with concrete, and then, walled off the anteroom for good with bricks and mortar.

The residence sold after only three weeks on the market. Two eager buyers launched into a bidding war. The result of the transaction was that even after realtor fees, the sale price would cover their outstanding mortgage and provide a small profit.

One of the prospective buyers that toured the home had asked their realtor what had happened to the architect who lived across the street. According to the local news, Jacob Parks had been declared missing, and had never resurfaced. The rumor, spread by neighbors who witnessed his revolving door of women over the past several months, was that he'd dropped out of sight to start a new life with a pretty young thing somewhere.

The home that Len and Olivia purchased was located in the

Virginia Highland neighborhood. It was a two-story Craftsman built in the 1920s, with loads of authentic period details. They personally met the sellers, a charming couple in their mid-sixties who were pulling up stakes to retire to Arizona. They had lived in the home for twenty-eight years and raised three children within its walls. They tearfully promised Len and Olivia that the residence would be everything they could possibly want.

They moved in over Labor Day weekend. That Sunday morning, they were having a breakfast of turkey sausage, eggs, and grits, when the doorbell chimed.

"What's that?" Kennedy said, a spoonful of grits in her hand.

"That, little girl, is the doorbell," Len said. He set down his coffee mug and checked his watch. "It's a quarter to ten. Sort of early for an unexpected visitor."

"A solicitor, maybe?" Olivia said.

"No idea." He felt an uneasy flutter in his stomach. "I'll check it out."

He navigated through the maze of unpacked boxes, to the window at the front of the house. The window gave him a partial view of the veranda.

An elderly black woman stood at the door. She was elegantly attired in a yellow dress with a matching ornate hat, as if she'd just left Sunday morning service. She held something in her hands.

She rang the doorbell again.

Len pulled in a shaky breath.

He had to release the past. It wasn't easy, but otherwise, they would never find peace.

He opened the door.

The lady held a large aluminum platter with a plastic lid. Inside lay a generous slab of peach cobbler topped with a golden crust.

The visitor's smile was warm.

"Good morning," she said. "I'm Mrs. Constance Perry. My husband and I live across the street. I'm sorry to drop by unannounced, but we wanted to welcome your family to the neighborhood."

Shaking his head, Len chuckled at the foolish ideas he'd entertained.

"Thank you," he said. "I'm Len Bowden, and it's a pleasure to meet you. Please, come inside and meet my family."

About Brandon Massey

Brandon Massey was born June 9, 1973 and grew up in Zion, Illinois. He lives with his family near Atlanta, Georgia, where he is at work on his next thriller. Visit his web site at www.brandonmassey.com for the latest news on his upcoming books.

Made in the USA
Columbia, SC
22 June 2020